Recipes

for a

Perfect Marriage

Morag Prunty

New York

Recipes

for a

Perfect Marriage

{ *A Novel* }

Epigraph reprinted with the permission of Simon & Schuster Adult Publishing Group
from THE ROAD LESS TRAVELED by M. Scott Peck, M.D.
Copyright © 1978 by M. Scott Peck, M.D.

You To Me Are Everything
Words and Music by Ken Gold and Michael Denne
© 1976 (Renewed 2004) SCREEN GEMS-EMI MUSIC LTD.
All Rights for the U.S. and Canada Controlled and Administered by
COLGEMS-EMI MUSIC INC.
All Rights Reserved. International Copyright Secured. Used with Permission.

Library of Congress Cataloging-in-Publication Data
Prunty, Morag.
Recipes for a perfect marriage : a novel / Morag Prunty.
p.   cm.
ISBN 1-4013-0197-5
1. Food writers—Fiction. 2. Married women—Fiction.
3. New York (N.Y.)—Fiction. 4. Commitment (Psychology)—Fiction.
5. Grandmother—Death—Fiction. 6. Ireland—Fiction. I. Title.

PR6066.R86R43 2006
823'.92—dc22   2005050367

Hyperion books are available for special promotions and premiums. For details contact
Michael Rentas, Assistant Director, Inventory Operations, Hyperion, 77 West 66th
Street, 12th floor, New York, New York 10023, or call 212-456-0133.

Book design by Nicola Ferguson

FIRST EDITION

1   3   5   7   9   10   8   6   4   2

In memory of Hugh and Ann Nolan

With love to my husband, Niall

True love is not a feeling by which we are overwhelmed. It is a committed, thoughtful decision.

The Road Less Traveled by M. Scott Peck

Contents

Prologue

The heart of a recipe, what makes it work, is a mystery. Taste is such a personal thing and yet the right recipe can open a person's mind to a food they thought they didn't like. Then again, you can put all the right ingredients together, follow the instructions exactly, and still have a disaster on your hands.

That's how it has always been with me and my Grandma Bernadine's brown bread. I would do exactly as she showed me, but it would always come out a little too crumbly or doughy or hard.

"You're too fussy," she'd say. "Put some jam on and just eat it anyway. It'll be different again tomorrow."

And it was always different. But it was never right.

Like my marriage to Dan.

THEY SAY you just *know* the man you are going to marry. That's how it's supposed to work. You date guys, sleep with them, live with them—get through your twenties having fun falling in and out of love. Then one day you meet this man and you just know he is "The One." He's different from everyone else you have ever met. You feel happier, more special, more alive when you are with him. So you get married.

For two weeks you are Barbie and Ken. There's a big show-off wedding at the Plaza, and you wear a white meringue of a dress even though you are over thirty. You spend what should be the down payment for your first home on fourteen days in the Caribbean.

Then, when you get your "Ken" home, you realize he was an impulse buy. You wanted the "married" label so badly that you didn't think it through, and now he doesn't look as good as he did under the spangly lights of singledom. He doesn't fit you properly, either; although you convinced yourself he'd be suitable for every-day use, you now find him uncomfortable and irritating. He has cost you your freedom; he is the most expensive mistake you will ever make. You have been married for less than three months and everything he does and everything he says makes you scream inside: *For the rest of my life! I can't live with this for the rest of my life!*

But you don't say it out loud because you are ashamed of hav-ing made such a terrible, terrible mistake. Even though you de-spise him for the way he clips his toenails in bed, you know it is not grounds for divorce. You know that this silent torture you are living with is entirely your fault for marrying him when you didn't really love him. Not enough, certainly. Now that you think back on it, did you ever love him at all, or was it all just about you desperately wanting to get married? Because surely love is too strong to allow these petty everyday annoyances to turn it into ha-tred. Love is bigger than that. Love doesn't make mistakes. Not real love. Not the kind of love that makes you marry someone.

BY THE seventh week of married life the statistic that one in four marriages ends in divorce cheers you, and you have decided that six months is a respectable amount of time to be seen trying to make it work.

Except that you know you haven't. Tried, that is. And you can't help thinking that perhaps you are just part of a generation of women who finds marriage a challenging and difficult state of being.

Or perhaps there is no universal group, no zeitgeist-y cliché to hide behind.

In which case I am just a woman who married the wrong guy and is trying to find a way out.

Chemistry

*It either works or it
doesn't work.*

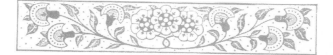

Gooseberry Jam

Jam, in itself, is not difficult to make. But the quality of the fruit is important, and key to the quality is when you pick it. Fruit contains its own thickening agent, pectin, which is only present in the fruit when it is just ripe. Too early and the fruit will thicken but there isn't enough sugar to make it sweet; too late and the fruit will be sweet, but the jam runny and weak.

Gooseberries are ideal because they grow wild and in abundance in this part of Ireland. Add 4lbs sugar to 3lbs gooseberries and boil them hard in a metal pot with one pint of water for a matter of minutes. It is important not to turn the heat down; the fruit must keep boiling throughout the process, otherwise the jam will be no good. To check if the jam is ready, decant a spoonful onto a cold plate. As it starts to cool, gently push with a spoon to one side. If it wrinkles on the top, it is ready. Put into a jar sterilized with boiling water and seal immediately.

Manhattan, New York, 2004

One

Jam is so simple to make—just fruit, sugar, and water—yet the success of it hinges on chemistry, which is quite tricky to control. The jam has to be heated to a ferocious boil, then kept there for just the right amount of time, until it is ready to gel.

If the heat is not right to start with, the thickening process will never kick off. If it overboils, the jam becomes cloying and too thick. And sometimes you can have the best quality ingredients, apply just the right amount of heat, and, for some reason, the chemistry just never kicks in at all.

Sound familiar?

Dan is an ordinary guy. I don't mean that badly; being an ordinary guy is a good thing. What I really mean is that he is ordinary to me, and that is the problem.

Was I ever in love with him? I just don't know anymore. I made the ultimate declaration of love on our wedding day and somehow, in the hugeness of the gesture, I lost the clarity of what love was. Lost faith in the feeling that made me say "yes" to him in the first place.

Dan is great. Really. Just not for me.

I met him about a year and a half ago (if I loved him, I would be able to remember exactly when), although I guess, in a weird way, he had been knocking about on the edge of my life before then. He was the superintendent in my apartment building. "Don't sleep with your building super!" I hear you cry. Basic rule of being a single woman in Manhattan. If things don't work out and your water pipe bursts, who are you going to call? You stay friendly with the super, you flirt with him when you have to, and you tip him at Christmas. It is one relationship you *don't* mess with.

Unless you are so sad and desperate that you are afraid of turning into one of life's conspicuously lonely: the lingering huggers, the abandoned wives who book a lot of aromatherapy and have begun to actively crave a human touch.

The New York singles scene was tough.

There were the players: high maintenance, competitive husband-hunters; manicured, buffed, styled-up peak-performers. Then there were the rest of us just bumbling through the bars, forgetting to change out of our work shoes, borrowing a friend's lipstick as an afterthought, knowing that we were never going to meet a man if we didn't start making an effort. All of us were trying to look as if we didn't care, pretending that what really mattered to us was our friends. Maybe I'm cynical, but behind the glimmering cosmetics and the carefully poised insouciance, I always saw just a lot of brave faces. In the eyes of my closest girlfriends, I knew that, ultimately, I was just an emotional stand-in for the man they hadn't met yet. We were co-commentators in one another's lives, important to one another's emotional survival, but not integral. Men, marriage, children; as we buffed and polished and shone through our thirties, this life cycle was turning from a birthright to a dream.

I was bad at pretending.

Reared by a single mother, who swore it was by choice but was never entirely convincing, I held up my maternal grandparents as my role models in love. James, my grandfather, was the local schoolteacher in their small village and my grandmother Bernadine was a wonderful housekeeper and cook. I visited them for at least two summer months each year as a child and benefited from the warmth they so clearly felt toward me, and each other. Their marriage provided my childhood with a structured, traditional environment so different from the permissive, unpredictable upbringing I had with my bohemian artist mother, Niamh. The long summer days spent with my grandparents were taken up entirely with simple household chores. James tending to his vegetable garden; Bernadine baking bread and allowing me to dust her kitchen in flour. My grandparents were not physically demonstrative, but their love was obvious in all the little things they did for each other.

Bernadine and James were married for fifty years, and I remember as a teenager wondering at the miracle of love that would keep two people together for almost three of my lifetimes. My grandmother outlived my grandfather by eight years. The legacy they left in my heart was an ambition to find a man with whom to have a relationship like theirs. A romance so strong that it could last out half a century.

I always knew that I wanted to be married. I dated losers and bastards and nice-but-not-right guys, but marriage was too important a stake to compromise on. I knew that much. Once or twice I fell in love and had to pull myself back from the brink of a big mistake. Although, looking back now, I realize that in love it is always better to follow your heart than your head.

In the end I married one of the nice-but-not-right ones because my head told my heart that this could be my last chance. Biology and opportunity conspired and conned me into a feeling like love.

With Dan, it was never "The Real Thing," and it needs to be. Fake love won't last the course. It's naïve to believe you can make it otherwise by wishing it so.

I was having one of those indulgent afternoons that you can have when you live alone. And I don't mean the pampering "home spa" type that you see in the magazines. I mean the phone-off-the-hook, feeling-sorry-for-yourself kind. It didn't happen very often, but maybe once a year (often around my birthday), I'd take the day off work and stay in bed feeling miserable. It was nothing as serious as depression—just my twisted version of "me" time. Other girls did meditation and yoga. I took to my bed with a quart of Jack Daniel's and a six-pack of chocolate muffins. After twenty-four hours of watching off-peak TV, I would always emerge longing to see my friends and generally more content with my lot in life.

Being self-employed meant that sometimes I could indulge myself this way, without a boss to worry about. After a lucky break early on, I had worked my way up the food-magazine ladder: from kitchen assistant to recipe tester and food stylist's assistant to senior food writer and stylist. Somewhere around five years ago, I became tired with the politics of publishing: the suits and the schmoozing and the drill of having to go into an office every day. I took a chance that I would get freelance work and on my thirty-third birthday resigned my post as senior food editor at America's top food magazine. Within days I was approached by an agent and have since published three moderately successful cookbooks. I also design and test recipes for food manufacturers and enjoy a peculiar but nonetheless lucrative sideline as a kitchen design consultant for wealthy housewives. Tressa Nolan has always had a good reputation in the food industry, and there's even been some interest in me from the Food Network.

So I was the archetypal child of the baby-boomer generation. Brilliant career, brimful of confidence, loads to offer—love life an unmitigated disaster. My decision to hibernate the day I met Dan had been triggered by the tail end of a hurt perpetrated by yet another jerk. After fifteen years as a food writer, you would think I might have learned about "up-and-coming chefs and photographers syndrome." Those men whose delicate egos lead them to want to reveal any female colleague as flawed and weak. The only comfort to be had from being shit upon by male food "talent" was that there were so damn many of them they weren't as unique or individual as they believed. Oh—and very few of them had talent. Except at getting unmarried thirtysomething women into bed, which, in my own sullied experience, took little more than two vodka martinis and less charm than I could ever admit to.

However, it is sobering for a woman to realize she is old enough and powerful enough to be career-climbed. Sobering enough, in any case, to justify a day off work getting drunk.

Ronan the chef was a classic nonromance. We had sex, I thought he would call, and he didn't. He turned up two weeks later at a restaurant opening with a model on his arm. I tried to be cynical, but when you get to your late thirties, bitter looks too ugly so you have to absorb the hurt. It had been a petty puncture, but I was feeling deflated and sad when Dan walked into my life.

"Fire drill, ma'am . . ."

Our building supers changed every couple of years, largely because their allocated apartment was a dingy, windowless hole in the basement. Dan had been on the job only a week, and I had yet to meet him.

"Ma'am, I am going to have to ask you to participate in our fire drill."

I hate to be called "Ma'am." It makes me feel old and cranky.

"Ma'am, it is for your own safety."

So I become old and cranky.

And in this case, also drunk.

I flung open the door, swayed for a moment, and said, "Can't you see I am *busy?*" Then I waved my pajama-clad arms and closed the door on him.

As I was doing so, it hit me in a vast swell that our new super was incredibly handsome. Not just those acceptable looks that combined with personality can turn an average man into a real prospect. No, he had those ludicrous, chiselled, shaving-cream ad looks. The kind of looks you sweat over as a teenage girl, then grow out of as soon as you realize that male models are way out of your league.

Of course, an intelligent woman in her mid-thirties knows that looks are not important. Especially as she brushes the crumbs of her fourth chocolate muffin from the ridges of her Target flannel nightgown. It is what's on the inside that counts, which, in my case, was apparently a lot of bourbon.

I must have seen something in Dan's eyes during our few-seconds exchange, some germ of desire because—for no apparent reason—I decided to clean myself up a little. Not a full leg shave or anything as extreme as that, but through the drunken haze a bit of tooth and hair brushing went on and the nightgown got exchanged for something sexier, which, let's face it, didn't have to be much more than a clean pair of sweats.

Dan came back an hour later when the drill was over, and while I was not surprised at him calling back, I remember being shocked that he really was as handsome as I had first thought. More shocking still was the way that these melting hazel eyes were gazing at me with some undisguised lust/admiration combo. Like I was the most beautiful woman on earth. Nobody had ever looked at me like that before—well, because I am not a conventional beauty—and it made me feel like laughing. I invited him in and he hesitated by the door, like household staff at a duchess's cocktail party.

Seducing Dan was the easiest thing I have ever done. Normally I sit back and wait to be asked. I don't take much persuading, but I had never taken the lead before. This guy looked so nervous, so smitten, that it made me feel certain of myself. Confident.

The sex was fantastic; I won't go into the details but he loved every inch of my body in a way that astonished me. He was heartbreakingly handsome, and there was something comforting and safe about being with him right from the start. I was deeply flattered, but I knew, deep down in my gut, that Dan was not my type.

I am attracted to intellects, not bodies, and we had nothing in common.

When I look back on it now I worry that I seduced Dan for no other reason than I felt dirty and drunk and lonely. Oh, and of course—because I could. A toxic combination that was eventually legitimized by our marriage.

Hardly grounds for a happy one.

Two

That first afternoon of sex with Dan somehow extended itself into the comfort of a convenient relationship. It was good news or bad news, depending on how you looked at it. In the short term, Dan patched me up and made me feel better. But my feelings for him were always sullied by the bad guy before him. Even if the chef was a jerk there had been some chemistry between us, albeit the poisonous kind. Dan didn't have that power over me. Although I knew he would never do anything to hurt me, sometimes I wished he would. Because surely it is better to feel hurt than to feel nothing at all.

Perhaps I am making things sounds worse than they were. I did have feelings for Dan—of course I did. When I married him, I thought I loved him.

Dan made me feel good. He was great in bed; I had confidence in my body around him. He thought I was gorgeous. He desired me and, I'll be honest, that was something different for me. I love to cook and I love to eat, so I am on the heavy side. Not in a bad way—at least I don't think so. But Dan was the first guy who I felt I didn't have to hide from. He was always telling me how sexy, how smart I was; what a great cook I was, what a hot body I had.

Right from the start, from that first afternoon, Dan Mullins was stone-mad crazy in love with me. He was so sure about marrying me, so clear and certain that he could make me happy, that I believed him.

After just three months he said, "Marry me."

Not "Will you?" or "I think it would be a good idea if we got married."

Just "Marry me. I know I can make you happy."

No one had ever asked me before and part of me knew that no one would again. I was thirty-eight and I wanted to believe in something: in happy ever after, in him. So I said "yes."

I allowed myself to get caught up in the arrangements even though I knew that they were not the point. The dress, the cake, the venue, the canapés: Getting married was the biggest, most glamorous photographic shoot I was ever going to organize. If I was using details as distractions, at least I had that in common with every other bride-to-be. It was such a big deal. Such an *event*. Everyone wanted a piece of me.

Doreen, my best friend the fashion editor, had her whole fashion team on me and they went into meltdown.

"A European bride—I mean, it'll be *so* this season."

"She's Irish. It doesn't count."

"Why? Ireland's in Europe? Isn't it?"

"Physically, yes. Style-wise? It's Canada."

"Oh."

"Get on to Swarovski; I'm thinking crystal choker to distract from that size ten ass."

"And the rest!"

"We'll have to get her down to an eight if she wants to wear white . . ."

I enjoyed playing the princess, all the fuss and frivolity. And it turned out to be just like in the magazines: the happiest day of my life.

Part of that was due to the bonding I experienced that day with my mother. Niamh flew into J.F.K. from London to be there. I had always wanted a conventional cookie-baking mother and she had always wanted a friend rather than a daughter. We didn't clash; we just inhabited parallel worlds. Niamh and I had little in common. I was pragmatic and conventional, an inverted rebellion against her chaotic, promiscuous nature. She had followed her lecturer boyfriend to London five years earlier, where he took up a position at Oxford University and she played the part of his eccentric partner: all hippy clothes and dyed-purple hair, hoping to shock the unshockable English. I was hurt she had left me behind so easily—that there seemed to be no place in her life for a single, soon-to-be-middle-age daughter, and there was a minor estrangement. We spoke every couple of months on the phone, but I never had the urge to go and visit her and she always had an excuse not to come home on vacation. Five years had managed to pass without us having seen each other.

I had almost considered not inviting her. It wasn't that I didn't want Niamh there; it was just that I guess, underneath the bravado of seeming not to care about her, I was afraid that if I invited her, she might not turn up. My mother stridently disapproved of marriage on principle and that she came at all was a revelation in itself. The night before the wedding, she met Dan, and after he had departed to his apartment my mother and I stayed up drinking in my suite in the Plaza.

"I like him," she said once we were both tipsy enough to be honest, but not so drunk that we wouldn't remember. "Although I know it's not important what I think."

I argued briefly before she said, "Bernadine would have approved."

I wondered if she was right or if she was just saying it because she sensed some uncertainty.

"He seems solid," she added.

It was a cop-out understatement. The wrong thing to say and the wrong time to say it. While I knew Niamh meant well in that moment, I longed with a fresh grief for my grandmother. It had been ten years since she had died, but my love and need for her still felt so alive. I wanted her to be there, not just so that I could get her approval of Dan but also because it did not feel right for me to be taking this big step without her.

Niamh seemed to sense that and said, "I miss her, too."

Her eyes drowsy with drink, my mother reached across and took my hand.

"She still loves you," she said, "and so do I."

Niamh was into this afterlife stuff, which I had always believed was nonsense. But the soft tone of her voice led me to do something that I can remember doing only rarely as a child. I lay my head on my mother's chest and waited there until the strange smell of her perfume and the unfamiliar touch of her blouse on my cheek faded, until everything dissolved but the comfort of being held by her. As Niamh stroked my face, I felt the instinctive care of generations of mothers before her seep through her hands. For a moment, I believed the strong arms of Bernadine were embracing me again.

I don't know how long I lay there, but when I sat up I knew, ten years after her death, that I had finally accepted that Bernadine was gone. My grandmother had been such an influence on my life, especially on my love of cooking. As a child, Niamh and I existed on takeaway scraps and whatever she could rustle up out of a tin. I certainly would never have become a food writer without those holidays spent in Bernadine's kitchen—crumbly homemade bread straight from the oven with jam dribbling over its salty crusts, lamb shanks made impossibly tender from slow stewing, carrots as sweet as apples, and soft potato fluff bursting through skin so soft it hardly needed mashing. The changing consistency of butter as it melted, pastry as it browned, bread rising—the chemistry of cooking seemed like a miracle to me. A thrill would shoot through me when I saw her take down her worn cotton apron from its hook on the kitchen door and determinedly lay out her ingredients on the long pine table, and I longed to join in. Bernadine taught me to cook methodically. It was never a game to her; there was no throwing flour around, and if I dropped an egg or spilled a cup of milk she would lecture me briefly about the sin of wastefulness. But I didn't mind. My mother had never been interested in cooking, so my grandmother made me the recipient of her skill and experience and I was a devoted student. My grandfather was an intellectual man, a reader, and he influenced my decision to study English literature. But it was Bernadine who had been my true mentor. I never understood or appreciated that as fully as I did the night before I got married and suddenly knew with certainty that my next project would be to adapt my grandmother's recipes into a traditional Irish cookbook.

What I still did not feel certain of was my decision to marry Dan the following day. I told myself it was pre-wedding nerves, what everyone experiences. I was afraid if I vocalized them, Niamh would tell me to pull out and I would not have enough conviction to act against her advice. If I pulled out at this stage I would have the drama of a cancelled wedding on my hands, and I am not a dramatic sort of woman. Under that lay the fear that had put me in this position in the first place. The fear that Dan—even if he wasn't "The One"—was the closest I was going to get to sharing my life with somebody. If I was afraid I was doing the wrong thing in marrying him, my fear of being alone was greater.

We had a traditional Catholic service in Dan's local church in Yonkers, and Niamh walked me down the aisle and gave me away. Doreen was my maid of honor. As I stood at the top of the aisle in my big dress, I knew that this was what I had always wanted. At the same time, there was a disbelief that it was really happening. Looking back at me, smiling, was everyone I knew. It was the most overwhelming moment of my life. Better, bigger than anything I had ever experienced. I was part of a fairy tale I thought I had left behind long ago, and now realized had just been lying dormant inside me. Hope had been growing bigger and was buried deeper with each passing year. It all came flooding out as I sobbed my way down that walkway to the rest of my life. Dan was the man who had made that happen for me.

DAN WAS sure he could make me happy, but he was wrong. You can't make other people happy; they have to make themselves happy. Dan loved me, but I now know that it wasn't enough. I needed to love him back.

And let's face it—you can't force yourself to love somebody if the chemistry just isn't there.

Faliochtar, Parish of Achadh Mor,
County Mayo, Ireland, 1932

Three

When love is pure, it is easy. It comes as fast and hard as a shower of hail and often passes as quickly. It fills your heart and when it's gone you feel as hollow as an empty cave.

Then there is the other kind of love. The one that comes so slow that you think it isn't love at all. Each day it grows, but by such small measure that you hardly notice. Once your heart is filled with this perennial love, it will never be empty again.

I have known both, and still I would not like to choose one over the other.

Although for the longest time I thought I had.

THE MOMENT my eyes fell on Michael Tuffy, every love and loyalty I had experienced up to that point was rendered meaningless. I could feel the heat of my own blood just looking at him. The first time his eyes met mine they branded me; from then on I would be defined by my love for him.

In all my life—which has been long and textured with the emotions of wife, mother, grandmother—I have never forgotten what it felt like to fall so immediately and so completely in love. I would have followed him to the other side of the world. It all but destroyed my youthful optimism when I realized that I couldn't.

Our first meeting was at a *spraoi* in Kitty Conlan's house. Kitty had the knack of matching, and there was nothing to do in Achadh Mor back then—only work and wait. Bad, unyielding land, and a hard history blighted with famine and the messy, bloody politics of occupation meant that emigration to England and America from our area was an almost foregone conclusion. Those of us left behind were half a community, not knowing whether we were lucky to be still at home when the greater number of our family and neighbors were in New York or London. Sometimes it felt as if the hundreds of thousands who had left since the famine had each brought a handful of Mayo earth with them and unsettled the very ground from under us. We waited for our men to return from summer's potato picking in Yorkshire, adventure implied in their new jackets, and affluence in their shiny brown wallets. In the meantime we had to draw whatever entertainment we could from looking at one another.

I didn't mind being looked at. I was brazen by nature. Some people thought me spoiled, even my own mother at times.

"She wants jam on everything!" I remember her saying it to Aunt Ann the summer her sister returned from America.

"Nothing is good enough for her. She wants everything her own way. I keep telling her, Bernadine, life is *hard*. She has her head full of silly notions."

Falling in love certainly came under the banner "silly notions." People made romances all the time but they rarely ended in marriage. Marriage was about land and security and money. To marry for love was considered reckless. Looking back, I suppose my mother was worried that my idealism would lead to disappointment and eventually despair.

I was the only daughter among three brothers, and my father drank. In those days nobody had anything. A woman was at the mercy of how hard her husband was willing to work. A lazy man, no matter how much land he had, would end you in the poorhouse. A drinker was worse again, for he might work hard and then spend every penny in the pub and believe himself entitled to do so. That is how it was with my father. And so my mother, in addition to running the house, worked like a slave on the farm. She reared pigs for a Ballyhaunis butcher and sold eggs to a grocer in Kilkelly. Both men were careful to have business dealings only with my mother. They understood what type my father was and that they were providing our only source of income. They were decent, and doubtless the good price they gave her reflected my mother's desperation. Hardship had made my mother bitter at home, and she was a slouching, distant woman with barely the gumption to nag her children. She was unhappy. I could see the miserable circumstances that had turned her that way and I was determined to avoid them.

Mam's sister, Ann, was my savior. A confirmed spinster, Ann had gone to America in 1910 and become a seamstress to a wealthy American socialite. She returned in the thirties a "millionaire"—the description in our poverty-stricken times of someone who owned more than one coat.

My aunt told me stories of New York. She read books and had an easy life with plenty of money and no men to look after. She was always glad of my company and often asked my mother if I might stay with her the night. In the evenings, we could suit ourselves entirely. Making dainty potato cakes and spreading them with butter and my mother's tart gooseberry jam, eating them greedily as we discussed the news of the neighbors in intricate detail. Ann told shocking stories of their relations in America: This one's son married a Jew, another was killed boxing bare-fisted in a bar. I embellished duller tales of arguments over field boundaries with gory details. To me, Ann's house was a palace filled with exotic and beautiful things. A vase made of heavy glass the color of a cat's eye to hold a single rose, an ermine stole, two red cushions with gold braid trim, a silk kimono lavishly embroidered with peonies and chrysanthemums.

My relationship with this glamorous aunt elevated me above the hoi polloi of our village—in my own mind certainly, and in the minds of many of the lads roundabout, who considered me one of the finer-looking girls among the diminishing supply of would-be wives in our parish.

It suited me just fine to be placed high on a pedestal, with my long black curls and my delicate pointed nose stuck high in the air. Those brave enough to approach me would soon find themselves withered by my indifference. I had the idea of leaving Achadh Mor when the summer had passed. Aunt Ann still had contact with all of her friends in America and would surely pay my passage across. I was a brave and adventurous young woman. I would not have emigrated for survival, but, with Ann as my role model, for success. It would have happened but for my falling in love.

Love changes everything, but not always for the better.

Ann did not come with me to Kitty Conlan's party that night. She thought the widow a foolish woman, indulging the young people of the parish with silly matchmaking games. Also, the men were allowed drink even though the company was mixed, and Ann didn't like that at all. She was prudish in matters where drink and romance were concerned. Looking back as an older woman myself now, I believe Ann was less committed to her spinster status than she let on. Perhaps she had been let down by a sweetheart in her younger days. Certainly that would go some way towards explaining what happened between her and me.

Kitty's parlor was small and her fire roaring, and the crowd kept having to disperse into the cold outdoors, so as not to roast themselves alive. Joe Clarke had come back from his break and was starting up the squeezebox again. Cousin Mae and I were giggling over some trivia when she prodded me in the ribs and nodded towards the door.

Then I found I was both floating and sinking.

The room grew huge as crowds of people receded into the white walls and Michael alone walked towards me. With each step he took, I knew he was the braver, stronger of us because I could not move. For a moment I thought perhaps he did not care for me at all, otherwise he would be paralyzed as I was. He did not speak, only held his hand out to mine so he could take me to dance. When we touched, a thrilling heat shot through me and I thought the feet would go from under me. But they didn't.

We danced, him holding my eyes all the time and not speaking at all. I, drained of my usual brazen huff, blushed scarlet throughout, so that every neighbor could carry back as far as Kilkelly, Knock, and Kiltimagh news of our big romance. That Bernadine Moran of Faliochtar in the parish of Achadh Mor and a young American lad by the name of Michael Tuffy, whose mother had returned to claim the estate of her deceased husband, Michael Senior—tragically passed away in New York City some six years past—were doing a line.

People talked, but as I said, I never minded that. Gossip and truth feed off each other. If our romance was great, then it was made greater by talk. In a townland, talk brings pressure to bear.

Let them speculate; and the fireside ruminations of a thousand old biddies added fuel to our burgeoning passion.

Michael and his mother were strangers to Achadh Mor, but we welcomed them in a way we rarely welcomed our own. Returned emigrants, like Aunt Ann, seemed to goad those left behind with what might have been. They were expected to keep a low profile, sink back into the grim, boggy landscape as if they had never been away. The likes of Maureen Tuffy and her handsome son were different. The real McCoy—they had American accents and had not been born to the drudgery of our land but had come here by choice. We thought them marvelous for believing us worthy of their company.

I could not believe that Michael had chosen me to love, and yet when I was with him, I felt so beautiful that I might have been picked by royalty itself. My disbelief was tempered by a sense of having known him all my life; a certainty that I would be with him until the day I died.

What we did, where we went, what was said is as meaningless now as it was then. We walked fields, we took tea with my aunt, we attended the same Masses. We stood across from each other on either side of the main street in Kilkelly on market day, our views of each other interrupted by cows and carts. And we each wondered at the miracle of our matched souls meeting in this insignificant, squally corner of the world. We saw God in each other, and perhaps that was our only sin. What we had was rare, and still, after all that has happened since, I believe that to be true. It was the love that fools stand in wait their whole lives for, then die loveless and bitter when it evades them.

Perhaps that knowledge alone saved me in the end. Knowing that my love for Michael Tuffy could never be repeated.

We didn't marry, although it was fully intended.

Our parents met in a hotel in Ballyhaunis, at the suggestion of his mother. My father, for all his shaving and washing, looked like a boiled ham in his suit. My mother was already nervous, and taken aback when money was mentioned, although she could see herself the opportunity that was being offered her. It seemed a small price to pay for her daughter's eternal happiness. Mrs. Tuffy was clearly a woman of means and it was only a token of respect she was asking for.

In any case, we all knew that Aunt Ann would be happy to provide whatever money was needed. She, of all people, would be thrilled for me to marry into such a respectable household—and for love. It was every dream she could have had for me.

Ann did not poor-mouth over declining to pay my dowry. We all knew she could well afford it. Her first insult was to refuse to offer the money of her own volition, but instead to wait for my mother to ask her. It was a humiliation my mother had never had to endure before; Ann had quietly provided for our family countless times in the past.

My mother didn't give me any explanation; she just said that there was no money and that therefore I could not marry Michael Tuffy.

I begged my mother to go back and ask again, but she refused. I threatened to run away with him. Michael and I were destined. Nothing could keep us apart. What did our families—what did money—matter?

When I turned around to plan our escape, he was gone. Back to America.

I knew I would never see him again.

I howled and tore at my hair until my father and brothers were afraid of me. For months, I locked myself into the house with my mother and shredded potatoes until my fingers bled, scrubbed flagstones until my knees bruised black.

I never spoke to my aunt again and spoke of her to others only rarely and with caution.

As the next five years passed, the pain softened. I came to understand that I had been privileged to experience such a rare love at all, yet cursed because it had ruined me for anything that would come after. As for marriage—the very idea of it became an insult. Although part of me knew it was inevitable, there was one thing I was certain of: No one or nothing would ever match my love for Michael Tuffy.

He was gone but the memory of him had marked me forever.

Compromise

*You can't always have as much
sugar as you'd like.*

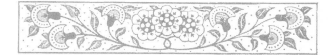

Rhubarb Tart

Head and tail the rhubarb and cut it into small pieces, about a quarter inch—your eye will tell you. When the rhubarb is young, you can put it raw into the tart. In late August when it is tougher, I fill a pan with water and leave it to warm over the fire with a little sugar while I am making the pastry. Sift 10oz flour with a half teaspoon salt, then mix in 2 dessert spoons sugar. Chop 4oz butter, then crumble into the flour with your fingers. Beat 1 egg into 2 tablespoons milk and work the mixture into a dough. Line a well-floured pan with a half inch of the pastry, then put in your rhubarb and as much sugar as suits. I like it sweet and could take up to 3 tablespoons. James prefers it sour, but I'd put in an extra spoon anyway so as not to poison him. Cover with a pastry lid then put in a medium oven and watch for up to 1 hour.

Four

You can buy anything in New York, except rhubarb. Oh, you can buy the forced stuff all year round. Creamy-pink, firm, fat rods, but as far as this cook is concerned, they are a watery waste of time. What I wanted were the spindly sticks that used to grow wild in the field behind my grandparents' house. Bitter green leaves and a sore scarlet stalk gradually giving way to a white tip. They were shockingly sour, but with the addition of sugar they took on a unique, exotic flavor.

I started reviving my grandmother's recipes. It was painful, bringing all of her old dishes to life again. As I worked through my memories of her cooking, I could hear her talk me through the measurements and methods as if she were there. But she was only able to answer questions I already knew the answers to, like how many grams equal a cup of sugar. She was not there to give me the answer to the one question I really needed to ask her, which was what she thought of Dan. I wondered if Bernadine would have put Dan and I together, and when I was feeling unsure, I longed for her to be there. If she could only have given me her opinion, I think it might have helped. I guess I needed someone else to feel certain on my behalf. I knew that was not possible, and maybe that's why I chose to value the opinion of the one person who would, let's face it, never be able to give it to me.

NOW THAT I had reorganized my apartment and sorted through the pile of storage junk I'd avoided for years, I needed to get lost in this cookery project so that I could ignore the fact that Dan wanted us to move to Yonkers.

The Hamptons? Of course. Brooklyn? Yes. The Bronx? Maybe. But Yonkers?

Dan owned a house there, which he had been renovating on and off for the past five years. I had never been to see it because as far as I was concerned, it was just an investment. It was nice to know that I was marrying a guy who was a property owner, but it had never occurred to me that he intended for us to live there. It was a weekend building project that he would scurry off to when I was away on press trips. Dan and I really did our own thing a lot. I didn't bring him to work functions and I was good at avoiding socializing with his Irish American drinking buddies.

Out of the blue one day, when I was doing my day's recipe prep and Dan was putting a plug on the stereo, he started this clumsy conversation about how the city was getting "real busy" and "real crowded" and "real dangerous." It was an obvious attempt to ease me into his dumb idea of moving out of the city. I didn't know which was worse. His wanting us to lose two prime apartments in Upper West Side Manhattan, or the fact that he thought I would consider moving to Yonkers.

But then, that was just number one on my "things I hate about Dan" list.

The list had been growing in my head so fast that I found writing it down helped to lessen its power over me.

* He wants to move to Yonkers.
* His toenails are too long, and they scratch me in bed.
* He wears tartan shirts.
* He keeps fishing catalogs in the bathroom.
* He's too big and noisy—he lumbers around the apartment so that you always know he is there.
* He shuffles and uses hillbilly words like "real" when he gets nervous.
* Instant coffee. He prefers instant coffee? Explain!
* He gets up before me in the mornings, and wakes me with tea. It makes me feel guilty.
* He forgets to put sugar in my tea.
* He purses his lips just before he says something that he thinks is clever.
* He thinks he's clever. He told me last night that he does not think that he missed out by not going to college.

Actually—that stuff about the list losing its power when it was written down? That's bullshit. The only power I had was in the list itself, which was hidden under my side of the bed. When Dan moved toward me in the night or when he leaned in to me in the mornings, I knew it was there. The list said more about what a bitch I was than anything else, which didn't help me either. I hated everything about Dan. The only time I looked at him and didn't think, "I hate you," was when I would look at him and think, "What have I done?" Poison or panic. Take your pick because that's all that was on offer in my head right then.

Dan had been more or less resident in my apartment since we came together, but when we returned from our honeymoon we had a ceremonial him-moving-his-stuff-in evening. There was a mountain of stuff I hadn't realized he owned: crates of old records, piles of cheap dishes, nasty acrylic linens, magazines dating back to the early eighties, to name but a few. As I watched it all piling up in the hall of my perfect minimalist palace, Dan happily hauling up another box of dusty videos, I honestly thought I was going to be sick. In the end, intuiting that I was unhappy with the mess, Dan moved most of it back down to the super's apartment again. But it couldn't stay there forever and we both knew it.

When we were dating, it was comforting to have him in my home. But now that Dan had the *right* to be there it felt wrong. I felt suddenly robbed of my privacy, and intimacy isn't supposed to feel intrusive, surely?

I was possessed by this person I could only pretend not to recognize. May I introduce to you—my worst self: the discontented, bitchy, I-know-everything teenager. She was back, she was living in my brain, and no, she was not paying rent. What she was doing was complaining and criticizing and laughing sardonically at Dan and the sad, thirtysomething desperado who married him. She was vile and I hated her. But she was the only company I had. I couldn't tell anyone else what was going on. My single friends would all say, "Gasp! You don't love him! You must leave at once!" My married friends would say, "Love? Get real girl, this is *marriage*."

This was not what I wanted when I got married to Dan. This was not who I thought I would turn into.

Virtually everything I said out loud was a petty complaint disguised as a question. "Is the dishwasher still full?" "Did you forget to buy toothpaste?" "Are you wearing that?"

Sometimes all I could do was make a statement.

"These are the wrong washing tabs." "I take one sugar in my tea." "Close the bathroom door." Then he would say he was sorry, and I would say, "It's OK," in this clipped voice that made it quite clear that it wasn't OK at all. Without meaning to, I had joined the Passive Aggressive School of Noncommunication. All calm on the outside saying, "Everything is fine; everything is lovely," when any fool could sense I was a simmering concoction of hatreds that, sooner or later, would come spewing out of me in a shower of lethal bile.

Nice.

I was scaring myself and I was scaring Dan. I could see him waiting for the argument he knew was impending, but couldn't start himself because he hadn't the first idea what was wrong. His truth was, we were newlyweds and in love. But my truth couldn't have been more different.

I HAVE never made rhubarb tart except with the vegetable grown from my grandmother's garden, and it's been ten years since I was last home in Kilkelly.

Granddad James had planted a single root bulb the year my mother was born. My grandmother hadn't wanted the untidy, ferocious plant in her pretty back garden, so he planted it away from the house, but near enough that she could access it. By the time I was a young adult, the single root had reproduced so that it stretched out across a quarter of an acre, a mass of broad umbrella leaves hiding the scarlet underneath. It is an unremarkable and unruly looking vegetable—yet when prepared right, it is truly delicious.

During my summer vacations in Ireland as a child I ate rhubarb tart every day. I returned to live full-time in Ireland as an English literature student at Galway University when I was eighteen. The memories I treasure from those three years of living in Ireland are not the late-night, giggling, staggering walks up cobbled bar-lined lanes; losing my virginity to a beautiful, wild-haired philosophy student; or even the books I studied and the passionate professors who dissected them. It is the time that I spent with my grandparents that resonates with me now. I would carry one of my grandmother's rhubarb tarts all the way to Galway on the bus from Kilkelly, carefully double wrapped in two tea towels so as not to be crushed. Once back in my digs, I would hide it in my room, safe from the afternoon munchie attacks of my dope-smoking housemates, and have a slice of it with a cup of sweet tea before going to sleep. That daily ritual and my weekends in Kilkelly gave some order to my crazy student years and got me a first in English Lit. Although I was born in America, rhubarb tart was the taste of Ireland, of home: not the New York loft that my mother and I lived in, then filled with Andy Warhol prints and work-shy boyfriends, but her parents' home in Kilkelly, which smelled of smoldering turf, beeswax, and camphor. When I would visit each summer, I knew from their faces that they had been waiting ten months to see their only grandchild again. They adored me, and they adored each other. From July to September, I was the center of their world and rhubarb tart was always the first thing out of the oven. Tressa's favorite.

So if I couldn't get the right type of rhubarb, I decided, I might have to leave Grandma Bernadine's tart as a fond memory rather than tarnish hers with a tasteless look-alike version.

When you are really attached to an ideal, it is just not possible to compromise.

Five

I had no interest in James Nolan. I respected him. We all did. He was a local scholar, but since he was thirty-five when he returned from his studies to take up the post of teacher in Faliochtar school, he wasn't anyone I had socialized with. The only contact I had with him was in the Friday evening Irish classes he taught. It was the fashion at that time to learn Irish, and on Friday evenings James opened the school and taught us local people the native language that had been beaten out of our grandparents. There was dancing and singing and great *craic* after the classes, and some nights we mightn't leave until after eleven. Within weeks of starting the classes were packed; people were walking three miles and back from Achadh Mor to attend.

James was a member of the Gaelic League, and along with that, there were rumors that he had served us all in the Irish Republican Army. Nobody knew the whys and wherefores of his ten years away, but there was nothing unusual in that. The smart man knew how to keep his mouth shut. In any case, he had not been shirking because Kitty Conlan noted that his five sisters had been successfully dowered, two into the convent, and he had helped to finance and build a smart new house with a slate roof on the site next to their family home.

Mr. J. Nolan was in danger of becoming something of a champion, except that he was local to our small, humble parish and would therefore never be allowed to consider himself anything other than unremarkable. Certainly his appearance gave nothing away of any alleged heroics or romantic activity abroad. I barely remember the first time I saw James, except that I might have thought him ordinary beyond belief. More truthful is that I didn't think about him at all.

There had been some small speculation about who, among the women still available, might fancy him. He was respectable and kind with children by all accounts. There was the new house, which remained unoccupied—his brother and his wife having recently moved to England and the old mother refusing to budge from her old cottage—and a teacher's income, which was nothing to be sniffed at. He was, if you were pushing thirty, a good prospect. However, I was only twenty-three.

I may have had no interest myself, but there was some sport to be had watching the older women fall over themselves to get at him. Mae and I would be in kinks laughing at them; the lipstick drawn on like a clown's hanging around after Mass on Sunday to enjoy the *cupla focal* with the *Muinteoir*. The worst of them was Aine Grealy. She had a face as pale and plain as bread, but she had brains. She had won scholarship after scholarship—gone as far as university in Dublin, and was back that summer to decide what she was going to do with all her education. I didn't like her.

My cousin Mae and I were the prettiest girls around the place. Aunt Ann had given me all manner of beautiful things when we had still been friends and Mae also had excellent Yanks who regularly sent home packages. The two of us turned out in public like something you might see in a film. I had a yellow blouse and a matching yellow scarf with which I tied back my long black hair. Mae had a pair of cream-colored shoes with a leather bag to match. Aine was the type who would look down her nose on shows of glamour. She never spoke to us at the Irish classes, and I knew she thought us stupid. I didn't mind, as I thought it better, at that time, to be stupid and pretty than clever but plain. We were there for the dancing afterwards and spent most of the class scanning the packed room to assess who was going to give us the greatest *craic* for the night ahead. Mae was on the lookout for romance, but I wasn't.

I only went after James Nolan to upset Aine Grealy.

It was childish and nasty looking back on it now, but she had riled me terribly. Aine had been talking away to James after Mass this Sunday, and I had greeted them both in Irish as I passed by. Aine had corrected my pronunciation in reply. I thought it was a vile thing to do—and still do to this day—so I decided to put a halt to her gallop. Even if I broke his heart, I told myself, I was doing James a good turn. There was clearly an understanding developing between the two of them and I believed Aine to be ugly through from the inside out. He seemed an easygoing type who would be happy for anyone who'd have him. James Nolan might have been a scholar, but I had him down as a *ludarman* in matters of love.

I was wrong about that. It was the first and last time I was ever made to feel a fool in front of James, but it was the first time of many where I had read his character wrong.

The next Friday, I was wearing a lavender cardigan, which I fully knew set off my long black curls to beautiful effect. The class was over and everyone made busy pushing the chairs around to the edges of the room. Mae was talking to Paud Kelly as he was unpacking his accordion. Aine had made a beeline for James and was stuck to his side before the last of his pupils had stood. She was determined all right.

But now she was up against Bernadine Moran. I might not have been good at Irish, but I knew something about love. At least I thought I did. I could look at any man and make his heart melt. It was cruel entertainment perhaps, but as far as I could see the men around me had it all their way. You had a few short years to tease them before you'd be darning their socks and tolerating their drunken abuses. That's how it was for my mother in any case. Except that I could see James was a harmless type, I might have been more careful at setting myself on him like I did.

All I did was look. I looked across the room at James in the way I had looked at Michael Tuffy some five years before when I had fallen in love. Except this was an imitation. When I had looked at Michael, I'd felt my knees buckle and the color rise in my cheeks in a fountain of pain and joy; this night I looked at our ordinary teacher and pretended. I cannot say how I did it, except that I stared hard at him until I knew he had noticed me. I knew, or believed back then, that I had something worth noticing.

He stayed by Aine's side that evening and walked her home as usual. I was irritated to have failed, but my resolve in the matter did not stretch to further action.

The following week Aine was not there, and James asked me up for a dance. He was a tall man and made an awkward, gangly dancer. I was mortified as the other girls, including Mae, clapped us on as if there was something in it. As we were leaving, Mae nodded over to him, pointing out that he was loitering after us as if he had the intention of accompanying us. I scurried out quickly and she behind.

I thought that was that, but before the week was up, I would get the greatest shock of my life.

Six

I came in from late Mass that Sunday and found James Nolan sitting in our kitchen. He was at the table with my father and there were papers in front of them. I was immediately confused; although my father was a brutish enough character, he could read and write sure enough. He wasn't like some of the poor unschooled who needed to get the local teacher in to help them draft a letter.

Father nodded at the kettle for me to make them tea, then at a rhubarb tart I had made in a hurry the night before. I had left it aside because I had already put it in the oven before I realized that I had put no sugar in it. Rhubarb tart is bitter beyond belief without sugar, and so I made our guest tea and deliberately placed a slice of the rotten tart in front of him. My father took none, as he was not in the habit of eating in front of anyone, save his family. I thanked God for that, as he would have thrashed me if he found out what I had done.

James ate every last crumb and declared it the most delicious tart he had ever experienced. I was about to test his endurance and acting skills with another slice, when my father stood up and said:

"Take James and show him around the place, Bernadine."

My father always called me Bernie.

James was quiet—sheepish, I think now with the benefit of hindsight. I remember that he tried to take my hand, and I pulled it away with the utmost rudeness to deter him. I must have had some inkling of what lay ahead. I gestured my arms at the hens and the hay shed and we were back at the house within ten minutes. My parents had cleared out and I made busy around the kitchen, rolling up my sleeves and walloping pots to make it clear it was time for him to leave, which he did.

When my father came back in and found James gone, he went mad—shouting that I was a useless strap. Still I didn't understand, until my mother ushered him out and sat me down at the table. Her voice was gentle, the sharp, busy tone gone out of it. She looked worried.

"Do you like James?" was all she asked.

I knew then that they had come to an arrangement, although I could scarcely believe it of them—or, for that matter, him.

THE SORDID details only came out later. How James had come calling with the intention of walking me out and my father had pinned him down to a marriage commitment there and then. After the family had shamed itself in not being able to dowry me to Michael Tuffy, the old bastard was afraid he would be stuck with me forever. James and his mother took me on with no dowry, and they never told a soul or sinner in the parish to save my family name.

James had written and signed an informal contract with my father that afternoon, buying me like cattle, though no money changed hands. A worthless piece of meat, that was how I felt myself. This man didn't love me, nor I him. My parents clearly did not love me; otherwise they would never have done this terrible thing.

When Michael returned to America, I thought my heart had torn asunder. My loving him, my missing him, that terrible wrenching longing to see him came upon me again that day, and with terrible force.

I ran from the kitchen, and walked fast across five fields and five ditches to a place we called Purple Mountain. It was a small hill, no more than a mound of heather, and below it on the other side was the "lake." In reality, it was a pond of water that changed from a large brown puddle to a deep pool depending on the rainfall and the time of year. Beyond it stretched miles of black, treacherous bog. No one owned this land and no one cut turf from it, although there were plenty of stories of men who had tried and disappeared. We were told they were dragged down to hell itself by the bony paws of the demons that lived beneath the bog's surface. It was to deter us playing there, but also played on our terror, as the demons surely didn't choose their prey at random.

I was full of sin and had gone past caring. Michael Tuffy and I had sinned ourselves senseless on several occasions. It was that, and the knowledge that I could not endure the rest of my life without him, that made the fact of our not getting married so terrible. We had been so certain of our fate together that we had enjoyed each other's bodies.

On the day of my father's and James's arrangement, I stood on the top of that filthy mound of earth and I thought about flinging myself into the lake. There had been heavy rainfall for weeks, so it was deep. I could not swim, and I knew the demons would be ready for me after what I had done.

I opened my arms and I swayed, but I could not do it.

So I thought about what I was left with.

I could flee, but I had nowhere to go. I could not stay at home, that much was clear. And then I realized I had no choice. I had to marry James.

AS THE weeks crept towards the wedding I tried to keep up a front. It didn't help anyone for me to be surly and sad. My mother and Mae sold him hard to me, and I took heed of them the best I could. James Nolan was clean, respectable, and kind. A tall man, he may have been more than ten years my senior but he was well built and strong. Not handsome, but his fine features gave him a gentle, intelligent appearance that was not entirely unattractive. His mother was decent, and we would have our own house. I could do a lot worse.

But this route of thinking wasn't mine and while I went along with them, all I could think about was how this was supposed to be happening with somebody else. Every inch of me burned again for the young man who had gone to America five years before and taken with him my heart, my soul, my spirit: the tools I thought I needed to love.

On the morning of my wedding, I wore the cream gown my mother had worn. It was silk and smelt of lavender. Cousin Mae put rouge on my cheeks and on my lips. As her fingers touched my mouth, she slipped her hand around the back of my neck and held my head so that I could weep. I shook into the silk of her shoulder and thought of how nothing would ever be the same again.

When I had finished, I determined then that I would not cry again over any man. James Nolan was supposed to be good, but here he was dragging a young woman into a loveless marriage. So if he was happy with a wife who didn't love him, then that was exactly what he was going to get.

I smiled and charmed my way through the day of celebrations. I was, everyone agreed, the most beautiful bride Achadh Mor church had ever seen and James, being the popular teacher, drew out every neighbor in the vicinity to wish us well. It was gone ten before the last of them left the house and we settled into our first night alone together.

Two complete strangers—and I was determined that we should stay that way.

Seven

Dan was great the day we went out to Yonkers. He said that if I didn't like it, we didn't have to move there. He just wanted me to look, as it was something that we had to decide about together. He was trying so hard and with the patience of a saint, but the joint ownership thing hit me like a brick. Another complicated layer of commitment kicking in.

It's not that I never travel out of Manhattan; it's just that I prefer not to. I have lived on the Upper West Side most of my life, except for my university years in Galway. I found my apartment back in my twenties. Everyone was renting, but I had enough of my grandparents' Irish insecurity gene to push myself financially and purchase.

The thing that I love about the city is that it is always changing. You don't need to move because it moves around you. Restaurants transform themselves from Indian to Italian overnight; neighbors replace themselves every couple of years. If you redecorate, then sit still for a while and a new neighborhood will join you.

Since then, I have lived in this two-bedroom apartment on West Seventy-seventh every which way. Lived with a single futon until my job as a magazine editor yielded enough for me to decorate in late-eighties chrome and white leather. Then Parisian purple and gold-leaf chic through the self-consciously stylish nineties until, after years of lobbying the board, I finally got to knock down that wall and get the huge open-plan kitchen and living space I'd been dreaming of forever. My apartment is finally home. *My* home. First and only problem right there. I am not alone anymore.

The superintendent's hole in the basement was never an option, so Dan had been more or less living in my apartment since we met. Out of pure necessity, I paid lip service to the quaint "what's mine is yours" principle. I tried to restrain myself when he put his boots up on my original Eames chair and terrorized my much-loved kitchen implements with his clumsy ham-size hands. He put my Edwardian potato ricer in the dishwasher, where I found it rusting, devastated by the careless attack.

I didn't know if I could accommodate Dan in my life forever, but I did know I couldn't accommodate him in my apartment for much longer. It sounds dreadful, but I was beginning to think I would feel more in control renting it out to a high-paying tenant and living elsewhere with my lumbering husband.

Perhaps Dan putting my potato ricer in the dishwasher was part of some Machiavellian plot to move me to Yonkers?

Whatever.

Almost as soon as we got onto the Henry Hudson Parkway, I felt the agitation that fusses through me when I move too far out of the city. There is this snobbery, a superiority complex I have from being reared in the most cityish city in the world. No other city can quite match the cool island sanctum of Manhattan, but nowhere falls as glaringly short as some of the areas that surround it.

The roads yawn out from four lanes to eight and the landscape makes that subtle shift. I started to see four-wheel-drives, the occasional pickup, strip malls, aluminum siding, and patches of grass that are not public parks but owned by individuals. To me, this has always been a place with more space, yet less room to breathe; more churches, but less soul; more light, more sky, yet less to look at.

All the while, Dan babbled on and on about the area and the friends he had there. He was painting truly awful pictures for me of barbecues on decked patios, with jumbo packages of chemically spiced meat from price clubs frequented by people named Candy who have feathered bangs and use ketchup as a cooking ingredient.

His thought process is spoken out loud and along the lines of happily ever after in the suburban outback. Mine is a terrified implosion of panic. I knew that all I had to do was look at the house, say, "I don't want this," and things would stay as they were. But this is what Dan wanted. It's who he was, a man of simple tastes, conventional in that everyday, unremarkable way. I wanted something, someone different, a soul mate, and Dan wasn't it. With the right person, I could share Yonkers in an ironic, postmodern way. But with Dan, clearly, that was not going to happen.

We had been married one month. Dan bought me flowers. A mixed bunch in cellophane from a deli. It's the thought that counts—yet I just kept getting caught up in all these ways in which we were not right for each other. I don't need expensive flowers. I like simple but stylish. So buy me daisies from a florist, not roses from a deli. It's a small distinction, but a significant one to me. Shouldn't the right guy just know? Of course, it doesn't matter. It's a detail. Except that now that I was wedded to this person for life, a detail, barely discernible in the heady fog of our early romance, became intolerable once it had the weight of a lifetime attached. I know that it is hard adjusting to living with somebody else, but it just seemed like there were too many things: plaid shirts, fishing catalogs, the wrong flowers. Then the basics, which I hadn't chosen to notice before. Every day I seemed to become fixated on a different one. He blows his nose at the table. Once I noted this, I could see nothing else; he appeared to be blowing and wiping his nose continually. Dan was a professional nose-blower. How had I never seen this before? I wanted to say something, but I didn't. Because even though we were married, I didn't have that right.

I didn't love him. You have to love somebody before you can scream bloody murder at him for something as stupid as blowing his nose.

So I was living with this frenzied monologue in my head continually bleating on about all the irritating little things he did. He left the bathroom door open and talked to me while he peed. He needed a nasal-hair trim. He left his knife in the open jam jar. He put the butter back in the fridge, so it was always hard. I was boring *myself* with my endless list of petty complaints.

Dan and I were not made for each other, I knew that. He had no idea what was going on in my head. If he did, then it would undoubtedly be the end of our marriage. Perhaps I'd find the courage to come clean and do the right thing by both of us. Maybe I was just not cut out for marriage at all. Unable to compromise, or uncompromising. The former was bad, but isn't the latter a compliment? It means sticking with it, holding out for the real thing.

I wanted to be married. I wanted children, or at least one child. I am a food editor and writer. I create a feeling of home in magazines that people aspire to. I wanted to create something special with somebody else. But there has to be something more. You can't spin a lifestyle out of nothing. Otherwise it is just style with no life. You need love to build a home with conviction. And that crucial ingredient was missing for me.

I got married because I didn't want to be alone. Yet driving away from the city, my old life behind me and the possibility of a new one in front of me, I never felt more alone in my life.

Eight

hated James that first year. I thought him arrogant, the way he carried himself in public, as if he were equal to everyone else. I felt I knew my place and I remember him introducing me to the doctor and his wife and being annoyed that he thought we were suitable for such grand company. The lady invited me around for tea and it irritated me even more that they both appeared to like James. I told her I didn't have time for such niceties as my husband worked me too hard. I could see she was shocked by my brashness, but James laughed at my attempt to embarrass him, as if I was the wittiest woman around.

He was always in his element showing me off. Everywhere we went, he attracted people like a magnet, and the first thing he would always do was introduce me as his wife, his face flush with pride as if to say, "Look what I've got."

Although we both knew I did not belong to him. Not in any way that mattered.

Kilkelly Church had a long aisle and was rather grand. James and I had a place in the second row, just under the pulpit, where, as teacher in the local school, James was expected to sit. As he ushered me into the church pew before him each Sunday, he would place the flat of his hand gently on the small of my back. And for the first full year of our marriage, that was the only time James touched me.

FROM THE first night we spent together, I made it quite clear that if James Nolan wanted his marital rights, he was going to have to take them. I would not fight him off, my body was his property and it would be against God to deny him. But he knew how I felt. While I never said it, my dislike for him permeated our home. I made sure I was an exemplary wife in every way around the house. Up at six every morning with the hens fed, fire lit, and his shaving water warmed and waiting for him before he rose at eight. He ate hot porridge with cream and there was meat with two vegetables on the table at one o'clock each day. For tea, there was always a choice of cake, tart, or bread and jam. His shirts were starched and pressed and every item from his socks to his felt trilby hat were darned and steamed until they were restored to a better condition than the day they were bought. The house was so clean that a visitor might feel awkward putting a boot on my shiny flagstones, or dragging a dirty coat on one of my chairs. I was so scrupulous in my housekeeping that the very ashes in the grate held themselves in a tidy pyramid for fear of me.

If I worked hard, I knew that no one being, not even God, could question my honoring and respecting my husband. Only James and I knew that he did not want my honor or my respect. He wanted my love. I was withholding it and angry, and I did not have the love he wanted in me to give to him. I had already given it all away to somebody else.

Only when our bedroom door closed at night did the truth of our loveless arrangement emerge. James continued to sleep on the settle at the side of our bed that I had made up for him on our wedding night. I remember shaking with fear that first night in a stranger's bed, terrified that a man with whom I was barely acquainted would suddenly leap on me in the darkness. As the hours progressed, I almost wished his brutality upon me, so that it could be done with and the terrible waiting over.

It was only in the morning that I realized he had crept silently out of the room not one hour after lying down and spent the night sitting up in the kitchen, reading. I was nearly angrier with him over that than I would have been over the other. I felt deceived in expecting this barbaric ravaging when my Viking perpetrator was adjusting his reading glasses over *The Capuchin Annual.* This I didn't understand.

Night reading was something James did often in that first year. He never asked or suggested or cajoled or made any attempts on me whatsoever, except in often telling me I looked beautiful. I was not grateful for the way my husband was managing his passions; in my ignorance, I thought him weak. I think now that if he had taken a firmer hand to me that first year, our marriage might have been a more balanced affair.

But then, how suddenly we become saints, willing to give all our hearts once we know our sacrifice is no longer needed.

Against all expectations, what got me through that first year was James's mother, Ellie, who insisted from the first that I should call her by her Christian name. Widowed young, she had reared seven children, educating the older ones until they were old enough to help support the younger. She was a resourceful, extraordinary woman. Refusing to accept charity from her neighbors, she had farmed her children out to various relations while she spent several summers working in England alongside our local men. The fact that this had earned her respect and status among her neighbors, as opposed to scandalizing them, laid testament to the type of person she was. Ellie Nolan was not a craw-thumping, clergy-worshipping Catholic. She was a hardworking, generous woman who did not care what people thought of her. And it was a credit to our community that she was thought of so highly. I did not know or care about any of that when I found myself living next door to my new husband's invalid mother. All I knew was that, despite myself, I liked her and she was kindly towards me, which she certainly need not have been.

A routine developed quickly between us. After James had opened the school at nine o'clock, I would cross the short field with a tray for her breakfast. I would cook to please the old woman quicker than I would for her son. I found his praise cloying and false, given the strained situation between us. Ellie's praise was always genuine though she had no reason to give it. She confided that she was a poor cook and would go into ecstasies over my boxty pancakes, asking for the exact method, then laughing at the idea she would ever make them herself. Ellie could afford to make jokes against herself as she was so very easy to love. Her house was higgledy-piggledy, and as I would start to fuss around the place cleaning, she would call out for me to sit and read to her. It felt decadent somehow to be reading novels and poetry at eleven o'clock in the morning when there was work to be done, but Ellie insisted we feed our minds as well as our bodies.

Her favorite was Sir Walter Scott's dramatic poem "The Lady of the Lake." There was still plenty of fire in Ellie, and she loved the bloody descriptions of combat on the Scottish highlands, repeating every syllable alongside me:

Fell England's arrow flight like rain;
crests rose, and stoop'd, and rose again,
Wild and disorderly.

I waited for the women wailing over their perished loves, and while my voice quivered over some exaggerated declaration of love, I always felt that Ellie knew I was thinking about Michael. She certainly knew about us in the way that everybody knew I had been doing a line with the Yank. I always felt Ellie knew more still—that I did not love her son, despite the fact that I would leap up from my seat before midday and rush back to prepare his dinner.

I believed that Ellie loved James with the fierce, protective passion every mother has for her sons. But she befriended me anyway. She was in my life for such a short time, and yet she had a huge influence. Perhaps because she made me feel that I was not so bad a wife as I pretended to be. Perhaps her unconditional approval made me less cruel than I might have been towards James. Maybe this was her way of asking me to be a good wife to her son after she was gone. Certainly a direct request would not have worked. Or maybe she just liked me and was glad to have me related to her. I don't know—nor will I ever.

But this is what I believe: Ellie Nolan had more wisdom than I ever earned in the whole of my marriage, or will ever in the rest of my life. In losing her husband so young, she learned how little value we place on real love while we have it. The poetic passions of fiction are just that, a fiction. And the realities of love, the way it fades when you try to grab it, then clutches your guts with a painful squeeze of grief after you have lost it, reach so much further than a young girl's romantic dreams. Ellie struggled in the aftermath of her husband's death to feed, clothe, and educate seven children on her own. She understood that poetry and passion were for reading by the fire. But a woman who could cook well and keep a clean house for her working son was a good enough start.

Ellie knew that the love that starts strongest often weakens with time, giving up before the race is ended. It is often the slowest to start that will finish the race.

But this is not a lesson that anything other than time can teach you.

Nine

"This," Dan said as we pulled up at a small grocery store, "is McClean Avenue."

He said it like we had finally arrived at our destination. Not in Yonkers, but in "life." McClean Avenue is where you can buy last Sunday's *Irish Independent* and "tayto crisps," enjoy a cup of Barry's Tea with your imported sausages and bacon, or get drunk on Irish beer in an Irish bar with people who also *wish* they were Irish.

Dan's whole "Irish" angle really made me crazy. It was the only thing we truly had in common, yet our perception of what it means to be Irish couldn't have been more different. Although I wasn't born there, I spent much of my childhood and student years there. For me Ireland is the brooding brown boglands, lit up a thousand shades of purple and gold by a temperamental sun. It is the sour smell of burning turf on a wet day, and my grandmother's rhubarb tart. It is Joyce, Yeats, Behan, Patrick Kavanagh—a complex, creative heritage too vast to attempt explanation.

For Dan? It was green beer and rubbery brack cake.

I knew this because Dan came back out of the shop with a carton of milk and a cellophane-wrapped package claiming to be "genuine, original Irish Barm brack" made by a woman called Kitty. The sell-by date was the following fall and the list of ingredients a roll call of chemicals.

"This is crap," I said, and he looked hurt. Like I wasn't just talking about the cake. There was an atmosphere building between us. He knew he was doing something wrong but was afraid to ask me what it was. Then the guilt kicked in, the arbiter of my honesty. As soon as things got close to the truth, guilt always stepped in to create a smoke screen.

"I'll bake you a better brack than this, baby. A real Irish porter cake."

He leaned over and kissed me even though he was driving, and I wondered how it was possible I could turn myself into Doris Day so easily, and that, more unbelievably, I had married a man who believed me when I did.

As we wove our way upward, the houses got more affluent. It seems that money can buy character, and the higher we went, the more interesting the houses became. My cynicism toward Yonkers was temporarily quieted by a three-story Redbrick with beautiful wrought-iron balconies. Dan stopped the car and said, "Here we are."

I was stunned.

"Here?"

"This is it, baby."

"This? The Redbrick?"

"You like it?"

He was doing that thing that I couldn't bear: wagging his tail with boyish enthusiasm. Looking for my approval, my praise. "I love you" by another name.

"It looks OK."

Actually, I loved it already. But I couldn't tell him that. Dan had bought this house five years previously as an investment. Not just a financial investment, but in his belief that one day he would meet the right woman and have a proper home to put her in. If I said "yes" to this house, I was saying "yes" to so much more. It was idiotic to say that I did not feel ready to move into Dan's house, when I had already agreed to spend the rest of my life with him. But as long as we had our separate apartments and a temporary à-la-carte living arrangement, I could still see my escape door.

There was no escape door on Longville Avenue. Inside there were exposed beams, aged-oak floorboards, a basement full of cranky bits of furniture that needed polishing, upholstering, loving back to life. There was an original cast-iron bathtub languishing in a hallway, and a dresser with an enamel worktop and broken hinges. The house was a set of a dozen rooms waiting to be cast in their roles as nursery, kitchen, living room, bedroom.

Dan was directly behind me shuffling, gawking, hoping.

He started, "It's a real mess but . . ."

He wanted me to finish his sentence. To tell him I could see what he saw: that with his work and my eye this house could be a wonderful family home. I could see his dream, and I wanted to share it. Just not with him. The faded floral curtain over the back door shivered in a breeze and the sadness of my secret washed over me. I didn't answer but walked toward the back door, rattled it open, and stepped out into the garden. It was a wilderness.

I picked my way down a stone path that seemed to go on forever, then reached a bank of ivy and budding clematis that told me I had reached the end. To my left were young, green nettles, which, I made a mental note, would make excellent soup. To my right, I could see a stone cherub peering at me from behind the weeds. As I brushed them aside, the mossy figure fell with them. I leaned down to rescue him, and saw that he had fallen onto a bed of voluminous frilly leaves sprung with narrow red stalks.

It was rhubarb, growing wild.

Ten

We were married one year to the day when Ellie died.

James had made a small fuss over our anniversary, presenting me with a brooch in the shape of a swallow. I thanked him politely, and then placed it to one side of my dressing table, not bothering to try it on. As I prepared Ellie's breakfast, my mind was occupied with my shiny new trinket. If I wore it, it would give James a message of love. If I left it aside forever, perhaps he would not bother buying me another. I decided on a compromise. I would wear it across to Ellie's and show off what her son had given me. It would please her to see that James had made me happy.

It had taken me a full year to be willing to sacrifice a small corner of my pride for somebody else's happiness, and it was too late.

When I found her, Ellie was lying on her back with her rosary beads arranged on her lap. She had died peacefully in her sleep. She must have known herself she was going to die. There was no surprise in that; Ellie had seemed to know everything.

I wept over her cold body for one hour before fetching my husband. There are lies in tears. The ones we weep most loudly are usually for ourselves, yet how easily we can pass them off as grief.

I was fond of the old woman, but I allowed her to turn cold while I contemplated my own troubles. Ellie had provided a distraction, and now it was James and me alone. How was I going to cope?

Honesty, in my experience, is seldom an act of kindness; more often it is a brutal, selfish need to purge, thinly disguised as morality.

So I buried my face in the gray wool of Ellie's blanket, clutched at her hard, knotted fingers, and wept for all my misfortunes. I told her I did not love her son, but I promised I would never stop trying. And even as I said it, I knew that I had not tried to love him up to that point, beyond keeping him and his house clean and tidy.

After I had cried myself dry, I went to the schoolhouse and I told James that his mother had passed. He was stoic and kept the school open until lunchtime. Ellie was old, and when James was seen leaving the school stony-faced, the neighbors guessed at what had happened. The funeral began with barely an instruction from us.

The wake went on for three days and two nights. As was the custom, Ellie was laid out in her kitchen. It was the first funeral I had ever been directly involved in. The neighbors brought in their best crockery and laid out scones, sandwiches, tarts, cooked hams, chickens. For those few days, the house belonged to them, and they came and went as they pleased. Their message was clear: They had known and loved Ellie all of her life, and I was an interloper. An obscene amount of food and ten full bottles of whisky were consumed by a host of friends and strangers who came to pay their respects. James welcomed them all as if they had been as close to Ellie as he had been. He offered them food and drink as if they were as deserving of comfort as he.

I stayed by his side and together we nodded and accepted condolences until we could barely stand. It was the first thing in our marriage that I can truly say we did together. I had respected Ellie, and for those few days I admired James for how he was handling his grief and for the generous way he received his guests.

For the burial, I wore my fitted black coat and a smart woollen hat that Ellie had once said she would like me to have. On my lapel I wore the swallow James had given me. It was inappropriately decorative, but I didn't care. Neither did James, and I felt Ellie would have been pleased at our small rebellion. It did not rain down on us, but stayed dry for the Sorrowful Mysteries, the final decade of the Rosary. I held James's arm throughout the service as a public show of support. As the clay clattered down onto the coffin, I felt James's hand reach for mine and I did not move it one way or the other but let him hold me. His fingers felt as cold and dry as his mother's had two days beforehand.

We arrived home, the two of us alone again as we had been on our wedding night. James was in the footless, disbelieving grief of the adult orphan. A mother draws a map for her child and places herself at the center of it. Her death wipes that map clean. She leaves you knowing you must redraw it to survive and yet not knowing where to start. James was left staring at a blank page and a young, foolish wife who did not love him as he wanted her to.

Our house seemed strange after spending all of our time up in Ellie's, as if we had been out of it for months instead of only three days. That is death's dirtiest trick; the way it plays with time so that the funeral seems to go on forever, yet when it's over, you are placed back in your first moment of shock, as if it hadn't happened at all.

I asked James if he wanted food, and he declined. Although it was barely past four in the afternoon, I went into the bedroom, closed over the curtains, and lay down in the bed. My eyes were like lead, but as sleep began to pull me down into its velvet black-ness, I suddenly felt something behind me. I sat up in the bed and called out in terror. My voice was so loud that I hardly recognized it, and that served to frighten me even more.

James had climbed into the bed next to me. Although he was under the covers, I could see that his arms and shoulders were bare, which I took to mean he was naked. I did not know whether to laugh or cry, but I wasn't afraid. The room was light and he was looking at me.

His eyes were stuck on my face. Love being too much to hope for, he was searching for the finest thread of feeling. Evidence to prove there could be some comfort in being married to me. He would not have expected much after the year we had had together. Just enough to get him through that night. Enough warmth for him to hide in; enough spirit to hold him up; enough strength for him to cling to. He found nothing and I knew then that he had seen my disdain for him, and heard it in my voice when I cried out in shock.

In that instant, I witnessed the depth of his grief. His face crumpled in on itself, and he turned his back to me. Our bed be-came a boat floating on the waves of his grief, as it rocked in rhythm with his sobbing. I might have lost patience, were these the petulant, self-pitying tears I was so familiar with in myself. But this was justified grief. He was a naked, rejected man unable to physically lift himself away from me, such was the power of his sorrow.

I was afraid, not of what James might do, but of what I could not do. Afraid of my own coldheartedness. So afraid that I tried.

I reached out my hand and I touched the top of his head. His hair was wiry and this surprised me. I had looked at it often and wondered, yet never touched it before. I had expected his body to freeze, as if a single innocent touch from me was enough to quell a mountain of passion. I was disappointed when he continued to cry. More than that, I wanted him to stop. I did not feel I was strong enough to bear witness to such pain. So I leaned across his back, and clumsily kissed the wet of his cheek.

He turned on me suddenly and kissed me hungrily on the mouth. I felt betrayed, as if he had tricked love out of me by weeping for his dead mother. I knew that was not the case, but that was how it felt.

When you are young, feelings are your truth; love is how you feel. The years have taught me that love is not an emotion that you feel about someone, but what you do for them, how you grow with them.

That night I gave James my body. I did not give with the feeling or the passion I had given to Michael Tuffy. Although I choose not to remember it now, I probably did not give with much good grace. But I gave.

In the years that came after, I never told him I felt only pity in my heart for him that first night. That truth was hard and I knew it would hurt him, so I kept it to myself. I compromised my own truth for his.

Yet the truth is not always as it seems. Many years afterwards, James told me that the person I had called out for in my fear had been him.

Sacrifice

*In sacrificing something we believe, we can be
rewarded with something we love.*

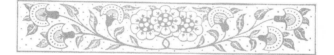

Honey Cake

Although I always had a sweet tooth, I never liked honey until I ran clean out of sugar one day and tried this.

Mix 1 tablespoon corn flour, 2 teaspoons baking powder, and 1lb flour and set aside. Cream together about 5oz butter with just short of a full jar of honey. Gradually add the dry ingredients, along with 3 eggs beaten into a ¼ pint milk, until the mixture is smooth and creamy. You can add 1 teaspoon of vanilla, or cinnamon to taste—but I always preferred it plain. Turn into a greased loaf tin and cook in a medium hot oven for up to 1½ hours.

Eleven

Replacing sugar with honey may seem like a straight swap, but it isn't as simple as that. Honey works best when used with sugar, not instead of it. Sugar does the hard work of sweetening, and honey acts as the top note. Of course, a lot depends on the honey—and as with all ingredients, some are better than others. Granddad kept bees, so the honey Grandma Bernadine used was unique and fresher than anything you could buy in a shop. I know. Westside Market stocks forty-six brands and I've tried them all. You can use a full jar of really expensive stuff and you still might not even be able to taste it. Generally, taking sugar out of a cake recipe for the sake of a little honey is a pointless sacrifice.

DAN'S PARENTS were Irish Catholics, and he came near the middle of eight children. He was the only one who wasn't married by age thirty-five, and the only one who didn't attend Mass each Sunday. By his family's standards, he was wayward and unconventional. A real wild card.

Eileen, his mother, was a substantial woman who turned every question into a barked instruction: "You'll have tea?"

She spoke in a Cavan accent distorted with a Yankee twang.

Her home was a shrine to marriage and children. It was crammed with trophies, china dolls, pictures of children in heart-shaped frames and frames with teddy bear motifs. More cherubic faces were emblazoned on mugs, coasters, and calendars. Every surface was groaning with wedding photographs surrounded by Waterford crystal or ornate gilt: nudging boys in navy suits, their seventies haircuts skimming their shoulders; girls with glittering eyes and toothy smiles in leg-o'-mutton sleeves. All of Dan's family were interconnected; they godparented one another's children, bought one another's cars, shared ownership of ride-on mowers. They shopped at price clubs together, passed on information about A&P specials to one another, visited the mall in hair-sprayed, buggy-pushing gangs. They decorated one another's houses and fed one another's children. Reigning over this car-pooling, baby-sitting, meal-sharing, mall-mashing industry was Eileen Mullins. She cooked and coordinated, but mostly she just presided. Inscrutable, indestructible, in charge. Dan was a little afraid of his mother, which I found disconcerting.

In contrast, Dan's father was a wiry, self-contained fellow who mostly just kept out of everyone's way.

I was with the father, hoping to stay on the outskirts, but it seemed I was not to get away with it.

DAN LEFT his superintendent's job in Manhattan when we moved out to Yonkers and started doing contract building work. With his vast network of friends and relations in Yonkers it meant that he was getting enough small jobs to earn him as much as he was earning before, with plenty of time to work on the house.

One Sunday at noon Dan said, "You better get dressed, honey—we're due over for lunch at one."

I was confused. This was a surprise and I didn't like surprises.

Especially when it comes to food, and especially when I was exhausted from unpacking boxes of junk in an effort to make our house home.

"What, have you booked somewhere?"

Dan raised his eyebrows quizzically, as if the answer was so obvious it didn't needed stating.

"Mom's place, of course."

Of course.

NINETY-EIGHT PERCENT of Dan's extended family lived in or around Yonkers. An only child, I was raised in a loft with a single parent. How was I to know that marriage was going to suck me into a vortex of relations? That saying "I do" would initiate me into a tribe of women who rummage in one another's handbags for tissues?

"Sorry, Dan, but you should have told me earlier. I have things to do."

The vastness of the understatement wasn't lost on him. We first visited this house just five weeks ago, and already we had packed up my apartment and prepared it for rental. Dan had knocked a wall through from the front to the back of the house, downstairs, and was preparing the plumbing and electricity for my new kitchen. I had planned pared-down Shaker style units with open shelves and an imported solid-fuel Waterford Stanley stove. Completely different from the high tech state-of-the-art one in my apartment, it was going to be a grown-up working kitchen for serious hands-on cooking. I could get appliances in as and when I needed them. But for the time being, I wanted to keep my cooking as simple as possible. Perhaps because my head was swirling with complications, my body craved the clarity of physical activity; the one-two-three order of mixing and beating and pouring. Only the sitting and waiting for it to bake disturbed me, so I turned to the garden and within days had a vegetable patch cleared and ready to be planted.

The day before, Dan had joined me and, without asking if I needed his help, begun to rake the soil while I remained on my knees crumbling it with my fingers. Mincing compost into the square yard of gray grit I had meticulously weeded the day before. He babbled on for a few minutes, asking me questions about what I was going to plant, then the two of us fell into a concentrated silence. We worked well together in those first few weeks in Yonkers. Dan was physical, strong—and so, I discovered, was I. We made a good team, and I found myself appreciating the way we could pass tools or make each other coffee without the other having to ask. It was a kind of intimacy, an easing into our marriage. I kept busy because when I was working, I was less aware of my guilt, the fear that all I was doing in creating this home was building more obstacles to hinder my eventual escape.

The following weekend was the Food Writers' Symposium in Chicago and I was looking forward to the break. It's bad to want a break from marriage after just two months, but I had decided it would give me time on my own to try to sort my head out.

Dan could have mentioned lunch at his mother's house while we were out in the garden the day before, but he didn't. I needed to draw the line. If I went with him, then we would be expected to go every Sunday, something he'd always been expected to do before meeting me.

"We only need to go for an hour," he said.

I was not aware of the kind of emotional blackmail that Eileen could inflict on Dan. My mother had always been an independent woman. She did her thing and I did mine. My grandparents longed for my visits to Ireland. I knew that, but they never made me feel obliged and always celebrated my career successes even though they meant less frequent vacations spent visiting them. This pleading was alien territory to me.

"Please, Tressa."

However, I was learning real fast.

Dan was a good man and he was doing all the right things. He could plumb a toilet, fix a roof, wire a stove—he never said "no." He was staying up all night to put together kitchen units to my (exacting) specifications. He had accepted my lies of being exhausted from the stress of moving and had laid off me in bed. I could see how he was putting everything he had into this marriage, and yet it was not enough. I knew it would never be enough because whatever it was I needed to make me feel fulfilled, content, *sure*—that mysterious ingredient that just said this was right— Dan did not have it. Not for me. No matter how hard he tried.

But because he was trying, I felt guilty. So I gave in.

"OK, I'll get dressed. One hour, then we come home—right?"

He was beaming like a prize-winning schoolboy and it was making me nervous.

I WAS not in Eileen's house five minutes when I realized what a monumental aberration it was that I had managed to avoid this Sunday lunch gathering for so long. There were a lot of people there, maybe twenty including the children. It always alarmed me when I saw how many there were in Dan's family; names and ages started whirring and they seemed to blur in front of my very eyes. They were all greeting me with the warmth one might reserve for somebody returned from the brink of death. Their relief was palpable, like *at last* Dan's wife has graced us. I realized that Dan's casual "we'll pop in for an hour" invite had come after weeks of intense family pressure. So now there was this layer of knowledge: that I knew that Dan knew that I didn't like his family, even though I had never said anything to suggest it. And now *they* knew that I didn't like them because it had taken us so long to respond to this ongoing Sunday lunch summons.

Basically—it was one of those buttock-clenching, awkward moments.

When we entered, Eileen grunted at me briefly, but that meant nothing. She was from the generation before hugging was invented. Stern matriarchs who provide shelter and food, but don't offer affection after your fifth birthday. No wonder her kids were all grinning at me like frightened rabbits.

I asked, "Can I help, Eileen?"

A sister-in-law, Shirley, caught my eye, and raised her brow a degree, although I knew that she didn't mean her fellowship to comfort me. Shirley was a cheap, competitive cow. She'd worn a white gauzy dress to our wedding—and no underwear. Nipples in the chapel. Classy.

The twins leaped up to help their mother. Kay and Connie are identical, right down to their square, straight teeth and their bubbly personalities. They were mercilessly upbeat and friendly. You had to like them, although their appearance was unsettling. Kay wore her bangs side parted and tucked behind her ears, Connie had a back-combed fan. It's sad to think that their senses of individuality were so crucially contained in a hair-spray can. The twins both seemed much younger than their thirty years and still lived at home.

There was no order to the meal. Cutlery was thrown onto the center of the table along with an open packet of napkins. Kay handed out (un-warmed) plates, which were supplemented by disposable party ones; men wandered to get beer from the fridge and women took the opportunity to call to them for a Sprite. Connie

and Eileen started to carry out platters of food, and guests haphaz-
ardly cleared away newspapers, bills, kiddie cups, Walkmans—
the miscellaneous stuff that gathers in a kitchen—to make room
on every crammed surface. The food was mostly fried meat—
drumsticks, steakhouse burgers—accompanied by man-made
variations of the potato—fries, waffles, wedges. Everyone grabbed
at it hungrily and started dipping into bowls full of various store-
bought condiments.

Shirley was picking at a bread roll with her curved fuchsia
nails and poking shreds of dough into the corner of her mouth
with the reluctance of the vocational slimmer.

"Bet this is different to what you're used to, Tressa."

I knew the comment was designed to make trouble and there
was no "right" response but everyone looked at me, waiting for the
new family recruit to make her reply. I smiled as brightly as I
could and said, "It all looks delicious."

With that, Eileen picked up a plate of ribs and stuck it under
my nose. I took one and she nodded toward a bowl of sauce. She
was going to police my eating, check the fancy food writer's response to her cooking. I was not, despite being a food snob, a fussy
eater. But this pressure was making me feel physically sick and the
vinegary smell from the dripping meat did not help. Dear God, I
was going to hurl. I could feel the shocked faces follow me onto
the patio.

Dan came straight out after me and when he laid his hand on
my shoulder, it released a breath I didn't know I had been holding. For no specific reason I could determine, I started to cry. He
led me to a corner of the patio where nobody could see us and
wrapped himself around my head and shoulders. He didn't care
that I was sobbing in the middle of what was supposed to be a
happy family gathering, and he didn't ask what was the matter

with me. This was just as well because I didn't have the first clue myself. It was a relief, briefly, not to think about it and just let myself go.

Dan held onto me until I managed to gather myself back together, then he took my chin in his hand and wiped my wet cheek with his palm. I felt about ten years old.

"I guess Mom's ribs are pretty bad, huh?"

I managed a smile and said, "Thanks."

"Thanks for jack shit, baby—that's my job," he said, then took my hand and walked me back into the kitchen. In a funny way, I think he was pleased that I had snapped; it showed him I was human.

"Tressa's got a bug, folks. I'm taking her home."

They were all concerned, although I could see Shirley smirking in the corner as if to say, "Welcome to Ma Mullins's Sunday Bonanza, bitch."

As we were walking out the door, she called after us, "See you at the first communion next weekend?" and I could feel Dan's hand weaken over mine.

Twelve

he years passed and brought with them the inevitable intimacy of routine. I knew James's footsteps on the gravel of the road, I could trace the pattern of his body in our bed, I grew used to the smell of his skin, so that I found comfort in it. Still, I would not let go of my ideal, and not one single day passed when I did not think of Michael. Over those early years especially, I remember walking out in the field at the back of our house late at night and looking up at the stars.

Michael.

I would say his name and imagine that he could hear me.

I still love you, Michael. I still love you.

In saying it out loud, I was able to make it real again. So I was not an ordinary country schoolteacher's wife, but that passionate young woman again, victim of that greater kind of love. A stream of whispers pouring out of me: *I still love you, I still love you*, over and over so that the words might make a line that would carry up and up, across the galaxies and find where he was. How many words would it take to get to America? How many to bring him back to me again? He would never forget me. Not Michael. Love like we had never dies. It never grows old or dulls with the bland, gray shades of familiarity. Love as vibrant as ours would live forever.

In those early years, my husband became my family. I visited my parents only occasionally and always out of duty rather than pleasure. The estrangement brought about by Ann's refusing my dowry never healed between my aunt and myself. I think now that by staying angry with her it was a way of keeping Michael alive in my heart. My mother's humiliation at being refused my dowry softened in time, especially once she knew I was settled with James. Although I did grow fonder of my husband, I could not say that I loved him. But I did come to understand that being married to him was not the disaster that I thought it would be. Although I did not fully appreciate it at the time, we had a good life. James, spurred on by my example, started to rise early and developed more of an interest in small farming, so we had a modest head of cattle in addition to his teaching income. I kept hens and reared pigs for the slaughter as my mother had done, and James took up beekeeping when war loomed and sugar shortages were threatened. Between us, we were virtually able to feed ourselves and sell any surplus honey and eggs to a shopkeeper in Ballyhaunis. With the spare cash, we made improvements to our house. We had running water in the scullery and a range built into the wall where the fire had been. I had the tailor, Tarpey, make me three suits a year, and I bought fabric from him to make my own dresses. One year, we had a four-day holiday in Dublin. We stayed in great style at the Gresham Hotel, took tea in Bewley's Coffee House. I bought cinnamon and coriander and all kinds of spices from Findlaters on Harcourt Street. We went to the cinema and saw *Random Harvest,* then walked up and down O'Connell Street into the late evening. I wore a lilac suit and James a long trench coat and a Trilby hat cocked over one eye. I had bought him the gift of an ivory-capped walking cane, and he swung it grandly as if he were an English gentleman. I remember thinking that I was lucky enough to be married to such an elegant man. Although I would always stop myself short, always pull back. I was afraid to let go and let myself love him. Afraid I would lose the bit of power I had, if I didn't keep him at arms' length. Those few days in Dublin, though, I felt as if we had everything we could possibly want in life. And we did. Except for the one thing each of us wanted more than life itself.

For me, it was Michael.

For James, it was a child.

James knew I did not want children early on in our marriage, and being an educated, sensitive man, he went along with my wishes and took steps to avoid impregnating me. There are ways that are not against nature or God, but they only work in tandem with luck. And we were lucky.

I had witnessed the birth of my cousin Mae's first son, and any idea I may have had about having a baby had been thrown out with the bucket of blood that she shed. When the midwife saw how shocked I was, she said, "It's the most natural thing in the world." So is death, I thought—and we spend a lifetime avoiding that.

I was not maternal by nature. Babies and children left me cold. Some women who don't love their husbands have children so they can have somebody to love. I needed to love the man I was going to have children with, if I was going to sacrifice my body, my dignity in that way. I was prepared to shrug off the snide comments as the years passed without our conceiving. The sideways looks in Mass when another infant was christened, their screams reverberating around the chapel eaves, drowning out the priest's murmuring. Neighbors and James's sisters looked at me with disappointment, disbelief, and latterly, pity. I didn't care. I thought they were all fools. Babies, as far as I could see, were selfish, squawking, sucking parasites.

No. I was not one of nature's natural mothers.

After six years, without saying anything, James stopped withdrawing from me during lovemaking. He was well over forty and I was edging ever closer towards thirty.

People would make assumptions if you remained childless, and one of the assumptions they made was that your husband was not a "real" man. James was educated, kept himself neat, and had married late. He was an easy target, and I felt for him because I knew people would be talking. Extra pressure came every year as his brothers' wives and his one married sister were having at least one baby a year between them. I could see James was hurt that we were seen to be not "producing," and I assumed his pride was taking a bashing.

I said nothing when he changed our routine. I just took myself from the bed immediately after we had made love, washed myself thoroughly, and prayed.

The tension we had experienced in the first year came back into our marriage as if it had never been away. James had grown more sure of me, but I was still no pushover, and we waged the second of our long-standing silent wars. I became physically elusive, which was my only weapon. James in turn started to behave out of character, which I found unsettling. When I scolded him (as I did almost every day) over some household trivia, I could see his chin set in anger, and once or twice I feared he might rise up at me. He became irritable, criticizing the priest and complaining about his job on an almost daily basis. One Sunday, I caught sight of him as he looked up from his book to check the weather through the kitchen window. Pure sadness washed across his face, an expression of devastated loss like there had been after Ellie died. James had a long nose and slim delicate features that gave him an erudite, refined expression. When that confident, sophisticated face became sullied with anguish, the extremity of it tore at me terribly.

I wanted to reach over as I had done the night we buried Ellie. Except that this time I knew exactly what words would make his sorrow disappear and I couldn't speak them because I knew I was not prepared to follow them through. If I were a different, weaker kind of woman, I might have lied his pain away.

I did not love James but I was not coldhearted and I could see that he was hurt. My mistake was in believing, after almost ten years of marriage, that I knew him. I thought that his pride was at stake. That it was his craving for convention, the respect of his peers that was making him want a child. You can live a lifetime in ignorance of a person if you don't put your own needs aside to give them room to show you who they really are.

It was only after our daughter was born that I came to truly understand how James simply yearned to be a father.

Thirteen

I was scheduled to go to the Food Writers' Symposium in Chicago the following week, when my agent, Roseanne, rang to discuss various business. It felt weird talking to her standing in the middle of the half-painted hallway in my wreck of a house. It was my voice, saying the same sort of stuff as usual, and even though it had only been the usual number of weeks since I'd gotten her bi-monthly "darling" call, it felt like I had been out of circulation forever. I often hide away, especially when I am working on developing recipes. But with the wedding, and the house move, and no kitchen to work in, it felt like I had gone into hiding from myself.

I was lost and started to think about who I had been before I met Dan: Tressa Nolan, thirty-seven, Irish American, single, successful food writer, living comfortably on the Upper West Side. My morning routine had been a ten minute walk in the park, followed by a Mocha Frappuccino coffee from Starbucks; my morning's work interrupted by delivery guys arriving with fish, meat, and organic dairy. Then I'd meet a girlfriend for lunch, or else think up an excuse to wander down to Citarella and splurge on chocolate or delicious olives, followed by a root around Westside

Market's vegetables, looking for ideas. All of the best ingredients I could possibly need were within a few blocks or could be ordered to the door.

I had liked my life how it was, and realized that I had lost it. Literally.

The house, Dan, his family, mall shopping, the two of us pushing a grocery cart around Farmers' Market with thousands of other Saturday supermarket couples, that was my life now. It didn't feel like it belonged to me, and I didn't know that it ever would. I had spent years creating a routine that worked and that was now gone. I had to find new shops, new suppliers, and I felt too set in my ways to be bothered. Truthfully—I didn't know that I felt committed enough to my new life to start over.

I didn't know what I was expecting from married life. Was the life I wanted just the life I had with the additional benefit of testosterone? The same of everything with somebody strong to put up shelves and demystify furniture instructions? Was I really that shallow? That cynical?

In some ways, I wished I was.

The truth was, the vision I'd had for myself was what I had: a good man like Dan and a big old house to renovate, with enough of a plot out back for vegetables.

But the important expectation, the only one that mattered, was that I would be happy. And I wasn't.

Happily ever after—so how does that work? Two months into my marriage and I was miserable. It was just not working.

I woke up in the morning and the first thing I thought was, "I don't love Dan."

I'd work like a dog all day so that I didn't have to think about it, then last thing at night it came back: "I don't love Dan."

I wanted to love him. I *needed* to love him, but I just couldn't. Couldn't, wouldn't, never would.

What the hell was I going to do? I couldn't stay married to a man who I didn't love because it was not fair to either of us. Dan had it all there on paper. He was handsome, a listener, affectionate— I knew he would make a wonderful father and a loyal husband. And he loved me. He really did.

So why couldn't I just love him back? I knew in my head that I had married a good man, but my heart just wasn't responding. It felt flat and underwhelmed and I knew that wasn't right. It was a mystery to me that I could see all of Dan's good qualities but I still could not drum up a feeling of love for him. But then I knew that falling and, more important, staying in love is a mysterious process. You just have to wait until it happens to you. Maybe I just should have waited longer.

Maybes aside, I knew that Dan deserved better than this. He deserved a woman who adored the ground he walked on. A woman who would do anything for him.

A woman who would give up the most important event in her work calendar to attend his niece's first communion.

HE HAD dropped hints about it, but he wouldn't ask outright. Dan knew that this conference was really important to me. I had told him that on Sunday, as soon as we had left his mother's. He had told me that his entire family was gathering afterward at his Mom's for an informal reunion with some cousins from Ireland. His mother's brother, whom she hadn't seen for twenty years, would be there. It was kind of a historic event really. Not just Deirdre's first communion. He hadn't mentioned it before because he knew it clashed with my conference.

I told him that was really understanding of him and gave him a kiss.

The following day over breakfast Dan mentioned in a voice that was meant to sound casual, but didn't, that actually, there would be quite a lot of people who weren't at our wedding coming to the first communion. I looked forlorn and said I was really sorry, that it really was, truly, a terrible pity that the two things clashed. That if it had been any event other than this, I might have been able to change it. He shrugged and said it didn't really matter, but he looked as if he had just been run over by a bus.

The theme continued over supper with the revelation that it was a real shame I couldn't make it to the first communion because his Uncle Patrick was kind of coming over from Ireland especially to meet me.

I kept my head. That was just awful, I said, but I felt sure I would get the chance to meet Uncle Patrick while he was here— perhaps your mother could bring him around for supper the following week? Not possible, unfortunately, said Dan, because Uncle Patrick was going to stay with his friend, the priest, in Los Angeles the day after the communion, and this really was our only chance to meet him.

A tragedy, I conceded. If only somebody had taken the trouble to notify me when Uncle Patrick was booking his flights, then we might have arranged our lives around his trip. It was a last minute thing, Dan rushed to inform me, he got a cheap deal. I was drawing breath on my final "Oh well, never mind," when Dan launched into a soliloquy about how his sister Kay had been really upset when he had broken the news that I might not be going. And poor little Deirdre, who had been telling all her friends that her new aunt would be at her party, was upset as well. Then he ended with the extraordinary information that his Mom hadn't made it clear how important this Sunday was to her because she didn't want to put us under any pressure.

So. No pressure then.

"What can I do, Dan?"

There was a pause. Check-mate. I didn't walk away because I got this terrible feeling that it wasn't over. It should have been. Important work event for his new wife versus lunch with aging distant relative? No competition surely.

Dan looked down at his feet and eventually said, "You could cancel your trip."

He said it really quietly and meekly. Like he knew he was wrong. More than that—like he was afraid.

I said nothing. I didn't know what to say. I had never seen him like this before. Vulnerable. Exposed. When he looked up at me, his chin was shaking and he was looking at me in that I-don't-care, defensive male way. The look they put on before the inevitable rejection, so they save face.

In that moment, I didn't care if Dan was afraid of his mother or me or his Uncle Patrick. I just knew that he had handed me something and was waiting for me to throw it back at him. I wasn't comfortable holding it; nobody had ever given me this kind of power before. Nobody had ever loved me enough to care if I turned up to some lousy family gathering.

Part of me wanted to find out the reason why he felt he needed me to be there so badly, then rationalize it away, so he could go without me. Isn't that what you are supposed to do? Communicate, talk about your problems, then reach an agreement about dealing with them. Except I knew that would have just been the scenic route to getting my own way. I thought the party was less important than my work. But Dan wanted me to go. He needed me to be there. Sometimes why and how just don't matter. Dan was afraid for some reason, and he needed me to be there. It was a straight yes or no.

"OK. I'll cancel Chicago and come to the communion."

I don't know what I was expecting—tears, declarations of heartfelt gratitude? An apparition of the Virgin Mary, come to welcome me to the fellowship of eternal martyrs?

Dan just said, "Thanks, baby," and gave me a squeeze. Then he drained his coffee cup, brought it over to the sink, and switched on the TV.

I sacrificed an important work event to make him happy and he flicked on the TV?

Suddenly I felt very, very married.

Fourteen

ames was very close to his brother Padraig, in age and appearance as much as anything else. We got along all right in the end, but we disapproved of each other for years. Padraig disliked the refined way of life I encouraged: trips to Dublin, elegant clothes, matching shoes and bags and their like. He found me ludicrous and shallow and I found him scruffy and too ardent in his politics—a subject that, as a younger woman, bored me to death. However, as the years passed, a grudging respect developed.

"No china today, Bernie?"

"And have you break every piece on me?"

"That only happened once!"

"Yes—and it'll not happen again."

"Such a strict mistress—James, I don't know how you put up with her silliness."

"He likes my ways well enough because my husband is a gentleman."

"Is that why he gets his tea in a china cup and I get mine in a tin mug?"

"Be grateful you're not drinking it out of a bucket with the dogs in the yard, Padraig."

Then my brother-in-law would throw his head back and laugh until the tears fell down his face.

Padraig was the only person who dared shorten my name to the commonplace "Bernie." I didn't like it one little bit but he was incorrigible, so he got away with it. Though I would never have admitted it, I got a certain thrill from my brother-in-law's light-hearted abuses, as I liked to think he did from mine.

Padraig and his wife, Mary, had seven children, and had been married only a couple of years before us. I liked Mary and we should have been great friends, except that we had barely exchanged a full sentence since the day we had met, much less a real adult conversation. Children constantly surrounded her. At her breast, running around her feet, calling at her from another room. There was not a moment of her day when she was not feeding, answering, scolding, or tending to one of them. Her house was a pigsty and horrified me at the time, although looking back on it now, it was just the home of seven children. Realizing what an easy life I had in comparison, every week I would call in with a cake and offer to help with her chores. Often, Mary would be sitting on the settle in the kitchen, surrounded by damp nappies and dirty dishes, reading to her children. It mystified me how she could be so calm in the midst of all this chaos, astonished me how she could be so patient as to occupy her children, play with them, when there was so much important work to be done in the house. She was an appalling housekeeper, there was no doubting that— but I admired her nonetheless because in her shoes, I knew I would surely have dropped dead long ago from nerves. Or—may God forgive me—buried at least two of the little so-and-sos and prayed that nobody would notice.

Some days, I would enjoy it. There was an adorable set of twin girls, Theresa and Katherine, who would call out "Honey!

Honey! It's honey auntie!" when they saw me walk up the driveway to their house. "A kiss for a cake," I would tease them and they would shower me with squealing kisses, their little hands grasping for my basket.

But the moments of pleasure were always outbalanced by the bloody knees and the relentless bawling. I liked the twins because they paid me some attention, but mostly my nieces and nephews were a moving, messy blur of noise and neediness. Mary and Padraig seemed happy in their life but the disorderly mess of their home was my most effective contraception.

Until the twins' first holy communion.

I decided to host a party for Theresa and Katherine's big day. The weather was warm enough for the children to play outside, and I enjoyed baking and preparing the house for guests. Hospitality was something that was generally offered in a casual drop-in way in those days, but entertaining James's family in a grander fashion was a way I had of making up to him for the way things were between us.

James loved people and took every opportunity to fill our house with them in all shapes and sizes. When we were first married, I scolded him constantly for bringing neighbors in, inviting his pupils' parents to call by, having an open house policy with his siblings. My own parents had been ferociously protective of our privacy and nobody ever came into our home. But James, with his unfettered, popular ways, won out and I rose to the challenge of being as organized as a priest's housekeeper, with a selection of fresh cakes constantly at the ready. I grew to like the flow of visitors. It broke the day up and kept me on my toes. Taking my apron on and off, always having to have tidy hair and smart shoes by the scullery door to change into, in case it was the priest or the doctor. It gave James and me something to talk about and stopped us from dwelling on ourselves. That was a trick I learned about marriage early on. Keeping myself busy.

I made a particular fuss over the twin girls and dug out special treasures for them both from my own collection. A pair of lace gloves for one and a set of mother-of-pearl rosary beads for the other. There would be in excess of eight adults and so many children I didn't dare count on the day. On the Saturday before, James killed and prepared three chickens, then he went to Kilkelly and collected ham, jelly, oranges, custard powder, glacé cherries, tinned peaches, chocolate, a bottle of sweet sherry, and a bottle of Sandeman port. He spent four shillings on toffee, so that each child would have a bag of sweets to go home with. It cost a small fortune, but neither of us cared. We had the money and it gave James pleasure to spend it on his family. With no children of our own, I saw my indulging him in this way as some small compensation.

Things had been cold between us for months, but in jointly preparing for the party, a temporary truce had been called. When James found me still baking at seven o'clock in the evening, he rolled up his sleeves to help. I felt relieved that my husband's dour mood seemed to be passing, and so I insisted he don my frilliest apron, then instructed him in measuring, beating, and mixing a honey cake. When I realized in horror that we had run out of sugar, James, in high spirits, tipped in nearly a full jar of the honey. He made an awful mess, trying to halt the sticky stream by turning the jar on its side, dripping cheeky wiggles all over the clean table. We laughed at his ineptitude at managing the honey, and my end-of-the-world dramatics over the sugar shortage. James finally declared that he would never complain about his job ever again, as a woman's work was infinitely more complicated and the stress of it unmatched.

I don't remember there ever having been as much warmth between us as on that night. Although there was no reason for it, there was an air of anticipation about the party. As if, in our own separate worlds, we felt like something magical was about to happen.

James made love to me that night. As I rose from the bed as usual, I could feel his arms weighing down on my breast to try and hold me there. When I pulled myself away, he turned his body with a suddenness that indicated his disdain.

The party was a success, although James had detached himself from me again. He did not comment on my outfit as we left for the church, which was his way of punishing me. While he laid his hand on my waist to guide me into the pew, all life had gone out of his touch. I felt a pang of sadness at how quickly our rift had returned, and although I was busy making gallons of tea and slicing mountains of cake and keeping legions of children out of my parlor, I don't think the disappointment of that entirely left me.

The honey cake was a huge success and gone within minutes. People said it was the nicest cake they had ever eaten, and asked what I had done differently to make it so special. I tried to find James and tell him of his victory, but he was deep in conversation and I was afraid to intrude. I had been feeding James's tolerance with these small shows of affection over the years, but he had moved onto a different level now, and I sensed that it was going to take more than a lighthearted compliment to bring him back.

Perhaps it was that realization that made me see what I did. Or perhaps it was just a moment of clarity that comes to us all when we know that something is right.

It was a small thing.

I had just given Katherine the lace gloves. She was so excited she ran off, without thanking me, to show them to her mother. Mary was distracted adjudicating some toddler scrap, and sent Katherine back to show her father. Padraig was sitting close to where I was standing, talking with James. Katherine put the glove on, her tiny hand swimming in it, and held it out for her father to look. As Padraig studied the lace glove, I watched his seven-year-old daughter's face and was taken aback by what I saw. Her eyelids were flickering in anticipation of what her father would think of the gloves, a look of such deep concern that you would not expect it from a child. After less than a minute he said, "They are beautiful, Katherine. You look like a real lady." I am sure Padraig gave me a flirtatious wink then, but if he did, I didn't see it. I could not take my eyes from young Katherine's face. Her eyes lit up with adoration for him, undiluted by age or experience or expectation. She was looking at Padraig the way I had looked at Michael Tuffy. With pure love.

I had never looked at my husband in that way, and I knew I never would. But James was a good man nonetheless, and he deserved to be loved in that same adoring way.

I knew then that I had to give him a child.

Fifteen

What do you wear to a first communion?" I asked Kay, Dan's sister.

Kay often dropped by on her way home from work. She was a schoolteacher and had that sunny, smiley disposition of the head girl that makes you think it must have been an easy transition from student to teacher. Kay said "fiddlesticks!" instead of "fuck," but I liked her. Knowing how relentlessly downtrodden she was by her mother made me believe she was tough behind that candy-girl personality.

The next three hours bore this out, as she bundled me into her car and marched me into a discount designer outlet on the outskirts of Yonkers. In and out of various pastel shades of awful suits later, we settled on a bias cut calf-length dress in slate gray and a fuschia wrap. I was waiting for my card to go through at the register when I looked at Kay and suddenly I saw Dan in her. The broad mouth, an imperceptible slant in the eyes, that wide-open expression. And it hit me: *This woman is my sister-in-law. I am married. To her brother. Dan.* There was a feeling of shock, like I was realizing it for the first time. *Oh my God! I am related to this person. Married! For the rest of my life! What have I done!* I can't

even say that it was a negative feeling. Only that it was a shock.
Like waking up in the hospital or winning the lottery. Shock is
like that. Neither good nor bad.

I got over it by the time I signed the receipt, but felt I had
somehow shifted into a different gear.

LITTLE DEIRDRE loved my sugar-pink iced cake with silver
baubles laced around its edges, and her friends were duly impressed with it and the fifty-dollar Gap Kids gift certificate. For
the adults, I made an understated honey cake, which I sliced, driz-
zled with lemon icing, and set on two large trays covered with
gingham napkins. Traditional, but not showy enough to intimi-
date Eileen, who grunted her acknowledgment and said she
hoped I was feeling better. I saw her hand the tray around herself,
and nod in my direction once or twice.

Uncle Patrick sought me out. I think Dan had told him to, as
he did not seem to have the first idea who I was and seemed a little overwhelmed to be there. He reminded me of the men my
grandfather used to bring into our house in Mayo. Seemingly
quiet, simple men, but once you got them talking, they had these
enormous intellects. Living among nothing but fields and cattle,
they became addictive, voracious readers of everything from
great Russian literature to magazines and local newspapers.
They knew about the Chinese state, and papal law, and ladies'
fashions.

"So you're Dave's wife."

"Dan's."

He ignored that. "And she's a grand wee thing," he said, nodding at nine-year-old Deirdre—her chubby, flat chest crammed
into a white JLo tracksuit.

He said it like he cared as much as I did. Which was not much.

"You made the honey cake?" He paused while I nodded. "Eileen told me."

His singsong accent rolled around her name with real romance. The point was not that I had made the cake, but that his sister had told him about it. That was nice, and we sat for a moment and let the brief fantasy of Eileen being nice float over us.

"There was too much sugar in it for me, girl."

I am used to this type of comment. Because I have a job that is creative and in the public domain, a certain breed of opinionated fool feels it is their "duty" to criticize me. In the interest of improving my recipes, of course. I always have an answer.

"Oh really? There was no sugar in it, actually."

And of all smart answers, I find that lies work the best.

"Well, you must have used really cheap honey then."

"Actually it was Wild Flower Organic Honey."

"The label was, maybe, but that honey was not wild."

"And you know this because . . . ?"

Dan had left me sitting talking to a stream of dull relations for almost two hours. I was tired and bored and I wanted to go home. Actually, I was quietly seething. Dan had made out like this day was going to be really hard for him to do alone, then abandoned me almost as soon as we got here. He seemed to be having a marvelous time, coping perfectly well without his loyal wife to protect him from whatever abuses he had blackmailed me into believing might befall him. He didn't look awkward or uncomfortable; from where I was sitting he looked like he was partying like a freshman. I felt a little conned. All right—a lot conned. And Uncle Patrick was an easy target.

Except he wasn't.

"I have been keeping honeybees for more than thirty years, and I am telling you that is not good honey in that cake."

Then he got up from his chair, disappeared upstairs and came back down two minutes later with a small brown paper package, which he thrust at me with an aggressive "There! *That's* wild honey—if you know the difference."

The jar was sticky, and as I prised open the jammed lid part of a comb came with it. The scent of it passed through me and the satin of unexpected memories brushed across my skin. Granddad, in the swell of summer, bringing in the first batch of honey; the drama and fear of seeing my first swarm; how he called my grandmother "honey girl" and kissed the wrinkled tissue of her aged hand. A vision of marriage that you don't know you've absorbed until you are married yourself, and looking for answers to questions you are not supposed to ask.

"I know the difference," I said.

Uncle Patrick was delighted.

"Eileen doesn't care for it. She says she'd prefer honey from the shop. She knows where it's from."

I said nothing about that, but we both knew the other was horrified.

"How much have you got?"

"Six jars."

"I'll buy them all."

Patrick laughed.

"Tell you what, lady. Have these ones on the house and next time I'm over, then we'll talk."

"You've been here before?"

He looked at me quizzically and said, "I come maybe once or twice a year."

Great. Not only is my husband manipulative, but he's a liar, too. Manipulative liar. Nice. A lifetime of joy and happiness right there. In a funny way, I approved.

* * *

THE NIGHT was drawing in, and I thought we would never get out of there. One of the kids had turned on the stereo and there was some terrible CD of disco hits banging away in the background. I had this horrible feeling that the party was just beginning while I'd already had enough.

Dan was talking animatedly to some cousin or other. I walked across and took his hand and he continued talking, interlocking my fingers with his to let me know he knew I was there. Then this seventies love song came on and, without explanation or introduction, Dan grabbed me and started to dance.

I would take the stars out of the sky for you
Stop the rain from falling if you asked me to

I was really embarrassed, but Dan held me tight in his amateur sway as if we were the only ones there.

I'd do anything for you
Your wish is my command
I could move a mountain
If your hand was in my hand

"Thanks for coming today, baby."

He whispered it with the solemnity of a wedding vow, like it really had made all the difference to him.

And then I got it. Dan didn't need me to bake cakes, or entertain his uncle, or dress up, or field his mother's expectations, or make his sisters feel important, or chit-chat nicely to his relations. He just needed me to be there. Because when I was with him, it made it easier for him to be with his family. To be able to point across a room and say, "She's with me," to his Uncle Patrick, his mother, his cousins, but most important, to himself.

My being in his life—sitting, walking, breathing, talking in the background of his day—made it better. Made him look and feel like he was a better man.

Dan had lied to get me there that day because he believed that was what he needed to do to secure my presence. Only I knew that all he had to do was ask me straight, and I would have said yes.

It felt good, and in that moment I knew I had taken one step closer to being Dan's wife.

Shared Joy

There is love in watching other people love.

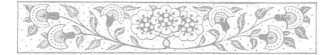

The recipe makes just over a dozen.

Cream 4oz margarine with 4oz sugar then add 2 eggs. If you beat them gently first, it lessens the risk of curdling. Mix in 8 heaped tablespoons flour (about 10oz) and a half teaspoon baking soda. (This is your basic recipe, but it's fun to let children mix in things at this stage for themselves. Your mother loved raisins, but I seem to remember one ten-year-old girl who made me mash in a banana! Imagine my surprise when it worked!)

Grease your bun tin generously, and cook in a medium/hot oven for up to 45 minutes. Leave to cool in the tin before turning out and leaving to cool on a rack. (Although if the little ones are around, they won't last that long!)

Sixteen

No change ever happened in me more absolutely or more immediately than that of motherhood.

I was crotchety and complaining all through the pregnancy. I dreaded the birth, the hardship and humiliation of it, with a horror I could barely name. Pregnancy did nothing to warm me to the idea. I did not like the feeling of my body being inhabited in that way. It felt intrusive and uncomfortable and, despite what everyone kept saying, completely unnatural.

Niamh was born in the early hours of a Monday morning, after my waters had broken during Mass. It was an ordeal, from the embarrassment of stumbling with wet legs out of the church to the excruciating pain and the midwife's cruel pragmatism as she urged at me to "Push, push," and told me to offer my pain up for the souls in Purgatory. I thought it would never end.

Then Niamh was here, and in the split second that I heard her cry, everything changed. I had carried her for nine months, and yet she was a complete surprise. I could never have expected something so pure and so magnificent as this child. Immediately that I held her, a sob rose up through me, grief that I had left this joy so long to experience. She was tiny and frail, like a petal, yet as complex as nature itself. The earth, sun, moon, stars—all the continents of America and Africa and the galaxies beyond—could not contain the love I felt. I wept, but with a joyful abandon. I wept in gratitude to God for her breath on my breast, and I wept because although I had made her, already I knew she did not belong to me and that one day I would have to let her go.

James must have been standing with his ear to the door because I heard him call out. The midwife told him that it was a girl and that we were not ready to see him, and I shocked myself by raising up from the bed and hollering at her to stop fussing around with her cleaning and let him in.

It was the first time I felt love in looking at James's face. Not pity, or concern, or grudging respect—but a passionate belonging. In the years we had been together, I had always felt apart from him. I knew now that as long as this child lived, we could not be parted. And in that moment I wanted to draw him to me. For the two of us to wrap ourselves around this new life to cherish, nourish, and guide her. James looked from my face to the swaddled cocoon in my lap and his eyes shone with a symphony of emotion I had never seen before: terror, wonderment, and a tender, tender love.

WATCHING SOMETHING you love grow is both pleasure and pain. Each new phase—crawling, walking, talking—brings shouts of pride, but with each also is the mourning of the phase gone past. Never again the cluck of her chin as she fed on my breast; never again small enough to carry in one arm while I stirred soup or carried turf with the other; never again an infant lying in a muslin-covered basket in the top fields while we worked. The soft down of her scalp, fingers the size of beads, the mysterious whispers before words come, behind the joy of each

new talent, I regretted the passing of the last. I had a secret longing to keep her small and precious, and a part of me. As miserable
as I had been during pregnancy I now often dreamt that she was
back inside my body and that the two of us were floating like that
forever, clinging to the other for soft comfort in some eternal
womb.

Time is impatient to take your child from you. So you learn
that each moment is precious, and that life is an inevitable clock.
The pleasure of rearing a child is just a prelude to the pain of letting it go, and I anticipated that with an ache every day of her
small life. I thought it would make it easier when she finally
reached adulthood. But it didn't.

No matter what wisdoms or tricks for happiness you learn, a
mother worries every day of her life for her child. A wise one will
pretend to let them go to keep them, but it's just a sensible lie.
Motherhood is a sweet, sweet suffering; a joy today is marked by
fear for tomorrow and a craving for yesterday.

James was a wonderful father. In those early years of our parenthood, I had the pleasure of feeling close to my husband. Often
we would both lie down on our iron bed and hum our child to
sleep at the tail end of a playful afternoon. Sunshine dappled
across our lazy bodies, hypnotizing us, and I would see what an
extraordinary man he was to lullaby his wife and child on a summer's afternoon, when other men might be gathered in the pub to
drink themselves daft. Perhaps it was because he was a teacher,
but he seemed to have a natural, easy way with Niamh that mystified me. How could you love somebody as completely and absolutely as we loved her and maintain such a detached fairness? I
guess he was a more natural father than I was a mother. I had been
surprised by my love for her but as Niamh's personality developed,
my relationship with her became fraught. She was feisty—like

myself—and we were both willful and petulant. James became arbiter and confidant to us both.

When she was a small child, Niamh and I often squabbled in the kitchen, as I instructed her in making her favorite fairy cakes. Flour and butter would be everywhere; eggs dropped lethally on the polished flagstones. I would get frustrated when I realized that she was too young for instruction, but she was having too much fun for me to stop the lesson. James stood for a moment at the door watching me frantically wipe debris off the table, the floor, my face. And in his quietly observing me, I would see myself as he saw me: in my everyday apron, dark hair wound to the back, a swirl of flour dashed across my cheek. I knew that I was more beautiful to him then, as mother to his child, than I had ever been in the beguiling days of my youth.

I knew also that James was loving us both as he just stood there. That in his teaching, his digging for potatoes, his tending the cattle, his reading, in everything James did, was hidden a eulogy to his two "girls." And I knew that I was a lucky woman to be able to take his protection and provision and paternal patronage for granted, and a blessed one for the luxury of all the little ways he found to love me.

At times like that, I would believe that perhaps loving James as a father was as good as loving him as a man.

Seventeen

I was on a creative buzz with my new kitchen.

I had designed and built kitchens for myself, for magazines, for friends, and for very rich people who wanted to pretend that they were going to cook in them. Kitchen companies employed me as a consultant; Tressa Nolan was—without wishing to sound egotistical about it—the living embodiment of the modern American kitchen. But the kitchen in Longville Avenue had taken my idea of the perfect cooking space to a new level.

It all started when I was flicking through some brochures trying to find the perfect Shaker look.

Dan had looked over my shoulder and said, "They look expensive."

I told him that all the companies would give me a deal and he said "Oh, right—it's just I thought you wanted to fix up this old stuff. There's this carpenter guy I know . . ."

As he trailed off, I looked around at all the broken-down stuff we had been living with for the past few weeks. There was the fifties larder unit with the tin work-top, a broken-down sideboard we had been keeping the kettle on, a small square table with turned legs and a devastated peeling veneer top. All this scruffy old junk we had been living with since we had moved in which, despite my craving for a pared-down Shaker-style kitchen, I had grown quite fond of. Did I want to throw it all on the scrap heap and replace it with brand-new stuff?

"Is he good?" I asked.

"Oh—he's good," Dan said.

Dan knew that our kitchen was not only the most important room in the house, but also a really important part of my working life. Still, I was not sure about going eclectic. But I told myself that if it all went wrong, I could always call in the heavy guns. In my line of work, kitchens were frighteningly disposable.

So Dan made a call to a guy, who made a call to another guy, who got his tattooed biker buddy to come over.

I took one look at him and my skepticism level soared.

"We don't need to save money on this, Dan, really," I said, which was code for "Get this saw-wielding Charles Manson look-alike freak out of my house!"

"Trust me, baby, Gerry won't save you money, but he's good. I know what you wanted from this kitchen and he's the best."

He's going to cost us money? My husband has a mother who buys her ribs frozen, and on sale—sure, he knows about kitchens. But I felt I had to give his friend Gerry a chance because—well, he was in my house and was, unbelievably, carrying a suitcase.

TWO WEEKS on and it turned out this Gerry guy was a genius.

Gerry had waist-length gray hair and four teeth. He had come to America on a holiday visa from Ireland thirty years before and had been working for cash ever since. He slept on the job or on friends' sofa beds and spent his money on bikes and dope and—I don't know—tattoos? He certainly didn't spend it on clothes or dentistry, but I didn't care because together, with Dan, we were building a unique kitchen more perfect than money could buy. Every shelf, every door was different—hand finished in a style fitting its job. The spice rack had ten pine shelves, each a different width to fit my higgledy-piggledy collection of jars. We restored the original fifties cupboard and replaced the old tinwork top. I found original tin containers marked "Flour" and "Sugar" to place on it. His brief for the dresser was "Nineteen-thirties Ireland." "Got that," he said. Then he went to the garage and came back five days later with, I swear, a replica of my grandparents' one in Faliochtar. I painted it buttermilk and pistachio and already it looked as if it had been there forever. There was nothing "finished" or even describable about my kitchen. I knew it would look like a place that had been created by and cooked in by three generations of women.

I had thought that having a stranger around the place was going to be a living hell, but in a way it turned out to be good for us. All the awkward tension lying beneath the surface of our life since our honeymoon had completely gone. It was like Dan was showing me off to his single buddy, and I found myself falling in with his game, as if Gerry was our audience and we were playing our roles of happily married husband and wife in front of him. I found it safer to be physically affectionate toward Dan in front of other people, and as a result he was doing more than his usual amount of waist hugging and neck nuzzling. We bickered in a playful way to amuse Gerry; Dan called me his "ball and chain" and I mocked myself by pretending to boss him around. Ironically, I found an intimacy in behaving like a text-book wife; in acting like I was completely at ease with Dan, I actually became more at ease with him. And myself.

The atmosphere in the house was resolutely male; I was allowed to do light work such as painting and polishing and, of course, providing refreshments without having a working oven. One day I made a dozen fairy cakes in the microwave oven, with Dan and Gerry gawking at me open-mouthed as if I had just performed a miracle. I split the buns and stuffed them with butter icing and white chocolate buttons for the pure amusement of turning two grown men into prepubescent schoolboys. As a joke, I gave Gerry the spatula and Dan the bowl to lick. They both regarded me with an adoring lust that made me laugh and feel like playmate of the month at the same time.

"Jesus, man," Gerry said to Dan, raising his eyebrows and shaking his head as he wrapped himself around a fairy cake and a homemade cappuccino.

"I know," Dan said, glowing with pride. "This was what it's all about, right?"

Mother, master chef, sex goddess, all rolled into one. Nobody ever made me feel quite that good before.

We took the rest of that afternoon off and Gerry cracked open a lethal bottle of tequila he had been carrying around. The three of us held an air-guitar contest. Gerry went hardcore with Black Sabbath, Dan went for the middle-American vote with Springsteen, but in the end, they let me win with Thin Lizzy's "Whiskey in the Jar." My trophy was the tequila bottle and Gerry presented it to me with great ceremony, while my inebriated husband grabbed his stomach with drunken mirth.

Gerry decided that we needed a little smoke to finish the party off properly and went off to score some. He was the kind of guy you knew you might not see again for a week and the second he was gone, Dan grabbed me with an uncharacteristic, "C'mere you."

We made love like casual, lazy lovers right there on the sofa, and it was nice. I didn't have to work at it or tell myself stories to get through it. It was like it had been in the beginning, except it was different; less exciting because I knew what to expect. For once, that didn't feel like a problem. It was easy. Maybe it was the tequila, but easy felt good.

At five A.M. the next morning, I woke up to an empty bed. I found Dan in the kitchen, hand-sanding some skirting board.

"I have to work today, so I wanted to get these ready for you to paint," he said.

I put on some coffee, and while it brewed, I watched him running the sander up and down the board. His face was set in concentration, although the job he was doing was pure manual, his arm muscles contracting and relaxing.

Without thinking I said, "Thanks for building me this kitchen, Dan."

Without stopping he said, "It's our kitchen, baby. This was as much for me as you."

For once I didn't balk at the "we" reference. We were doing this together, and I didn't mind. I liked it.

My happiness was as caught up with building my dream kitchen as it was with my husband—but it's still happiness, right? It still counts?

Enter Angelo and Jan Orlandi. Old friends, organic food impresarios and officially New York state's most fabulous couple.

When I say that the Orlandis are "officially" America's most fabulous couple, it's not a figure of speech. It's the gospel according to *Vanity Fair* magazine.

An outline of their lives: Jan and Angelo met in college, married young, developed a mutual commitment to food out of which they built successful careers as a food editor and chef, respectively. They bought a huge house in Irvington before it became chic to do so and started up a small organic garden and wholesale sauces business. Now they own many thousands of acres of prime California farmland, supply all the big supermarket chains, and have a dozen cafés and restaurants to their name as well as a beachfront boutique hotel in the Caribbean. Add to that two beautiful children, a house worth featuring in *Vogue*, and the fact that they are still grounded enough to want to hang with an old friend, even though they couldn't make her wedding—and the happiness goal posts start to shift. Put it like this. You'd want to be pretty secure in yourself to do a weekend in Irvington chez Orlandi.

I considered them good friends but they hadn't met Dan yet. They had another long-standing arrangement the weekend of our wedding and couldn't come, although they sent a generous gift. Jan and Angelo had always been my benchmark for a successful modern marriage.

That weekend was not just a test for Dan. It was a test for me. Things had been going so well, but I still needed to be sure that marrying Dan was the right thing for me. When we got the Orlandis' invitation, I realized that I had changed. I now wanted my marriage to work and hoped that a weekend in Irvington would prove to me, once and for all, that it was worth the effort.

Eighteen

erhaps the darkest secret I ever kept was also the most innocent. Deep in my heart, I longed for a son. Perhaps because I
imagined it would be a different kind of love from any I had felt
before. Perhaps I would have called him Michael and poured all
my dreams into him.

I will never know.

Month after month I waited, convinced that I had controlled
my own destiny before by conceiving on demand and certain that
I would do so again. As the months turned into a year, and one
year into two, my despair deepened. Each time the bleeding
started, I felt my disappointment as a cold crater in the pit of my
body, as if the child I did not conceive had been scooped out and
taken from me. With each month came the shock of theft, the
anger of betrayal, the pain of loss.

Gradually, it dawned on me that I had never been in charge of
my own body in the way I had thought. I did not "give" Niamh to
James. God did. Now that I wanted a child for myself, He was
denying me. I was being punished.

So I prayed and I prayed. I said Novenas, memorare to the Virgin Mary, went to Mass on the first Friday of every month, and

begged. I became obsessed. Neglectful of Niamh and James, even my own appearance. Lovemaking became a frantic ordeal—for both of us, I am sure. James was worried for me, although he never judged. Once he tried to reassure me by saying that Niamh and I were enough for him. I bit his head off, screaming that he didn't understand, that he was an insensitive fool.

Such is the intimacy of marriage. The irony of its familiar, relentless kind of love was that whenever I felt sad or afraid or alone, the first person I always blamed was James. He was the most faultless, most attentive, most caring person I could have had to carry me through such a hardship, and yet he became the focus of my anger. I was too afraid to blame God, so I blamed my husband. His age, his body, his indifference. James knew that I was suffering, so he ignored me when he had to, and forgave because he loved me. A man, when pushed to the limits of his patience, will usually show himself to be either stoic or violent. You will only discover which kind of man you have if you relentlessly prod and push, push, push. I was lucky; James was stoic. Still, if he had been hurt or disappointed about our not having another child, I wouldn't have noticed.

Eventually I lost my faith entirely. And as happens when a sadness is too deep to bear, it must find another, more familiar pain to distract from it.

I THOUGHT I saw Michael on the pier at Enniscrone.

The summer Niamh turned five, we took a taxi to the seaside village in Sligo and booked into a guesthouse on the main street for two weeks. James thought that the sea air would lift my spirits and Niamh was recovering from a spring fraught with childhood diseases: measles, mumps, and chicken pox in immediate succession. Our fat little girl had turned slim and frail, and needed the hot salty air to burn some color into her cheeks. James and I needed to escape. Our bed was polluted by our failures, we felt defeated, and my grief had turned our home into a prison. Although it was never said, I understood that this holiday was James drawing a line under my wish for another child. It was time to give up: go away, get over it, and come back as I had been before.

For those of us who lived inland, the sea was a miraculous, incredible spectacle. James would disappear early to fish, and as Niamh collected shells, I would sit on a blanket on the dunes and allow myself to become hypnotized by the sea. A glimmering mass of glass, the flat horizon turning into a gliding, moving hill until it lurched towards the land and dissolved clumsily into a sniggering mess in the sand. I'd imagine that there was nothing beyond the sea: no boats to carry off our neighbors, our families to England and America. To take the boy I loved and place him on the other side of the Atlantic.

I would look at the sun splash the sky with gold and a hundred shades of purple; gray rain clouds hovering over Killala on the other side of the bay while we briefly enjoyed the gift of sunshine. Steps and smooth rock seats etched into the land where children could search for dead crabs and shells and other seaside treasure. And I would think, *God has created all this yet he won't give me another child*. Sometimes I would succumb to my tears, let them mingle with the sea spray and allow myself the relief of weeping alongside nature. As the days went past, I felt the injustice of my not conceiving diminish, and my thoughts instead began to circle around an old grievance with new eyes.

Romance.

The gap in me where my imaginary son lived was the same place that was harboring my yearning for passionate love. I could feel the sea breeze whisper across my neck, the hem of my cotton skirt flicker on my knee, but I could no longer feel the touch of my husband, nor hear his voice, nor really see him. He had become an object, like furniture or bread. So my longing for a child was replaced by my longing for the thrill of that first forbidden kiss.

It was a more familiar pain. But it was still pain.

I was sitting on the rocks, when I thought I saw him walking along the pier. He wore a brown suit, his black hair licking his collar in glossy waves. He was the same in that way that young love never gets the chance to age.

I didn't see his face, but I knew it was Michael.

The shock did not paralyze me as it does in dreams, but propelled me towards the pier. My feet slid across the rocks; I did not even stop to think of taking the proper path up. That would have meant turning my back to him, and I could not let him out of my sight. I did not call out or think of what I might have said when I reached him. Barefoot and perspiring, I was driven towards him in a straight line.

When I heard Niamh cry out from the beach behind me, I am ashamed to admit I was torn.

I went back, of course, and rescued my child. I comforted her about the jellyfish sting, and carried her back to the boarding house, bathed her in salt, cajoled and placated her. But my head was on a wild swivel searching for a glimpse of him again. I was irritable for the few days left of our break, but in a way that I know comforted James, in that he could see my deeper sadness had dissipated.

The sea had taken one dream and carried it away, sending me back a more familiar one. For weeks afterwards, I dreamt of Michael. What might have happened when we met. What we might have said. How our eyes would have searched the other's

face for unlocked memories, a habit of love reborn in our eyes. How we might have brushed cheeks when we said good-bye.

We always said good-bye.

Michael meant everything to me still. I burned for him and would always, even as a wretched old woman. James was my husband; I hated him for it, reviled him often. But the years and a child had glued us together. Time and nature had bonded me to James against my very will, beyond what I wanted, what I felt. Although I often wanted to escape, I knew I never could.

Wife. Mother. The very words had become webbed into the fabric of my soul.

MANY YEARS later, when Niamh left for college, I realized that another child would not have been the answer. It would have been double the joy, but also double the pain of letting the child go.

I was a good mother, but I was not a selfless one. I gave and while I never asked, I was always waiting for something back. I craved those moments of surety a child's love gives you, was always ready for Niamh's reassurance and admiration and always disappointed when it didn't come on cue.

I was never destined to have more than one child. I know that now. I think my desire for another was just greed for the easy joy I had felt with James when Niamh was born.

Joy did not come naturally to me. I always grabbed so hard that I crushed it. Examined it until I found a flaw; or tried to make it more than it was. It would always turn too quickly to disappointment. I found that when happy, I held my breath and waited for it to fly away. I waited all my life for joy to come and kidnap me as it had when I met Michael.

The one place I never bothered looking for it was inside myself.

Nineteen

t all started to go wrong on the Thursday evening when Angelo rang and asked Dan if he wanted them to send us their driver.

Dan was furious. He thought Angelo was implying that we couldn't afford a car. I tried to explain that when you are as enormously wealthy as the Orlandis, you employ a full-time driver and that we would be doing them a favor in giving him something to do for the day. I consoled him with the fact that I often had a driver when I was working and that it was no big deal. Angelo had certainly not meant any offense and was just trying to be helpful.

Dan didn't buy it. I didn't really know how to deal with this sudden testosterone surge, but I knew right away that I handled it wrong by defending Angelo. Dan then spent the rest of the day washing and waxing the car, and I overheard Gerry encourage him to borrow a vintage Harley Davidson from one of their mutual biker pals, a plan that, thankfully, did not make it past the plotting stage.

The trip there was tense. Their house in Irvington was homey, rambling rather than grand, unlike the mansion on their farm in

California that made the Kennedy compound in Hyannisport look like a shed. I was looking forward to a quiet weekend, just them and us, as I really wanted them to get to know Dan.

"So what is this guy—an Italian?"

"Well, his parents are."

"Yeah right—a rich Italian. What is he—mafia?"

"No, he is one of the most successful organic food producers in the . . ."

"If these people are such good friends, how come they couldn't make it to the wedding?"

Dan was making it obvious that he did not want to go and I was getting irritated with his attitude. The Orlandis are fantastic hosts. *Anyone* would want to go and hang out with them for the weekend.

"They are incredibly busy people."

"Hell—so are we!"

"I mean important . . ."

As soon as I said it I knew it was wrong.

"So we're not important?"

"That's not what I meant . . ."

"Making our wedding was not important enough for these important, incredibly busy people?"

One part of me wanted to bury a pickaxe in Dan's forehead. But another part of me was thinking, *Wow! We are having a fight—just like a normal couple.*

It wasn't nice, but it felt like progress. Like we felt secure enough with each other to argue.

"At least they won't be feeding us frozen mystery meat."

I knew immediately that I had taken a step too far. Dan's expression froze and his hands tightened on the wheel.

"I'm sorry, Dan. That was out of order."

He waited before replying. In the face of my apology, he played down my bitchy comment about his mother.

"Family is different, Tressa. You have to stick by family, no matter what. These people are strangers."

"Jan and Angelo are very good friends of mine . . ."

"So you keep saying."

I wanted to tell him that no one on the planet felt stranger to me than his family, and that the Orlandis were more my kind of people—educated, stylish, erudite.

But I thought I'd better keep that to myself. We had the weekend to get through.

To keep myself calm, I tried to get inside Dan's head and decided that he was simply feeling insecure. These people were wealthy, they knew me and considered me a peer. That must have been very threatening for him and that was why he was being so defensive.

What he didn't know was that Angelo and I had had a brief fling before Jan and he had gotten married. My first job was as Jan's assistant. Although not quite five years older than me, she was a food editor and I admired her hugely. I guess I had a kind of a crush on her. When she and Angelo split up after five years together, Jan hadn't seemed that upset. "College boyfriends rarely stick—we've both changed," she had said. She had seemed to shrug him off like a teenage denim jacket you still love but know you've matured out of. Although I had only ever met Angelo with Jan, the New York food scene being as it was, it was just a matter of weeks before I bumped into my boss's ex at the opening of a new bar. It seemed only polite to join him for a drink.

There was instant chemistry between us. It was as if our mutual relationships with Jan had been a barrier to what had always been there. We laughed at the same things, we loved the same restaurants, food, people. We slept together that first night and sex was instant and easy and explosive all at the same time.

My instinct was to tell Jan right away—the next day. She might have felt weird about it, but I was convinced that she would get over it quickly once she realized how compatible Angelo and I were. I could see us all in years to come, still friends, looking back and laughing at our situation.

Angelo persuaded me to stay quiet, saying it was best to be certain about each other first before hurting Jan. Being young and confident, I assumed things would continue; I thought relationships were that easy. I got a shock when, a few days later, Jan came into work beaming and announced that she and Angelo were back together.

"We needed a break," she said but she looked relieved.

I was hurt but I didn't say anything and decided to stay friends with them both. After all, I was young and thought the world was bursting at the seams with "Angelos." It was ten years before I realized that men whom I could relate to intellectually *and* physically were thin on the ground.

Having said that, the affair itself was forever ago and was so very, very over that I forgot about it myself most of the time. Although sometimes, I have to admit, I would catch myself looking at Angelo and wondering what if. It's ridiculous, and it doesn't mean anything, but in the deep pit of my stomach, I knew that this weekend was about me lining Dan and Angelo up next to each other and hoping to pick Dan. Buried under that knowledge was the fear that perhaps Dan could smell that there was a history there, which was why he was acting like such a jerk.

The Orlandis could not have been more welcoming when we

arrived, although their housekeeper, Rosa, answered the door, which I could tell pissed Dan off. Dan is uncomfortable dealing with "staff" on this level. It comes from years of being staff himself and answering requests to unblock toilets and change lightbulbs.

We went up to our rooms to clean up after the journey. When we came back down we were slightly taken aback to see that there was a full dinner party awaiting us. Apart from our hosts, there was another food writer (whom I didn't really care for) with her lawyer husband, a food photographer I had booked once and never used again, and a publisher who was good friends with my agent. Dan had just been thrown headfirst into a clique of foodies.

The food was in season and unfussy. Perfectly prepared goes without saying. Haloumi with chili oil, then chicken wrapped in Parma ham.

"Simplicity is *the* new style buzz," the ghastly food writer blurted.

"Easy Entertaining?" Jan replied, her fingers flicking quotations over the statement.

We all laughed at the allusion to the title of her cable TV show. Except Dan. He looked nervously at me, waiting for me to explain the joke. I couldn't because, actually, when I thought about it, it wasn't very funny.

The rest of the conversation didn't improve Dan's comfort zone much. It was centered around the dilemma of flying first or business class, restaurant reviews—as in where to eat next time you are on business in London, Martha Stewart (of course), and, awkwardly, agents and their percentages. All the time I was worrying that my husband had no interest in these subjects, so I said, "Dan and I are building a new kitchen."

"How fascinating! Who are you using?" the food writer asked Dan.

"We are doing it ourselves," I answered for him.

Dan threw me a sharp look, then just to let me know I had blown my chance, looked away from the table.

"Really? How do you mean?"

"Dan has a friend who is a wonderful bespoke carpenter, and we are customizing and restoring everything back to a nineteen-thirties feel."

They were hanging on the kitchen guru's every word to see where she was going with this.

"It's eclectic."

And right when I said it, I realized that I had managed to reduce the heart and the feeling of home that we had been creating for the last three weeks into a fashion statement.

WHEN WE eventually got to bed that night Dan just said, "There's no need to talk for me, Tressa," and turned away. I didn't reply, just lay there for hours between Egyptian cotton sheets sprayed with English lavender water and wondered how the hell I had got myself into this mess.

These were my people. I did not like all of them, but they were my peers and I could certainly hold my own among them. This kind of dinner party; networking; discussing food, wine, restaurants, and enjoying each others' stylish hospitality—this is what I did. The language was ours, yet it felt strange to be doing it with Dan. Wrong. Clearly it alienated him, but did I really want to give this part of my life up for him? Or was I destined to spend every weekend drinking beer and eating junk food with his family, stifling this part of my life and career?

I knew the next day was going to be hell, but I thought, he put me through the first communion, he can cope with a day of macho insecurity with me and my "fabulous" friends.

*   *   *

IN THE morning, the publisher and photographer had gone, but the vile food writer and her drab husband were there for the whole weekend. She was all over Jan, doing an overpowering girl-buddy act in the kitchen. The lawyer was boring Angelo to death, but he was having no luck with Dan. My husband had taken to the great outdoors with Rosa and Jan and Angelo's kids, who instantly adored him. He was avoiding everyone else, but especially me. By lunchtime everyone was drinking and picking on an over-the-top brunch buffet brought by the food writer. It was self-consciously casual: twice-baked leek and goat's cheese soufflés, sunblush roasted tomatoes in a balsamic *jus*. We knew the names because she had written them in gold lettering on cards in front of each dish. Tacky beyond comment.

I took a king prawn that would have looked overdressed at the Oscars and gazed out the window at Dan. He had Juliana balancing on his shoulders while he swung baby Carlos around. Rosa was looking on, horrified, but I knew the kids would be safe. Dan was like that: a big bear of a man. Maybe not a neat, educated college guy, but you wouldn't come to harm while he was around.

"Hey," Angelo said in a dark, dangerous voice behind me, "wanna see something?"

He had some special kind of arugula he wanted to show me in the greenhouse. So he said.

It was one of those seductive film moments you can't resist. It hits you hard because you don't expect it. One minute you are fingering a fragrant herb, then your hands touch by accident. Next thing, your eyes meet, they lock, then you pull together into a kiss. You barely know you are doing it. It's an animal thing. An attraction you can't control. Chemistry.

I guess it had never gone away. That easy charm he has always had. The fact that we speak the same language; he always understood me.

We pulled away and didn't have a conversation about it. It was our little secret. We had kept our previous dalliance quiet for such a long time anyway and I'll admit: It was thrilling to have the flame relit. Albeit briefly.

It was a moment, a kiss. Something to remind us both that while we were married we were still capable of passion. We were still alive. No big deal. Like a line of coke at a cousin's wedding. Nobody knows; nobody gets hurt.

But the minute we got back to the house and I saw Dan's face, I felt sick. He had come inside to find me and this look flashed between us. He was querying and I was defensive. It was less than a second. I was a bit drunk and I can't even be sure I didn't imagine it.

Dan didn't drink for the rest of the day, which was his way of letting me know he intended to drive home that night. We stayed for dinner, and just before dessert Angelo followed me into the bathroom. He was drunk, but I suspect he was acting more drunk than he was.

"Come on, Tressa, you know you want to. Let's live a little."

"Are you crazy, Angelo? In the bathroom? With Dan and Jan downstairs?"

And the kids in the room next door, you disgusting dirt bag? But I kept that one to myself.

He looked at me hard and when he saw there was no persuading me he went instantly cold, shrugged his shoulders and said, "Your loss." Then he turned and left me standing there.

I was shaking and took a few seconds to calm myself down. In that moment I knew it was gone. Twenty years of friendship over. I didn't want to be part of it anymore. This glamorous, empty life where your seemingly doting husband tries to fuck your friend in a bathroom because he's rich and he thinks he can. Where you can't make it to your friend's wedding because you are too busy being fabulous. I had been part of this, too. I had enjoyed the kiss, wanted it, and now I felt corrupted. Now I had Dan.

I breathed in deeply, and in breathing out, I craved the simplicity of being sure again. Like I had been about my kitchen. Like I wanted to feel about Dan.

Jan was disappointed we had to leave, but Angelo brushed my cheek with his then gave me a nonchalant look as if he knew he'd never see me again and didn't care.

The drive home was quiet.

Gerry had left an empty pizza box with a note scribbled on the top saying, "Gone drinkin." He had left a small bag behind as evidence of his intended return but we both knew he might not be back for weeks, if ever.

Dan went straight upstairs for a shower, and I flicked the light on in the kitchen. I had been hoping the mood would lift when I got back to my project. But it didn't. I hadn't got the answers I wanted; in fact the weekend had just sent me away with more questions. Wretched questions that had been haranguing me for almost four months.

How could a few days have changed things so much? Those past few weeks had seemed as if they had been the halcyon days of a marriage that now felt all but over. I cursed myself for having broken the spell.

I realized that the joy was not in my grandparents' dresser or the kooky antique kettle or the restored larder, it was in the people who built them.

Without the love and the spirit, they were just cupboards.

Endurance

When it feels difficult to give, give more.

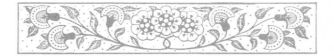

Everyday Bread

It seems foolish to be writing a recipe for bread because it was just something that had to be done every day, like peeling spuds or cleaning the range. Every woman found her own way of doing it, and the ingredients were certainly never measured except in the cook's eye for what looked right. You might be feeling generous the odd morning, and add a handful of fruit or a spoonful of cooking fat if you had it on hand. After a while, you learned how much flour would suit you and how much buttermilk would wet it.

As for method, it is so ingrained in my fingers, I would not know how to describe it. All I know is that as I got older, my bread improved in texture and became more consistent. I nearly poisoned your poor grandfather, your mother only barely survived, and you—my wee Tressa—got the best of it! If you really want to master an Irish soda bread, make it every day until it becomes as automatic as walking. There is no escaping its boring drudgery and only you can decide if it's worth it.

If you want to try, the basic ingredients are around 1lb flour, brown or white; a teaspoon of bicarbonate of soda;

and as much buttermilk as to make a wet dough, but not so wet as you can't handle it. To this you can optionally add 1 tablespoon butter or any cooking fat, dried fruit, up to a dessert spoon honey or sugar, a pinch salt, wheat meal, porridge oats—use your imagination. Cook in a hot oven for up to 1 hour, and tap the bottom, listening for a hollow sound, to see if it's cooked. Wrap immediately in a clean tea towel to stop it going hard on you and let sit for a good half hour before cutting.

Twenty

Life can be hard, but then we make it even harder by the way we look at it.

My mother walked across two fields to a well twice daily for water. She cooked on an open stove, the hem of her long skirts blackened with soot, her arms muscled with the strain of lifting pots. As she grew old, the palms of her hands were slashed with burn marks where she had grabbed hot handles without thinking.

I didn't notice my mother's hardship because I was never called upon to do so. Suffering was ingrained in her. Servile, solemn suffering—I never knew her any other way. Life was a slow penance, buying her time in the hereafter; it was not meant for enjoying, but rather meant for serving. Life was a sentence. The harder it was and the more quiet your forbearance, the more assured you were of eternal life.

My father often said cruel things to her when he was drunk, but she only ever took one beating from him that I know of. It was while she was pregnant with me, and her four brothers visited my father in our back field the following day and thrashed him with sticks to within an inch of his life. She told me this herself one day after he had hit my brother Patrick; sent him crashing to the floor during supper for some supposed slight. Patrick was extremely clever and this annoyed my father. He had won a scholarship to the local boys' school, but my father had refused to let him go on the grounds that we could not afford the uniform and books. The priest had been sent around to persuade him to change his mind and said that the church would provide any money needed to finish the boy's education. Patrick was devout and sensitive. My mother believed he could have been a priest. My father had refused out of pure stubbornness, saying that fourteen was time enough to leave school for any man and that he was needed on the farm. My mother saw her chance to have a priest for a son fly out the window, and while she remained respectful of my father to his face, she took up the habit of raging against him to me. She told me shocking stories of his cruelty, embellishing them at times, lest I should have any doubt of the kind of Godless animal my father was.

It was a small community and with her only sister, Ann, in America she had nobody else to talk to but her young daughter. Even if Ann had been around when I was a child, I doubt my mother would have told her how unhappy she was. Certainly when Ann returned from America, my mother never let her know how truly miserable she was. She was a proud woman, and in talking to her child at least, her pride would not be dented. Through confiding in me she found some release, and she needed that to survive. There was nothing she could do about her circumstances. Walking away from a marriage, no matter how full of hatred you were, no matter what indignities you suffered, was not possible in those days. You had to endure whatever came your way. Complaining all around you was weak and sinful and my mother wanted to be seen as neither. I was exempt from these conventions, however. Our own children give amnesty to all sorts of sideways cruelty.

When my mother told me about her brothers beating my father, her eyes glittered with pride. She defended the beating by explaining that my father would have killed me in the womb if they hadn't put the fear of God into him. It gave me a worse fear of my father than I had of him already, as well as a dread of any private contact with my mother. As the years went on, my mother's confidences stripped me of any loyalty I had for either of them.

For all that she was a helpless victim of my father's drunken abuse, she always held the Catholic Church above him. Above everything. Her devotion infuriated him but there was no arguing against it. Catholicism ruled her, but for all that she was a pious Mass goer and devoted priest worshipper, she seemed to get very little back from it. I have learned that a strong soul and a healthy dose of faith can carry a person through terrible hardships. My father's drinking, poverty, the effort of keeping us all alive, had broken my mother's spirit. She was religious, but she had very little faith. She clung to the candles and the ceremony like a drowning dog to a twig.

MY BROTHERS all left Achadh Mor. Declan and Brian to Birmingham, where they both found wives and started families, and Paddy to London. We never saw him again. In the nineteen eighties, I got a letter from the Metropolitan Police in London to inform me that Patrick had died in a hostel in Camden Town. They had found my name and address on a piece of paper he carried around in his pocket. Perhaps to remind him that he had a family, or perhaps in preparation for his death, who knows? His was a wasted life. He could have been a doctor or a teacher if my father had given him the chance of an education. In the end all he gave him was the bad genes and unhappiness that drove him to drink. Some people are just too delicate to survive.

My married brothers returned twice in twenty years. Their wives were strangers to us, and their children had English accents. We welcomed them, but it was an uncomfortable reunion. They had been away too long, and the gruff young men I had wrestled with as a girl had disappeared. They were overly polite, which is the worst insult a brother can pay you.

When my mother died, only Brian came home. He said he was representing the Birmingham contingent. They had tried, but could not find Patrick, which was the first sign that he was missing. It was an embarrassment to have such a small number of our immediate family present. My mother had suffered for us, but suffering does not buy you love. All it buys you is more suffering.

I had a dread of turning into my mother. It was why I had wanted to escape to America and why I had fallen so hard for the idea of falling in love. I never wanted to be trapped in the poverty of a loveless union. Even today, as I draw a picture of her in my mind to search for some common wisdom, all I can see is my mother's long, sad face. Mouth turned down at the edges, deep lines etched along her cheeks—her face a map of everyday misery. "My poor mother," I think, but I cannot conjure the same warmth as I felt for James's mother whom I knew for less than a year, or even for Ann, the aunt who betrayed me.

Knowledge is not enough, however, to stop a woman from turning into her mother. Except that my complaining was not tempered with the martyr's silent, pained forbearance. I could hear myself moaning over nothing at all: crumbs on the carpet, a broken cup. I was married to a hardworking man who loved me,

who would never let any harm come to me, yet I did not seem able
to silence the nag.

My need for constant change and improvement in our standard
of life was as much to do with boredom as anything else. I loved my
child, I had grown used to my husband, I knew I had a good life,
and yet part of me always felt cheated out of the dreams I'd had as
a young woman. As I got older, the fantasies I had nurtured
seemed more and more ludicrous, until, reluctantly, I had to let
them go. My young man wasn't coming back; I was never going to
work as housekeeper to a Hollywood starlet or twirl around a
lamppost on Park Avenue in a pink satin skirt.

All my life, I had been able to cut myself off and escape into
the world of my imagination, a place where I was eternally smiling into a warm sun, Michael's arms closing around my waist.
Sometime in my early forties I lost my ability to daydream. The
clouds that used to carry me off had grounded; when I closed my
eyes to conjure an escape, all I saw was my own stern face looking back at me, telling me not to be such a stupid fool. It seemed
that as I got older, reality was determined to own me. Perhaps it
is our dreams that keep us young. Older women who cling to
youth may look ghoulish, but perhaps they are happier than those
of us who grow old and crotchety before our time. Whatever the
case, the routine of life grated on me, wearing me down and aging me before my very eyes. I longed for something to shake me
out of it. We took trips to Dublin, changed the wallpaper, moved
the furniture around in the parlor, got electric lights put in, tiled
the fire surround. Always wanting more, more, more, desperate
for distraction.

Truthfully, I was bored beyond belief. This really was how it
was going to be for the rest of my life. In this house, with this

man. The only thing I wanted to stay the same was Niamh, and she was the one thing sure to change and leave. I could see it stretching on forever—the routine, the rituals of our lives. Housework, marking exam papers, meeting parents, mealtimes, Mass, bread making every day except Sunday: comfortable, cozy commitment. Marriage—forever and ever, world without end, amen.

I remember clearly looking at James over the supper table one evening—he was buttering his bread left to right, left to right—and thinking that I was so thoroughly sick of the sight of him that I wanted to scream. Day in, day out, buttering his bread left to right for how many years? I didn't dare count. I felt like hurling a plate at him for no other reason than to crash through his fog of contentment that was suffocating me.

If Niamh had not been around, I might well have thrown the plate, and who can say what difference such an unreasonable outburst of passion might have made.

I decided to paint the hen house instead.

My wish for dramatic change did come true shortly after, but in a way that was to test my tolerance further still.

Twenty-one

W hen you're around something every day, you stop seeing it. I can't make bread like my grandmother's and it drives me crazy. How many hours did I stand at the kitchen table in Faliochtar watching her make bread? She would do it every weekday, with the last loaf of the week baked on Saturday night, so that she would have the pleasure of rising late on Sunday morning with no other task but to prettify herself for eleven o'clock Mass.

For years now I have tried to draw up details in my mind's eye of how she did it, but my bread still falls so short of hers that I have all but given up.

I can remember the smell of the buttermilk on a summer's day as the heat from the range steamed the windows of their cottage; opening the back door to feel the freshness of the misty rain on my bare skin. I can remember waiting by her side, my chin barely reaching the tabletop, as she unfurled a linen tea towel from the fresh loaf; I can remember her favorite knife with the scorched, yellow handle, the blade concave from years of sharpening, slicing through the fleshy crumble, then the fresh butter melting to a salty dribble. I remember how the sweet jam mingled with its sour flavor and burst my baby taste buds.

But I cannot remember anything that will help me make the damn stuff. How she handled the dough or any of the little tricks she must have shown me. One thing I do recall is how, when she was finished, her fingers sped across the Formica tabletop picking up every last shred of errant dough to add them to her final loaf.

"Waste not, want not," she used to say.

I have already wasted a veritable mountain of flour and gallons of expensive buttermilk trying to replicate my grandmother's bread.

For punishment as much as anything else, I decided to bring one of my efforts over to Ma Mullins for Sunday lunch.

Yes. *Another* Sunday lunch party.

Part of me could not believe this was still going on.

That first Sunday lunch had been dreadful for us both, and I felt sure an understanding had been reached. Me and your mother just don't mix—so don't mix us. Little Deirdre's first communion was a one off.

But then it was some nephew's birthday, an anniversary, the first good barbecue day this month. One time, he begged me to go, saying his mother was "lonely" after the twins had left for a three-week vacation. I put together a special gift basket to cheer up this lonesome old lady and found the house full of the usual horde of relations. With one thing and another, that Sunday was to be the *seventh* time that we'd had Sunday lunch chez Ma Mullins. It had gotten so that going was the norm and not going was a big treat. It should have been the other way around.

My dread had turned into sarcasm. *Are we going to be treated to organic lamb, rack-roasted with rosemary and cracked black pepper and served on a bed of wilted spinach?* I thought to myself. *Are we talking pot roasted chicken with pistachio-buttered baby*

carrots and new potatoes? Or perhaps there will be traditional roast
beef, served rare with fresh horseradish and mini Yorkshire pud-
dings?

No.

There would be what there was every week: the usual revolting
platters of fried, bite-size bowel-blockers, with some ready-made
supermarket salads drenched in synthetic mayonnaise-based
dressing.

And I was worried about my bread not being good enough?

The really scary part was that I thought I might be getting
used to it. Dan was getting complacent and starting to assume that
we could go each week, and I was getting lazy about objecting.
Extended exposure to the awfulness of these family get-togethers
had upped my tolerance levels. The last time, I had skipped
breakfast so that I would have enough of an appetite to be seen
eating. I ate my own body weight in sausage and survived. I didn't
like going, but I could stand it. And it seemed that I needed to be
adamant in order to get out of it. But then, why should I have had
to get dizzy and nauseous in order to get my point across? Surely
just preferring not to be there should have been enough of an excuse not to go? I seemed to be running out of steam on this issue,
and frankly, I was really afraid that I was getting too used to Dan's
family. Once you become attuned to a family's dysfunction, it
means you have become a part of it.

I always thought that my background was really messed up:
wannabe artist weirdo for a mom, no dad. But now I was beginning to realize that it was just unconventional. There's a difference. I knew I was loved, my grandfather was a stable father
figure in my life, and, although my mother had her faults, I could
always talk to her. My school friends were jealous of the open

communication between us, and a mother can commit worse crimes than making you call her by her Christian name and having a propensity to tie-dye your wardrobe.

Dan's family gave good small talk, but there was a poisonous aftertaste that I couldn't put my finger on.

OK, yes, I could put my finger on it.

It was Eileen. She was cold; she was critical; all she did for her kids was get on them about coming over so she could shove junk food into them and glower disapprovingly at their spouses.

Hostess with the mostest, huh?

Dan's father was the nonevent in the corner; he just sat quietly in front of the TV hoping that no one would notice him. The twins were cute, but they were on vacation (otherwise known as escape from Alcatraz). Dan's younger brother, Joe, ran a car-parts shop and his wife, Sarah, was a small, plump, smiling woman— nice, but wouldn't commit herself, just nodded and agreed with everything I said. Tom was in real estate, just a year older than Dan, and his body double. A fact that appears to confuse his wife—braless Shirley—whom I had seen literally lick her lips when the two of them stood together. Shirley's age was blurred by collagen use and a body stuffed into the wardrobe of a teenage girl. She was the type of woman who would be buying *Glamour* magazine and experimenting with this season's makeup looks well into her fifties. I could rant about Shirley ad infinitum, but briefly? She gave me a pain.

ON OUR way over in the car, I decided to give it my best shot and have one more go at getting my point across.

However, it was a ten-minute journey and I took five minutes to work out what I was going to say. Which gave me two minutes to say it, a minute for Dan to think about how to respond, and two minutes to discuss and resolve the whole issue.

I took the self-help guide approach and said something rehearsed and diplomatic along the lines of: "I feel really uncomfortable with the number of Sundays we are spending at your mother's house."

"Why?"

He was just being aggressively obtuse. We had had this conversation before, and so he was goading me into saying what I really thought, which was, "I hate your mother!"

"It's not that I dislike your mother, Dan, but . . ."

Whoa. But. Not a good word on the end of a mother sentence.

Dan's face tightened into a worried scowl and I was starting to backpedal when suddenly it hit me like a brick: Damn you and your damn mother. That miserable old cow has been vile to me. She summons us to her house every single Sunday, then spends three hours ignoring me. She puts on this twisted, sarcastic face when I hand her over the cakes and canapés I bother my stupid ass to bring with me, and generally goes out of her way to make me feel like a worthless piece of shit. I hate her, and I hate you—you weak, stupid, hapless ape—for not standing up to her, but most of all I hate myself for having married into this awful woman's family!

But before I got the chance to edit my anger into a more palatable version that I could actually say out loud, Dan pulled up to his mother's house.

"But what?" he said.

Bastard! I was boiling inside, but there was nothing I could do about it. I couldn't explode there, in the car, outside his mother's house. I just had to keep it together, get inside, get through the next few hours—then go home and say it like it was. Because I was never, ever, *ever* going to put myself through the purgatory of that pretend-happy family fiasco again.

I plastered an unconvincing smile across my face, and sang, "Nothing!"

Then I unclicked the seatbelt, folded myself out of the car, and let him follow me up the path.

Shirley opened the door.

"Hi folks!" she said, all curly eyelashes and cleavage. Then she looked sideways at my husband and said, "Hi, Dan."

Dan looked delighted, and my rage rose another notch when I saw how easily he was distracted from the fight we almost just had.

They were all there, sitting in silence around the TV. As well as family, there was a middle-aged couple that nobody bothered to introduce me to and a woman in glitter capri pants with dyed orange hair who could only be a friend of Shirley's.

"This is Candice," Shirley flicked her nails in the woman's general direction. "Her husband just left her for her sister."

Candice spit, "Slut," but I took it she meant her sister and not me.

At that moment, I did not think I would make it through the whole afternoon. The key was to keep busy and not sit down.

So I went straight out to the kitchen to prepare some food that I had brought with me. It was one of my tricks to tolerating these events: preparing food, working. It kept me occupied and away from the TV-induced silence. Infiltrating Eileen's kitchen was never easy and she gave me her customary sideways grimace and shrugged when I said cheerily, "Brought some nibbles, Eileen—do you mind?"

I took as long as I could. There was sports on TV, and I could hear the men calling out occasional shouts of encouragement or abuse.

I worked as slowly as I could and took forty-five minutes to pile the soda bread with tomato chutney, shredded Parma ham, crumbled goat's cheese, and a drizzle of aged balsamic dressing. Eileen didn't turn to me once while I was working, out of curiosity or encouragement. She just kept shaking her bags of frozen hors d'oeuvres onto foil trays.

Holding on to my forced good humor as hard as I could, I started to work the room with my tray of canapés. Dan grabbed one and stuffed it into his mouth without moving his eyes from the TV; Sarah giggled a profuse "thank you," but looked uncertain as how to handle this alien concoction; her husband took one and put it to one side. But—surprise, surprise—it was Shirley who finally caused me to snap.

"Oh no," she said, pushing me away with her palm as if I were a waitress, "I hate that lumpy Irish bread."

If I was looking for a person to bury in my displaced anger, I could not have found a more deserving candidate than Shirley Mullins.

It was as if every slight I had ever received in my lifetime, from the cool girls at school laughing at my tie-dyed pants to a bad review three years ago, had all pooled together with my doubts about Dan and my reservations about his family. All those nasty little niggling gnomes I had been trying to keep under wraps had got dressed up in their loudest, fanciest gear and were holding a carnival. IT'S PAYBACK TIME! their banner read, and so I let rip.

I can't remember exactly what I said, but I could make a fairly accurate guess based on what had been simmering away in my head all afternoon. The starting point was calling Shirley a stupid slut and accusing her of coming on to Dan. I don't know where that came from; I certainly hadn't thought it was something that bothered me sufficiently to lose my cool like that. I threw the tray of canapés on the floor, declaring the assembled group "unappreciative ignoramuses." When I caught sight of myself losing it in front of relative strangers and three actual ones, I resorted to a teenage tantrum, shouted, "Oh piss off!," grabbed my bag from the table, and stormed out of the house.

Shaking, I rummaged in my purse, praying that Dan had slipped the car keys in there like he always did. As I started the engine and drove home in five minutes flat, I knew it was over, and I thought, *Good riddance, you bunch of messed-up freaks.*

But by the time I got home, the shaking anger had given way to the awful realization of what I had done.

I lay on our bed and bawled like a petulant child into the pillow.

Marriage was supposed to be the answer to everything, the blossoming of a mature love. It was supposed to dignified, civilized, supportive, nurturing. Marriage wasn't easy, but it shouldn't be a nightmare you couldn't wake up from.

That afternoon, I realized I didn't know what marriage was supposed to be like at all. But I was pretty sure it wasn't supposed to be like this.

Twenty-two

cannot say that what I felt for my father was love. I was afraid of him; yet worse than the fear was the way that I understood him. I felt responsible for his anger and guilty for his sorrows. Whether he was silent and sullen or loud and abusive, I always sensed that it fell on me to make him better.

While my mother's pretensions toward sainthood were often the catalyst to his anger, I was referee to his demons. In his worst drunken moods, I seemed to be the only person he could have around him. My mother could never fully understand my father because she did not have his blood running through her veins. So while his maudlin ramblings enraged my brothers, calming and placating my father out of a drunken frenzy became my job. They all ran like rats out of the house when they saw him coming, my mother wailing and wringing her hands in a way I knew would anger him even more.

He always professed a passionate love for my mother, and claimed that her coldheartedness was killing him. But my father did not want to be loved. He wanted someone to run alongside him and witness his pain, someone to drown in his anguish with him. So he would sit at the kitchen table, his coarse hands fumbling clumsily around the cigarette packet, and start to list his grievances: his brother getting the farm, bad price on cattle, some bastard this, some bastard that—working up to the climax of my mother's brothers giving him a beating. The betrayal of it! The humiliation! Then the fists would come down on the table and I knew it was nearly over and he was ready for some food.

I preferred my father angry because once the fight had gone out of him, he was just a vulnerable mountain of man. As a small child, it terrified me to see my father cry; as I grew older, it broke my heart. I spent my childhood wishing away my father's pain.

As a young woman, I assumed that treacherous trickery of fear and guilt, that compulsion to cure, was love. By the time my mother died, I was a woman in my forties and I had learned different. Or at least I thought I had.

When I saw my father help carry my mother's coffin up the aisle, I knew that he was not going to survive on his own. His ferocious frame confined in the black suit I had bought for him the day before, he shuffled his feet as if the ground were burning them. He had a look of anguish on his face, like an actor frozen mid-speech. It was as if my mother's death had been flung at him by an adversary. God. Punishment for all the bad things he had done.

When I looked at him, pathetic and broken like that, my heart disintegrated to dust. That was how it had always been. His anguish, his anger always dwarfed the feelings of the people around him. My mother's funeral became not about her, but about how my father would cope without her.

After years of marriage to a decent man, I came to believe that perhaps my father was not a lost soul deserving of my tolerance and pity, but a cunning, truly evil man. But it takes more than believing something to reverse the habits of a devoted daughter.

My mother was sixty-seven when she died unexpectedly, and

for their whole marriage, she had waited on my father hand and foot. He knew how to light the fire and he knew where the well was, but he could not boil a pan of water, and he did not know how many spoons of sugar he took in his tea. My family home was half an hour's bicycle ride away from our house, and I thought I would manage my father's meals and look after him sufficiently without having to move him in with us. As the weeks after she died progressed, however, I realized that it wasn't going to be possible. A neighbor was supplying Daddy with *poitin*, and he wasn't bothering to eat the food I was leaving for him or light the fire. Twice I found him asleep in the chair, having soiled himself. The second time I thought he was dead and, I confess, I felt a flicker of relief. It's over, I thought. It seemed so right, that death should come quickly and give him an early release.

It was perhaps only the shock and guilt I felt when he opened his eyes that made me bring him home with me.

That and James. My husband had been insistent from the first, "Your father needs the comfort of his family."

"Let one of my brothers take him back to England."

"Oh Bernadine . . ." His voice moved across my name in that disappointed tone he always used whenever I said something nasty; as if cruel words were so unlike the kindhearted Bernadine that he knew me to be.

James was a Pioneer—a nondrinker. As a young woman, I had thought his refusal of alcohol patronizing and unattractive. A man who did not drink was not a real man—no *craic*. As time went on, I began to realize that perhaps the only good thing my father ever gave me was a husband who didn't drink.

James occupied himself with his reading and always had plenty to keep him interested around the house: growing vegetables and keeping bees. He had more interest in Niamh than most men had in their children. As he got older, James did seek out the company of other men, but through the more gentlemanly pursuits of fishing and shooting. The pub was somewhere he went to pay his respects after a funeral, or perhaps buy his wife a bar of chocolate on his way home from town. In that way, I felt that James was innocent of the indignities and vulgarities of the drinking man. To him, my father was just the person who had given me to him. He knew that Daddy drank and could be rough at times, but he had never witnessed anything that would lead him to believe that my father was different from any other man. The idea of my refined husband being exposed to the coarse treachery of my father's drunken tongue terrified me.

I was not afraid of my father himself, but of who I became when I was with him. All my adult sense told me that Daddy was a drunken old fool not worth taking heed of. But in my heart I was still a frightened child, eager to make everything better. James had seen me tired, grieving—but he had never seen me weak.

MOTHER DIED in mid-August and my father moved in with us by early September. I was relieved at the timing, as it was the beginning of the autumn term, so James and Niamh would be at school all day and I would be left to deal with my father on my own.

Daddy was seventy, and should not have lived past sixty the way he abused himself. He was heavy, and grew out of breath after even the shortest distance walking, but he was still a strong man.

For the first few months, it looked as if everything was going to be fine. Daddy had got a fright when I had found him passed out for the second time, and promised his drinking days were well and truly behind him. He was still in shock over having lost my mother, but seemed to accept that a holiday in our house was a good idea. He was more outgoing than I had ever seen him before.

He declared that James was a charming man, saying that this not-drinking thing was very good indeed and that he wished he had taken his pledge more seriously as a youth. Niamh, who barely knew her grandfather and was used to living in the exclusive company of her parents, adapted quickly to having him around. They both reveled in the novelty of each other's company and after supper would sit by the fire in a conspiratorial huddle playing Old Maid or Snakes and Ladders while I cleaned the scullery and James tended the vegetable garden.

Those evenings, watching them from the scullery door, I could not help a feeling that my family had finally taken shape: three generations under the same roof. There was such warmth in seeing how the old man was with my child. It was as if the complications of parenthood had disappeared with a generation, and all that was left was his paternal love. If my own childhood had been fraught, then perhaps this idyll was my reward.

While my husband and child were at school, a cheerful working relationship opened up between my father and me. Eager to distract himself from drinking, but anxious not to step on James's toes, my father asked to be given simple jobs around the house. He cleaned the fires for me, and I even had him polishing furniture and cleaning windows. He seemed proud of finishing each task, and we argued playfully over his reward:

"That'll be apple tart and cream on the menu tonight, young lady."

"You'll have stewed gooseberries like the rest of us and be glad of them."

"What about a few blackberries then?"

"You'll have to pick them first, Mister."

I had never enjoyed a light banter with my father before and it was wonderful. He praised my cooking, and for the first time in my life I had the feeling of being my Daddy's little girl. I began to understand the carefree confidence that James gave to Niamh. This late blossoming of affection was my reward for enduring a childhood fraught with confusion and hardship. Compensation perhaps, perhaps, for losing the great love of my life and being married off heartlessly to the safest, cheapest option.

Although I was sorry my mother was dead, I was sorrier for the fact that I was enjoying the benefits of my father's sobriety and not her. Meanwhile a little demon princess was whispering that perhaps I had some power over him that my mother had never had. Perhaps I had the secret to stopping my Daddy drinking after all, and all the wishes I had wished and all the prayers I had prayed had finally come true.

The day you think you have the answers is the day life tells you that you know nothing at all. When you think you have suffered enough and the road ahead looks sunny and flat, you will turn the corner and find there is a mountain to climb. When you climb the mountain there are no guarantees that there will not be another, and another after that.

My father was seventy years of age. He had terrorized his family for the best part of fifty years and been forgiven, forgiven, forgiven. But with men like my father, it isn't over until they draw their final breath. And even then, you will carry them around forever like a stone in your heart.

Twenty-three

aiting for Dan to get back from his mother's house was insufferable. The longest and most dreadful half hour of my life. When I heard the front door bang, I thought I had been up in the bedroom for hours.

He came straight upstairs and found me lying face-down on the bed. Gently, he put a hand on my shoulder.

"Are you OK, babe?"

Call me a raving psychopath who doesn't know when to stop, but I turned from a weak, weeping kitten into a possessed madwoman as soon as I felt his touch.

"Where the *hell* have you been?"

"I came home as quick as I could—I had to get a lift off Tom."

"Yeah, I bet that bitch Shirley had something to say about me?"

"She didn't say anything, we were all just really worried about you."

That really finished me off. *"Worried about me?"*

Dan was looking right at me, and I saw his benign expression flicker for a second. I was still angry, but instinct made me draw back from ranting about his family and I finished with a frustrated, "Huh!"

Dan turned to go. "I'll go down and make us some coffee."

"I don't want coffee!"

He spun back around, looked at me straight, and said, "Well then what *do* you want, Tressa, because I am sure wearing myself out here trying to guess."

He wasn't shouting, but he was calling me out: eyeballing me in this calm, you-better-start-talking way.

And I did not like it one little bit, not least because the answer was, "I want to bury you and your family under twenty tons of shit, set light to it, then transport the ashes to outer space."

"I just want the two of us to spend more time alone together."

Where did that come from?

I had a fear of the truth. Not the obvious truth like Dan's family was weird, or even the next layer under that, which was that his mother gave me the creeps, but the next floor down. Otherwise known as gut level: the underlying truth. Why did I find his family such hard work? Why did I find doing what I didn't want to do for him so intolerable? If I loved him, I could endure the unendurable. If we were meant to be together, I would gladly have suffered boredom, indignity, awkwardness as part of my commitment to our marriage.

Within the confines of my own head, I obsessed about whether I really loved Dan enough to be married to him, and sometimes dreamed of escape. But as soon as I was given the chance to tackle this most fundamental of questions, an opportunity to speak my truth and thus put my hand on the handle of the "out" door, I would instantly teleport myself into a state of unswerving marital devotion.

Delusion devoured the truth, and made me say something utterly inaccurate, by which time it was too late. You can say something bad, then take it back like you didn't mean it—but it doesn't work the same for good things.

"Sorry, I didn't mean to say, 'I just want the two of us to spend more time alone together.' What I really meant was, 'I'm not sure if I love you enough to tolerate a lifetime of your awful family.'"

And, of course, once you start down that coward's highway of white lies, there is no turning back.

Dan walked straight over and folded me in a suffocating hug.

He said, "I have been so selfish, Tressa, putting my family before us." Then he launched into this story about how his mother had had a stroke when they were all very young, how nobody had explained to them all why their mother couldn't speak properly, and how the experience had made them all very protective of their mother. I wondered why he hadn't told me before, but was too self-absorbed to care. Too busy searching for the exit door on this dead-end alley of fake devotion. If it was there, it was blocked by my shame.

And so it was that I found myself standing at the front door of the house of a woman I loathed with a bunch of flowers in my hands, a rehearsed apology on my lips, and a heart that was thumping so hard it felt like it might jump out of my body and bite her.

Eileen wasn't going to make this easy, but knowing that didn't make it any more pleasant when she opened the door. She greeted me with expressionless silence, and then walked straight back into her kitchen where she continued her chores as if I wasn't there.

I put the flowers down on the counter and said my piece.

"Eileen, I owe you an apology."

It was unreserved, featured no "buts," offered no line of defense and was a text-book, perfect apology to which the only possible response was a counter apology.

When no response of any kind was forthcoming, I started to flail about with explanations and excuses. Eventually I tripped across something that got her attention.

"Eileen, I love your son and . . ."

I hadn't had a chance to finish whatever thoughtless platitude was on its way out when the old woman turned to me, and her eyes were raging.

"You don't love my son."

It was like a bolt had gone through me. I didn't know where to start. This sudden show of passion from a woman I thought was an impervious lump. Then there was the whole ghastly element of it being true.

"Eileen! How could you say such a thing!"

"Because it's true!"

I was taken aback. We were heading for a showdown very different from the muted, grudging apology acceptance I was prepared for. I was going to have to tread very carefully if I wanted to prevent my mother-in-law from beating me.

"I am not even going to comment on that, Eileen. Why would I have married your son if I didn't love him?"

"Because you are nearly forty and afraid of missing the boat . . ."

Thirty-eight, actually, but otherwise—good call.

Before I had the chance to formulate a response I was afraid I could not find, she added quite aggressively, ". . . *and* your brown bread is rubbish."

Was this an escape route she was offering me? A side turn off the truth route perhaps neither of us was ready for right now?

Whatever. Nobody criticized my cooking and got away with it, and I guess the old lady knew that.

"Oh really? And what's wrong with it?"

"It's too dry. You need to use butter."

"I always use butter," which was a lie.

"And an egg . . ."

"You don't put eggs in bread."

"Well maybe you should try, and a spoon of sugar might stop it tasting of cotton wool . . ."

"Thanks for your opinion, Eileen, but . . ." I stopped as I realized there was no but. She was right, my bread was shit. Then I saw what was really going on. We were two stubborn, self-righteous bitches standing in a kitchen arguing over how to make bread. It had been a long time since anyone had been anything other than deferential toward my cooking, so for chutzpah alone, I decided to rise to her challenge.

"Well, if you want to show me how it's done, Eileen, I am all eyes and ears."

She looked nervous—as well she might, the old cow.

"I don't have the ingredients."

"Oh, I'm sure we can come up with something . . ." I said, stridently starting to open cupboard doors. I didn't care now. The old lady despised me anyway, so I may as well trample all over her boundaries and be done with it. I had nothing to lose.

I found flour, bicarbonate of soda, sugar—then went to the fridge and removed a pat of butter, milk, and rather pointedly placed a single egg on the worktop in front of her. Eileen looked stunned, and for a second I felt sorry for her.

"We have no buttermilk. It's not the same without the buttermilk."

She was trying to cop out.

"It'll do," I said.

Eileen gave me one of her unnerving stares, then she did something extraordinary. She emptied the sink of dirty dishes, then rinsed out the blue plastic washing-up bowl, dried it with a cloth, and placed it on the work counter. Eileen rooted in a cupboard under the sink and came out with a sieve, into which she roughly threw handfuls of the flour and a large, unmeasured pinch of soda. As she shook the flour into fine downy peaks, the memories came flooding back. Grandma Bernadine's bowl was bright green and her sieve stainless steel, not plastic, but otherwise they could have been the same. I don't know that their methods were identical, all I know is that as I watched Eileen's worn, plump fingers swiftly churn the milk and flour into an airy dough ball, I was transported back to my grandmother's side. Like a child, I was transfixed by the speed with which the expert hands hoovered up every crumb and placed the perfect, crossed dome onto a floured baking tray and into the oven.

When it was over, Eileen was flustered, and could not untie her apron strings. I went and helped her and it was the first time (after an early aborted hugging attempt) that I had been that close to her physically. She smelled of sour milk and kitchen soap, of an ordinary old woman who never bothered with pretty things. I felt a snap of pity, but knew this was no time to let down my guard.

"I'm impressed, Eileen." Then, by way of an olive branch, "You make bread like my grandmother."

She gave me a cursory "thanks"—then disappeared into the drawing room. Just as I was wondering if I was meant to follow her, she came back, and thrust a silver framed photograph at me.

The image was an old black-and-white photograph of a kindly looking older woman with her hair swept back in a bun and small round glasses.

"She taught me."

"Your mother?" I asked.

"Ha!" she said strongly. "My grandmother."

Over the next forty-five minutes, I dragged Eileen's story out of her. Her mother had become pregnant, then run away to America, leaving the baby Eileen in the hands of her grandparents, whom she assumed to be her mother and father. Her grandparents sheltered her from the truth for as long as they could, but when she was seventeen, her grandfather died and a neighbor let slip her parentage at his funeral. Grief-stricken and furious, Eileen bullied her mother's address out of her grandmother and started to write to her, but her mother never replied. Finally, when she was twenty-three, her grandmother managed to scrape together her passage to America and Eileen went and found her mother living in Yonkers, only to be rejected in person. She had met and married a wealthy older man, who knew nothing of Eileen's existence. Her daughter's letters had all been destroyed without being opened. With no family, and no money, Eileen presented herself at the presbytery of the first Catholic church she could find and was given a job as assistant to their housekeeper. Dan's father was the housekeeper's younger brother and that was how they met. She continued to live in the same city as her mother and learned of her death through the local paper. She did not attend the funeral out of deference to her mother's new family.

All of this was delivered in matter-of-fact single sentences. Not a shred of embellishment or self-pity, just shrugging, that's-the-way-it-was pragmatism. When she had finished, I wanted to embrace her—this motherless burdened woman.

"The bread!"

We saved it just in time, wrapped it in an I LOVE ST. PATRICK'S DAY IN YONKERS! tea towel, the first clean one to hand.

I wanted to ask if she saw her grandmother or her mother again after that, but thought it best to let her finish reminiscing another day. There would, I knew, be other days to fill.

As I stood at the door, she handed me the loaf.

"Now," she said, "I hope it's up to your standards."

She gave me one of her sarcastic lopsided looks.

I looked into her eyes and saw they were soft with affection.

With shame, I remembered the stroke, and realized that Eileen had been smiling at me all along.

Twenty-four

I came downstairs to find my father sitting by last night's fire. His back was to me and his head was as still as a statue.

"I didn't light the range for you this morning, Bernadine."

His voice delivered the words deliberately, as if he had been rehearsing them.

Dread lurched up through my stomach.

I knew from his inflection that my father had been drinking. He hadn't had much, maybe only a sniff of whisky, but I could hear trouble in his tone. Knowledge of my father's mood swings was etched into my bones.

"I am missing your mother today."

"I miss her, too, but we have to get on with our work."

I spoke before I had the chance to breathe in and smell the heaviness of a storm brewing.

I was operating on a wing and a prayer, using the same harsh, pragmatic tone I used on my husband. As if it were the same thing; as if my everyday honest words would not antagonize him into a rage.

I had not lived under my father's roof for almost twenty years. This was my home. I was an adult with mature responsibilities. I had my own family; I was no longer a part of his world, but he of mine. He was staying in another man's house, and I was another man's wife. James was a respectable, hardworking, honest person. My father would not dare abuse me in my husband's house.

His voice was barely audible.

"You evil bitch."

I had heard him say it to my mother. Mutter an atrocity so quietly that you might think the devil himself was whispering inside your head.

"Pardon?"

The request to repeat it was out automatically.

He did not reply straight away, so I pretended that nothing had been said.

"I said, you evil bitch."

My hands were shaking as I scooped handfuls of flour into my basin and I repeated to myself, *Give us this day our daily bread, give us this day our daily bread.*

"Did you hear me, Bernadine? Are you going to reply to your father?"

Our Father who art in heaven.

I realized in that moment that I had no special skills for dealing with such a bully. No innate understanding running through my veins. What had protected me in the past was not my status as his blood relation or his child, but my mother. Now she was gone, he needed another victim to pour his rage into. Another "coldhearted" woman to justify his bitterness and depression. A reason he could give himself to explain the lump of pain inside, and help dilute it into something more digestible—like hate.

"Look at you—standing there making bread. My daughter, the coldhearted, evil bitch. Your mother lies in her grave and you

are standing there. Making bread. You don't give a shit about anyone or anything."

He had never spoken to me like that before, but when he had
spoken in that way to my mother, I had always been terrified because I knew it precipitated violence. And as he spoke, I knew I
should be feeling afraid, but I wasn't.

I felt angry. Really angry. And it didn't take much more than
that first outburst to pull this surge of loathing up from my feet to
my mouth. It was as if the *Titanic* had risen from deep inside me,
and I lashed out. A stream of obscenities I did not know I understood flew out of me, and I threw the basin of flour across the
room, narrowly missing my father's head.

Flour scattered around the fireplace, a cloud of it catching him
on the side of the face in a ghostly sheath. We both stood for a few
seconds, shocked.

Then he came at me. Silently, his mouth opening around a
half-created insult, drugged by his own anger, he flung his arm at
my head and swiped me to the ground. It was a blow as heavy as
if he had been holding a brick. As if he were a big man and I still
a little child. I fell like a weighted cushion and as my shoulder hit
the flagstones, I surrendered. My anger vanished in the impact;
defeat was instant and absolute. As my father lifted his leg to kick
me, there was a shout.

"Bernadine!"

James was at the door. The sound of his voice itself pushed my
body into a fetal curl.

"Get out of my house, John Moran, or so help me God, I will
kill you."

My father stepped away from me and turned to James. For a
moment, I thought he might hit him and I cried out, "No!"

As my father walked towards him, James put his hand to the back of the door and, in one discreet motion, took his hunting gun in his hand.

"I won't speak freely, John, but I know what kind of man you are. If you ever show such disrespect to my wife or lay a hand on her again, I will kill you. Now get out of my house."

My father looked back at me, and his parting shot was a look of pathos. As if he were the slighted one. As if the world were not big enough to contain the agonized regret of having hit me. As if I were the only person who could understand that it was himself, not me, who was the victim.

THAT NIGHT I woke under the bedclothes with my head buried in the soft flesh of James's stomach, sobbing "Daddy, Daddy."

James drew me up and held me in a protective knot, and I allowed the boundaries of father and husband to blur as he wiped my tears and kissed the top of my head. I cried without shame and the schoolmaster comforted the brave girl who had reared him a daughter and grown gray hairs at her temple. I never needed my husband's love as much as I did that night. It was as a replacement for someone else's, but he gave it willingly nonetheless.

Recovery from childhood traumas was unrecognized by my generation. They were not fashionable as they are now, but they were felt no less deeply. James was an intelligent, perceptive man, ahead of his time in many ways.

"You know that your father can come back and stay here at any time, Bernadine. You only have to say the word." James was a big enough man to play second best, to a runaway rogue or a brutal alcoholic. He would always walk two steps behind if he thought it would make me happy.

It took a few weeks for the ice to thaw, but I continued to visit my father and tend to his needs twice a week. That day was never mentioned again.

Within a year, the mild arthritis my father had been suffering from turned chronic. He became virtually chairbound, and, reluctantly, came to live with us again. My father remained with us for the rest of his life, another nine years. He drank, when he had the energy to get it himself, but there were no more violent scenes.

James found living with my father harder than I did. When someone loves you, you can see yourself through their eyes. I know that James never recovered from knowing that my father had hit me, nor from knowing that he had not been there in that moment to protect me. Until Daddy lost virtually all movement in his legs, it crucified James to leave me alone in the house with him each day. He was generous and polite to Daddy always, but he made it clear it was for my benefit and not his.

Daddy was not an easy patient, nor always a polite one. I cannot look back on the nine years he was with us and pinpoint moments of joy or familial revelation or intimacy. Even his playmate, Niamh, in time withdrew from him. My father had a way of pushing people away, especially those who loved him. In his lifetime I had watched him come to despise those who loved him as much as he despised himself, as if their love was never genuine but a cruel joke they used to taunt him. I was at pains to discourage my daughter from investing too heavily in her grandfather's affections, arranging for her to spend more time with her cousins and form closer friendships with children her own age. In fairness to my father, he never abused her or said anything to hurt Niamh, but the close tie they formed during his first stay didn't return once it wasn't encouraged by me.

My father grew weak and quiet, but I would never say he mellowed. Mellow would be too kind a description for the silence he gradually applied to his anger. There were times in those years keeping and cleaning and caring for my father's body when I was fraught, frustrated, disgusted even. I endured it because I had to, and I was able to because James was by my side. Every emotion, every hardship is endurable except fear. *What* we fear is endurable, it is usually the fear itself that is insufferable. I was never afraid of my father again after that day. When you have known real fear, to live without it can be a luxury; but you have to *know* when you are one of the lucky ones. That suffering is the destiny of some and the birthright of many.

I was spared my mother's suffering and that could be said to be due to one thing only: my marriage to James.

Respect

Complacency is the enemy of love.

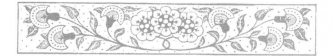

Porter Cake

I have been making this porter cake for as far back as I can remember. It's heavy with fruit and makes an ideal Christmas cake. Take 1lb and a quarter flour and mix in a bowl with one quarter teaspoon baking soda and whatever spices you have to hand—nutmeg, cinnamon, mixed spice—adding a flat teaspoon of each. Set aside. Mix up 4 eggs in a bowl and set aside also. In a heavy saucepan put the following: 1 bottle Guinness, 1lb rich brown sugar, 1lb each raisins and sultanas, 4oz mixed peel, and a half pound Stork margarine. Allow it to boil for five minutes then turn to a low simmer for a further ten. Five minutes into the simmer, add 4oz glacé cherries. Leave to cool until a good deal cooler than lukewarm. To the cooled mixture add your flour, and then the eggs— gradually and with great caution to avoid curdling. Pour the mixture into a nine-inch tin that has been lined with grease-proof paper. Cook in a slow oven for between two and a half and three hours.

Twenty-five

You should never take old favorites for granted in cooking. About the time a recipe becomes automatic and fail-safe is when it will let you down in front of an audience.

You've got to feel for these people who get dragged in as studio audiences. The sun is shining outside, yet they have been lured by the hollow promise of "entertainment" into a windowless, cavernous space with uncomfortable tiered seating to watch a nervous food writer panicking over a sunken fruit cake.

"I don't know what happened."

"Did you put in the raising agent?"

Great—my director bakes.

I did not dignify him with a reply, just said, "We'll have to do it again."

"I can't keep these people here any longer. They've already sat through two broken flans. They'll riot."

And charming, too.

This recipe was so simple, I had been doing it since I was, literally, seven years old. I had learned how to count measuring the ingredients out for my grandmother: one, two, three, four eggs; four, five, six pounds of butter.

When my agent called to say that I had been selected to screen test for a show on a cable cooking channel, I was pretty excited. If it worked out, that meant I could sell a lot more books, and get more TV work, and, well—suffice to say this was something I had hoped was in the cards for me and finally I seemed to be getting my moment in the sun.

Except I hadn't banked on the possibility that maybe television just wasn't quite the glamorous ride I was expecting.

The whole thing felt like an experiment in minor-celebrity humiliation. I had been plonked in front of a tired, rented audience, who for their ten-dollar paycheck and free lunch had already endured three hours of "oohing" and "ahhing" in front of Shelly, "the nail-care systems expert," before being subjected to me breaking two custard flans and almost causing fatal injury to a cameraman, thanks to his sliding on an undiscovered goose giblet.

It had not been my finest hour.

I was terrified of failing at this and had chosen Grandma's traditional Christmas cake because it is magnificent in an earthy, old-fashioned way. Fruit cake is substantial, no delicate confection liable to deflate with the slightest breeze through the oven door. So the collapse was a humiliation. People will forgive a deflated soufflé, but I could see them looking at me thinking, "How the hell did she do that?"

The director was not sympathetic to my being a nervous novice. This was a man who had been shooting pilots and screen tests for too long, and was obviously being paid a set rate to finish the job, so he wasn't running over on hours.

"I'm sending this crowd home. There's a fresh batch due into studio four at seven. We can prep now then film in there when the real chef is done."

Like I said. He was a charmer.

"What about continuity?"

I hated this director, and directors hate their integrity being questioned. As do I.

"The set's not exactly the same, but then, hey—you're not exactly Martha Stewart, are you?"

Except, it seemed, for this one, who had no integrity at all.

I wanted this day to be over.

In twelve hours I had gone from believing I was on the cusp of an exciting career breakthrough to the shattering realization that I was a lousy TV cook. Lousy cook, period, was what the director's face said.

The cake was finished by eight and came out perfectly, but the day wasn't over.

Just as I was finishing up, who did I see out of the corner of my eye but the "chef"? The one I had been seeing just before I met Dan? The one who had passed me over for a model? Well, his name is Ronan Robertson and though I had my eyes firmly trained on the camera, I could feel his eyes burning the back of my neck.

I somehow managed to close the show in one take and if the audience was pleased, and the director relieved, I didn't notice. As I turned and saw Ronan still standing there, staring, this rush ran through me. Something bad was going to happen, and there was nothing I could do to stop it.

"Ronan."

I walked over to him and I could feel my limbs start to weaken. It was as if my body had gone into recall about how much I had wanted him that one night we had slept together. The formality of our meeting through work, then suddenly being naked and intimate. My physical senses were in anticipation of reacquainting myself with him, without the permission of my brain.

"Tressa."

He was looking at me in a quizzical, intense way and—
oooh—the deep, grumbling voice. That was how he had gotten
me into bed. That and a lot of alcohol.

"I need a drink," I said, "how about you?"

It was OK, safe to flirt. I was an old married lady after all, despite what my body was signaling. Just glad of the opportunity to
let this egotistical jerk know what he had missed out on.

IT WAS all so different from how I thought it would be. Ronan
was subdued, not the consummate charmer who had seduced and
then dumped me. I suggested we go uptown. He shrugged,
"whatever," and there was an awkward silence in the cab that I
broke with, "Are you sure you want this drink, Ronan? You're
very quiet."

He shook his head and gave me a strange look.

"You are some piece of work, Tressa Nolan."

Though curious, I didn't ask what he meant because the mystery of his statement felt good. For the first time since we had got
into the cab I looked at him properly and instantly regretted it.
Ronan was no pin-up, not nearly as conventionally handsome as
Dan, but there was a quality about him that I found hard to resist.
I couldn't pinpoint it in what we said or his sense of humor or
what we had in common, although educated, erudite, witty chef
just about sums up his credentials for me. But Ronan feels familiar to me, almost a soul mate. I slept with him more or less a few
hours after we first met and it didn't feel sluttish, or wrong—it felt
destined. As if he had always been there.

We had made love like we were in love. Afterward, while I lay
folded around his body, was a night of understated emotion, of
comfort in just being with him, like hearing a sad song for the first
time and feeling like it was written about you. It sounds crazy, but

I had such a strong, instant connection with him that I almost believed we had been together in a past life. The funny thing is that I was sure that he felt it, too.

Then he didn't call and started publicly dating a model, so I pegged him as an arrogant pig.

I didn't think back on the night we had together or how special it had felt or how "different" or how "meant to be" it had all seemed. "All men are bastards" may be an old cliché, but sometimes you just need a line that works.

So here we were again.

His shirt was a faded blue, the same shade as his eyes by happy accident, his hands scrubbed like a good chef's should be.

"You never called."

Him, not me. I couldn't believe my ears.

"You never called *me*," I blurted out.

"You said *you* would call *me*, Tressa. You were like, don't call us, we'll call you."

"That is just not true, Ronan. You said you would call me."

"Other way around."

Then he gave me this big broad grin and shook his head again. His eyes were sparkling, he was suddenly filled with light, and somehow I knew I had done that to him.

"What's going on here, Tressa? We're, I don't know . . ."

"A couple of bickering kids?"

He leaned his elbow on the door window, put his fingers to his forehead, and shook his head some more. Then he looked up from under his palm, his eyes full of happy mischief, and said, "More than that, Tressa. I don't know what's going on with us. It's crazy, I just feel like—I don't know."

I didn't know either. Except of course I did. I just didn't want to say it. I was married now, so I said, "I need a drink."

We stopped the cab uptown and went to the nearest bar. Touristy, noisy, somewhere neither of us had been before. I ordered tequila shots, although I rarely drink hard liquor. I guess I was trying to pretend I was someone else, someone who was free to fall in love. The tequila was to help raise the stakes on the already intoxicating blend of adrenaline and emotion I was experiencing. Or perhaps it was just something to help me forget I was married.

We spent an hour clearing the ground. He told me how he was sick of screwing models. He made a very convincing case (even though it takes very little to convince a slightly drunk woman in her late thirties that men prefer "real women"), and when he talked about having screwed up by not pursuing me more assertively, there was genuine resignation in his voice.

"So you're married, Tressa."

"Yeah," I said, beaming at all this adulation, "I'm really happy."

As soon as I said it, I knew it wasn't true. I wasn't really happy with Dan. If I was, I wouldn't be sitting here. Ronan looked deep into my eyes in a way that only he could and said, "I've thought about you a lot."

He faltered over the words as if he had more to say, but couldn't. We were both holding back. Ronan because it was too crazy for him to say out loud, and me because I was afraid it was too late.

I wasn't just afraid it was too late. It actually *was* too late. I was married. I had Dan.

I had to linger in the moment because it felt too good to let go, and so I allowed the inevitable to happen.

We leaned, we kissed.

It was soft and slow and perfect. I was instantly sobered with the shock of how right it felt. With Angelo, the emotion had been strong, but it had felt wrong.

I thought I had been safe with Dan, but that was before I knew what *sure* felt like.

Now I knew. I can't describe it except that there was a deep, deep knowing.

They say there is one man for every woman, and mine, I felt more certain than I had ever felt anything in my life before now, was Ronan Robertson.

And I had married somebody else.

It was tragic.

So I ordered another shot, drank it down, and realized the bar we were in was part of a hotel. I called to the bartender and said, a little too loudly, "We want a room."

"No, no. No way!" Ronan was up off the stool. "This is too much, Tressa, you're married and . . ."

I could see the longing in his eyes. We were playing out a scene from our own movie.

". . . and what?"

I could feel that my face was flushed, and vaguely wondered if I looked as beautiful as I felt. He certainly seemed to think so, as his face collapsed in defeat.

"And I want you," he said. And that was it.

The room we entered was small, orange, irrelevant except for one detail.

We attacked each other in a passionate frenzy, separating briefly for Ronan to tear his shirt off and as he did, I caught sight of myself in a wall mirror I hadn't previously noticed.

My face was devoid of makeup and slanted with drink. Briefly, I didn't recognize myself and thought I was looking through a window into another room. It gave me a jolt.

This *wasn't* me, in a hotel room about to commit adultery. Immediately, I tried to turn it around. I wasn't doing anything wrong, just following my heart. Passions this strong cannot be ignored. Movies, love songs—irresistible, certain, destined love at first sight. It must mean something that I felt this way. Dan would understand, wouldn't he?

And in the millisecond that my husband's smiling honest face flashed through my mind, my uncontrollable ardor disappeared. I had to do the right thing. I'd resisted Angelo, though now I was behaving as badly as he had. This wouldn't be a "no commitment" fuck. It may have felt right—but I knew it *was* wrong.

"I have to go."

I buttoned my blouse and grabbed my bag.

"I'll pay for the room on my way out."

"Tressa. You can't go. You can't leave me like this."

I let my eyes flick across him with a brief apology. I was afraid to look at him properly, in case I changed my mind.

"This isn't right, Ronan."

"I don't have your number. Please, not like this . . . I'm begging you . . ."

As I was waiting for the elevator, I gave in to the impulse to go back and leave my number with him. When I reached the room I held my ear to the door and listened. Ronan was talking on the phone to somebody.

I took a business card out of my purse and quietly slipped it under the door.

Twenty-six

When big things in our life start changing, we rely more heavily on small certainties to make us feel secure.

My body changed early. In my late forties, it began to act against me like a rebellious teenager. I started to heat up like a furnace at irregular, unpredictable times. My palms became sweaty, my skin erupted in blotches and spots, it felt like there was some energy anxious to escape through the ends of my fingers and toes, so that I would sew and knit and run around frantically all day, then collapse in the midafternoon, exhausted. Often, I felt like weeping for no reason, and that was possibly the hardest thing of all. I was never given to easy displays of emotion. When I cried, it meant that there was something powerful and terrible going on. I considered the misty-eyed sentiment of older women to be a weakness. Now, here I was leaking emotion against my will and I did not like it. It made me bad-tempered.

So I flung myself into the certainty of my own proficiency as a housekeeper.

My house was already being run with great efficiency, so I sought out new ways to express myself as an exemplary homemaker. I took every tired or unworn piece of knitwear in the house—from old hats to holed socks and threadbare sweaters—and unpicked and reknitted them into a dreadful hodgepodge of multicolored sweaters and cardigans, which my husband wore without demur.

I crocheted antimacassars and doilies until every surface of the house was covered in lace, and then invented new things to cheer the place up. Among the more ludicrous of them was a monogrammed linen wallet for James's daily newspaper and several decorative sacks to hold his gloves, hat, and shooting scarf.

I made tea cozies, drawer tidies. I took every unused item in the house and turned it into something else; old mackintoshes into gardening aprons, felt hats into kettle holders. On one frustrated afternoon, I attacked the baby clothes that I had lovingly kept, and cut them up into tiny triangles for cushion stuffing. When I saw the decimated pile, I wept with sentimental longing to have them back.

It was around then that I developed the habit of using a different cloth to polish every surface in the house. In latter years, Niamh called it my "rag habit," as I never was able to let go of it fully. Cotton for cleaning, silk and nylon for polishing. Each rag then developed a special purpose in the house: this one for washing cups and everyday crockery, this one for china only, and another again for wiping and another for drying. This one reserved for saucepans and this one for floors. If you should use the wrong rag on the wrong surface, I would have to go back and start again.

This neurosis developed in tandem with the disintegration of my aging body. As I watched my childbearing years vanish behind me, I tried to fill the barren void with pointless fripperies. I had no purpose in life and was frantically searching for a new one.

In another age, I might have studied for a university degree. As it was, my legacy from that period was drawers full of doilies and a kitchen full of rags.

It was a terrible time. Just when you start to look forward to the wisdom of your maturing years, nature suddenly turns the clock back on your common sense and forward on your body.

It's unsettling and makes you do things that you would never normally do.

Like insult a bishop.

AS CHAIRMAN of the board of management in James's school, the local priest was James's boss. And the bishop was *his* boss.

You had to kowtow to priests, that was a given. A bishop expected any manner of response, but only as long as it came within certain boundaries. These ranged from the standard respectful kissing of his out-stretched hand to barely contained, simpering groveling. Basically, unless you were higher up in the pecking order, like a cardinal—or the pope—you were barely worthy to breathe the same air as a bishop. For most of us, the local bishop was the closest we'd get to God without actually dying.

James thought their pomp and the petty rules ridiculous, because he was too political and too educated to believe otherwise. But his school was run, like every school in Ireland, by the Catholic Church, so he had no choice but to go along with it all.

Monthly, the priest stood up and roll called the parishioners' exact contribution to the parish funds. Top of the list was some wealthy trading family with "a generous ten shillings"; bottom always some poverty-stricken unfortunate who could barely feed his family, the priest's eyes raging with the disgraceful insult of their "half a penny." It was a barbaric practice, and I had watched James's cheeks blaze with shame and fury each month. But I never brought the subject up. To do so would have been to question his integrity, and I knew that his first priority was the education of the children of our area and the security of his own wife and child.

In all of the forty years he worked for them, James never derided the church or its hierarchy and we never discussed our feelings about his bosses and their treatment of him as being just or unjust. James did not grovel because he did not have to. His education, reputation, and standing in the community evened the ground between himself and the high-ranking religious. He treated the clergy with a quiet respect. No more or less than that which this gentleman showed to the dogs on the road, but it was respect nonetheless.

Needless to say, I was expected to do the same.

Every year, Bishop Dunne honored Kilkelly with his presence when he came to confirm the young people of our parish into the Catholic Church. As a local schoolteacher's wife, I tagged along with my husband and contributed refreshments to a reception afterwards in the parish hall.

This particular year, I decided to pull out all of the stops and make the confirmation reception a special event, for no other reason than to make extra work to occupy myself. The trestle tables were laid with linen tablecloths, some of my own crockery was added to the humble parish stock, and I prepared a veritable banquet.

I went into a cleaning frenzy, scrubbing and polishing the rough wooden floors of the parish hall and running a knife along the edges of the Formica table trimmings, scraping out years' worth of crumbs and gunk. I scrubbed the toilets and polished the taps and swept the front steps, so that the place was, truly, fit for a bishop.

I barely slept the night before. James was confused as to why I was going to all this trouble, but he said nothing. Which was just

as well because I did not know myself. Secretly, I feared I might
be losing my mind. And so, in the way that madness perpetuates
itself, I woke on the morning of the confirmation and dressed
myself as if I were going to meet the Queen. I rarely wore
makeup, excepting a little lipstick on a Sunday, but on this day for
reasons I am still at a loss to explain, I applied rouge to my cheeks
and some blue eye shadow (which was still new in its box). I agonized over what to wear—so much that I ended up in a purple
two-piece which was slightly too small for me, and I had to wear
the jacket open.

When I arrived at the hall to finish the preparations, I thought
the other women working were looking at me strangely. When I
went to check that the bathroom was as I had left it the night before, I saw in the mirror that rivers of sweat had run down my
cheeks and made stripes of my rouge, which is what they would
have been staring at. I wanted to weep, but girded myself instead
with a terrible determination.

I was so angry that afternoon. Angry at having gone to all of
this trouble, angry at the way I imagined the other ladies were ex-
cluding me from their talk. Angry at my runny rouge, my incur-
able symptoms, and my uncontrollable, incontinent emotions.

But mostly I was angry with the bishop. Every year he swanned
in here in full dress regalia like some shrunken, aged bride. Not
bothering to talk to the parents or to thank the fawning ladies of
the parish for all their hard work. When he arrived, nervous children were swept aside in the triangular magnificence of his train,
while he glided up to the refreshments table and gave me a haughty
nod of the head to indicate he was ready for his tea and cake.

Odious man. I cut him a slice of my rich fruit cake. The recipe
I normally keep in reserve for Christmas. It was always my spe-
ciality and he didn't deserve it, but I handed it over anyway.

Well. He looked me up and down with the disdain that seemed to be his permanent expression, then picked a corner of the cake and shoved it into his mouth.

"Eugh," he said, "this cake is dry."

Bishop Dunne was famed for these rude, thoughtless outbursts. He had great trouble keeping a housekeeper for that reason. But I wasn't his housekeeper. I wasn't his servant any more than this ignorant, greedy gremlin of a man was God's. And my cake was *not* dry.

"Perhaps it's *your* mouth that's dry, Father."

Your Lordship was flummoxed with horror. At the implication that he was a dry-mouthed old bastard, but most of all at my not using his proper title. Bishop Dunne put down the plate and, in a silent but incandescent rage, he walked out of the parish hall.

In the second he turned his back I felt an absolute terror wash over me as I realized what I had done. But as the last of his skirt disappeared out the door, the relief in the room was palpable. There was a sense that a round of applause might start up. Bridie Malone actually came up behind me and said, "He's had that coming for years—well done, Bernadine!" In that moment I felt proud, and a smile was about to break on my lips when I saw James standing in the kitchen doorway.

There was a look of angry disapproval on his face.

Twenty-seven

an, there's something I need to tell you."

If he felt even a tenth of the dread in hearing that statement as I did in saying it, that was bad enough.

"You're leaving me."

I was taken aback. Did he know?

"No, I'm not leaving you."

"Then phew for that . . ." he said, laughing at his own joke. "Gotcha! Say, what time is it, baby? Gerry said he'd be here round about two to help me fix up the bike."

This was going to be harder than I thought.

After twenty-four hours, I had more or less decided that perhaps Ronan Robertson was not my soul mate after all. When I got home that night, I couldn't sleep, so I went downstairs and pottered around the house, trying to keep the infatuation going, recall the lust and longing I had felt that first night. How he had looked at me, how much I had wanted him. The "rightness" I had felt. But when I crawled into bed in the early hours of the morning, I was aware of Dan sleeping peacefully next to me and I became completely overwhelmed with guilt. I struggled with my conscience all of the following day, trying to put a romantic spin on what I was increasingly beginning to suspect had been simply my own unforgivable behavior. Part of me—the creative, whimsical Tressa—was saying, "True passion is beyond your control." The other—sensible, pragmatic Tressa—was saying, "Married women don't mess around. You did a bad, bad thing."

The two conflicting voices were fighting like hell cats in my head and my blood felt poisoned with my own adrenaline. By early evening I couldn't stand carrying it around with me anymore, and I knew I had to tell Dan what I had done.

I figured out my story and bit the bullet.

"I'm serious, Dan. We need to talk."

He was covered in grease, fiddling around with some Harley bike parts on the table. A huge boy, toys out in front of him, making a mess. "I'm sorry, Tressa. I'll clean this all up later. Once Gerry gets here and . . ."

I coughed. "I *nearly* had an affair." I looked him straight in the eye. Just like I promised myself I would.

He changed instantly from boy to man. I thought he would be shocked, hurt. I was ready for tears.

"What do you mean '*nearly*'?"

He looked angry in a way I hadn't seen before. I faltered. "I don't know, I . . ."

"What do you mean 'nearly' had an affair, Tressa?" he repeated, wanting an answer.

"It was this guy at the shoot that I used to go out with and we went out and had a few drinks and then . . ."

"Did you sleep with him?"

"No."

"Did you *want* to sleep with him?"

"Yes, no, yes . . . I don't know . . ."

"Did you kiss him?"

"Yes—sort of—I can't remember."

"Don't bullshit me, Tressa—did you kiss him?"

"Ye-es!"

I half-screamed, half-wailed it, like the drama queen I never knew I was. This was a scene I was not enjoying playing out.

"Did you enjoy it?"

He said it in a tone of voice that was so cold and disgusted, empty of any tenderness, that he didn't even sound like himself.

He went on. "Was it—I don't know—sexy? Fun?"

I was afraid of the way he was being and I was surprised at the fear I felt in the pit of my stomach in response to his anger.

"You don't get it, Dan."

"Don't get *what* Tressa? That my wife is out there nearly having an affair—kissing, maybe fucking other men? What's not to '*get*'?"

"Stop it! Stop talking like that. Be yourself."

"What the hell does that mean, Tressa? Myself? Slushy Dan, the big uneducated ape, who's too stupid to see what's going on under his nose? The gentle giant who'll forgive anything . . ."

"Stop it! Stop it!"

"What do you want me to do, Tressa? Do you want me to get down on my knees and beg you not to leave me?"

"I'm not leaving you, Dan . . ."

"Do you want me to do this?" And he picked up a coffee cup and hurled it toward the back window.

I screamed, and that shocked him into silence. He stood in front of me, his lips curling into the beginning of a tight snarl, hands shivering with rage, eyes huge and sad and terrified. For a split second they seemed to be pleading.

"You are clearly not happy in this marriage, and you know what? You are making me really miserable, too. Maybe we should call it a day. Whatever. I'm outta here."

Then my devoted husband walked out of our house, slamming the door dramatically behind him.

I was shaking, shocked. I had never seen Dan angry before, and I realized, to my own horror, that he was right. I did think he was a big soft fool who'd roll over and take anything. What I was taking in, more than anything, was the possibility that Dan would leave *me*. After all my uncertainty, all my hemming and hawing, he was holding the cards.

After maybe ten minutes, I heard Gerry knock at the door.

There was no point in hiding from Gerry. He knew he was expected.

He walked straight through the kitchen toward the back door.

"Is he out in the garage?"

"He's not here."

"Oh right . . ." and he started to rearrange the parts on the table.

"What's cooking, Tress?"

Gerry always sniffed the air when he came into my kitchen like a homeless dog.

"We had a row. I think he's left me."

"Shit, no. Coffee'd be good."

Gerry started moving the parts around awkwardly, as if he really didn't want to be there. I hadn't thought that I needed to talk, especially not to Gerry, but sometimes you don't know you need to do something until you need to do it.

He sensed he was expected to ask me questions, and although he clearly didn't want to he said, "What happened?"

"I told him I nearly had an affair."

"Whoa!"

This was way more than he had bargained for, so he took a step back and started waving his arms like a landing crew warning off a crashing plane. "Not my business, Tress—don't wanna know."

But I was bringing this baby down. Dan wouldn't listen, so I was going to make sure I got my message across to his friend.

"I met this guy I'd known before, I thought we had something, and then I realized he was *nothing* next to Dan, nothing. My love was challenged, and I chose Dan."

I felt triumphant. That sounded so good. No harm done, a dilemma sorted. Excellent work. Gerry let out a half-laugh and raised his eyes to heaven. He looked at me with a mixture of pity and amusement.

"You already made your choice, Tressa. You're not in the market for those kinds of decisions anymore."

Then he picked up a greasy carburetor from the kitchen table and headed out to the garage to wait for his betrayed friend.

REALITY IS just an interpretation. Some people believe only God really knows what's going on, we mortals just make up our own versions of it.

Reality one in my interpreted world was that Ronan and I were soul mates whose love was thwarted by misunderstanding, bad timing, and ultimately my marriage to somebody else. We met each other again, and in knowing that we could not be together, our souls found the freedom to express themselves honestly. We'd fallen in love—maybe. He was devastated when I didn't come through for him, and spent the rest of the evening on the phone to his therapist.

Reality two is that Ronan, on a day off from the live-in model, bumped into a vulnerable ex and, having overdosed on twenty-year-old beauties, fancied an evening of earthy, no-strings sex with somebody else's wife. He is the type of man who would say anything to get a woman into bed, hence all the faltering, soul-searching bullshit, which he figured (correctly) I needed to hear. There is also the ugly possibility that, having got the room paid for by yours truly, I had caught him in the act of rifling through his address book looking for a last-minute replacement, so the bed didn't go to waste.

The real truth is, I will never really know.

The only thing that I feel absolutely certain of right now is that I have hurt Dan in the worst way. You can hurt another person by being true to yourself, but in the long term you are doing both of you a favor. You can also hurt a person by just being a selfish bitch, and there is no excuse for that. Sometimes, it is quite difficult to tell the two situations apart.

However, next time I'm not sure if I'm following my heart or my hormones, I'll be checking in with my new friend, Conscience. She may not be as pretty as Creativity, but at least she will always tell me the truth.

I guess it's like the sunken Christmas cake. If you take good-will for granted and get sloppy, you might get away with it once or twice, but you won't get away with it forever. You should always treat the things that treat you well with respect.

And if you don't? Well then you have to be prepared to take the consequences.

Twenty-eight

James had never shown anger towards me before.

Twenty years is a long time to set a habit, and I knew my husband as a placid, mild-mannered man. He never raised his voice, or, God forbid, his hand, to any human or animal that I had ever seen. I knew he had been a captain in the IRA before we met, and although I was occasionally curious about the part he had played in our cruel war, I was largely content to think of my husband as a harmless soul. I knew of the way that other women were treated at the hands of bullying husbands but I never saw their misfortune reflected as my own good fortune. Perhaps that is the way it is when women marry men whom they have not chosen themselves. They had no hand in making the match so they never consider themselves lucky. Perhaps those who choose their partners can see the other's good qualities more clearly and will therefore forgive their faults more easily. Although I wonder if twenty years might erode such idealism. Perhaps it is better not to fall for a person's good points in the first place, then have time expose them as hollow charms.

I will never know because I was never given that choice. Now I think that romantic love should always stay the way I knew it.

Locked away, like a precious jewel in a chest in the attic, to be opened occasionally when in need of distraction, so you might marvel at its beauty, but never to be exposed to the harsh light of day. Perhaps romantic love is too delicate, too beautiful to withstand the weight of the ordinary.

James never looked more plain, more unlovably ordinary than the afternoon we got back from the confirmation. Yet the disappointment with which he looked at me was unfamiliar.

"You upset the bishop, Bernadine."

I knew I had done wrong, that I had put my husband's reputation, our very livelihood at stake. I knew that had I been in full control of my senses, I would never have let such a thoughtless insult spill out of me without considering the consequences. I knew I should have bitten my lip, smiled in silent decorum, and offered my intolerance up to a decent saint, who might see to it that the miserable weasel burned in hell for all eternity. I knew I was entirely at fault, and that just made it all the worse. I married a man I had not chosen and clambered hard all of my married life to make sure I stayed one inch above him on the moral high ground. I was not an affectionate wife, but I was always hardworking and diligent in carrying out my responsibilities. I was respectful. I did not love him in the way that he wanted me to, but when push came to shove, I had never failed him. Until now.

"You upset the bishop, Bernadine."

James said it in a patronizing, schoolmasterly tone that irritated me. But my anger was rooted in my own failure as a wife. If he was raging, I did not notice. Anger was not something I had to watch out for in James. There was no reason to be ever alert to it. If his voice shook over the words, I did not think it any reason to hold back. Twenty years is a long time. Long enough to know what to expect. I had started now and I could not find a way of stopping. I did not think there was any good reason to.

"How dare you speak to me like that? I have sacrificed twenty years of my life to be your dutiful servant." And then I said it, the unforgivable. "We both know I was destined for greater things than the dull life of a schoolteacher's wife."

The devil darted out of his eyes and towards me in a pin-sharp flash.

"Greater things?"

Still, I did not believe there was anything to be afraid of. I stuck my chin in the air, although probably a fraction too high, as I was beginning to feel unsure.

"Yes. A certain Michael Tuffy that I was doing a line with? We were matched?"

"Oh, I see. And that match never came to fruition because?"

There was a nasty slant to his face. A tight look to his mouth, such as you might see on a bitter old woman. I had turned my gentle James into a monster. But I was no quitter. I had to see this through.

"Don't you try and torture me, James Nolan. You know very well my parents did not have the money for that match. If they had had a penny, they would never have settled on you . . ."

"But your Aunt Ann had the money."

This sick dread descended on me like red mist. I had to make him stop.

"Didn't she, Bernadine?"

I had one more rage in me, a cruelty that I spat out. "You will never be *half* the man Michael Tuffy was . . ." Even as I said it, I knew it was my last stand. Tears were already streaming down my face, my veins coursing with the heat of my confession. "Michael was *my world*." Perhaps if I had not hurt him so badly with the awful truth, James might have let it go. But I was *his* world, and he couldn't stop himself. James knew I loved Michael over him, and he had found a way to live with that. It was the telling of it that he could not bear.

So he punished me by telling me the truth about Michael Tuffy.

MAUREEN TUFFY was, indeed, the widowed wife of Michael Tuffy Senior from Achadh Mor, but it seemed that was the only true thing that could be said about her. She never made legal claim to her husband's land, and it was assumed that was because it was of no great value to her. But the truth was that the land had never been her husband's, but his brother's, who was living in Chicago. He got wind of her scheme to embezzle him out of his inheritance. Arguments over land rights at that time were forgivable, but bigamy was not and Maureen Tuffy's greed had made a bigamist of her son.

He had already married one other young woman who was from a wealthy New Orleans Catholic family. The girl had run away to New York at the age of eighteen in search of adventure and immediately she arrived in Grand Central Station she had met and fallen in love with Michael Tuffy. He took the girl back home to meet Maureen, who immediately got the measure of the girl's wealth and contacted her parents. Relieved that their daughter was safe and in respectable company, they rewarded Mrs. Tuffy with a generous allowance to cover rent and board. Within months, the girl was pregnant, and a marriage was quickly arranged and a dowry negotiated. However, as time went on, the girl began to miss the trappings of her wealthy Southern life. Weeks before the child was due to be born, she said she was homesick for her parents and tried to persuade Michael to go back to New Orleans with her. By this time, it seemed, Michael had tired of her rich-girl whining and told his mother he did not want to move from New York. The girl was put on a train back to New Orleans, her dowry was pocketed by the Tuffys, and no mention was ever made of a divorce.

In any case, state divorce was meaningless to our generation. You married once and for life as far as the Catholic Church was concerned, and that was the only kind of marriage there was.

When Maureen Tuffy came to Achadh Mor to claim her brother-in-law's land, she quickly discovered that there might be a bigger fish worth hooking in my Aunt Ann, and set about after her cash.

I was the bait.

Ann was suspicious of the Tuffys from the first, and had her vast network of New York biddies check them out. It took but a return telegram to warn her off.

Ann told my mother, and was punished for being the bearer of bad news by my parents estranging themselves from her. Catholic shame cut a strange path through the conscience in those days; my mother would have blamed Ann for carrying that information, and herself for merely receiving it. Although they made it up again, I know the rift hurt them both. Even if I had known the reason for Ann refusing my dowry, I don't know that I would have forgiven her anyway. The pain of losing him had affected me so deeply that I had needed somebody to blame, and even in knowing the truth I found it hard to blame him. My parents never told me Ann's side, and I understood that their silence had been a misguided testament to their love for me. As my future husband, they would have felt duty bound to tell James. He was well-connected and if he had ever found out about Michael Tuffy, it would have broken their moral contract with him. After all, he had agreed to take on their daughter with no dowry. His silence on the subject up to that was testament to his tolerance.

I don't know what hurt most of all: the fact of Michael's betrayal, or James having kept the truth from me for all these years.

It came out of him in a short, spiteful stream. How my parents had virtually fallen to their knees with relief when he had approached them; their relief when he had been dismissive of my shocking history. My mother had sold me to him as a hardworking, gentle prospect. Even as he said those words, I could hear his voice break over his regret in having hurt me. He paused and added gently, "And you have been that."

James's fury crumbled away into the dry air, but I would not wet it with my tears, and so went about my business.

Late that night, I walked out to the back field and I looked up at the stars and I tried to make myself believe that my husband might have lied. I wanted to hate him, but I couldn't. I knew him too well, and a lifetime of courtesy and affectionate kindness in the face of my cruel indifference would always set the balance in his favor.

I wanted my Michael back. Not the man—he was so distant from me now that he might as well be dead—but the dream of him. The daring, handsome young lover with the furious blue eyes and the black, black curls. I wanted to close my eyes and be able to see myself in a soft lavender dress spread out on a pea-green hill and my lover spinning in the breeze ahead of me, his eyes flashing sapphire splinters against the sun that would cut a girl's heart asunder. I wanted the fresh, vivid colors of youth that my dreams of love had brought me.

Soon I was going to be old, and everything seemed so gray.

Acceptance

Acceptance is the first step
to unconditional love.

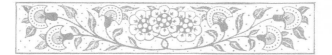

Boxty Pancakes

Peel and finely grate some large potatoes, then put the mush into a sieve and squeeze out most of the excess water, but not so much as to leave them bone dry. To each cupful grated potato add one level teaspoon salt and between a quarter and a half cup flour. I favor less as I don't like a doughy consistency, but the flour binds, so the less you use the harder the mix is to manage in the cooking as these pancakes have a terrible tendency to stick. Add sufficient milk to make a stiff pancake mix, one that will drop from a spoon rather than pour. Heat lard or bacon dripping in an iron pan to smoking point, then fry the pancakes until darker than golden brown on both sides.

Twenty-nine

I nearly burned the house down making boxty pancakes last night. Bacon dripping in an iron pan—hello? Is there any more dangerous kitchen feat I could perform late at night, while feeling as on edge and nervous as I am now? What does a girl cook when her husband of eight months has threatened to leave her?

I told myself it was just for work, but in some old-fashioned part of me, I was hoping that the smell of my crispy cakes frying in bacon fat would bring him puttering down the stairs for a late-night tasting session. It was what he always did, lumber into the kitchen in his jocks and grab a tidbit from the top of a carefully prepared pile. Dan treated my cooking as if it were just for him, and while he had that in common with every single person who has ever come into my working kitchen, it annoyed the hell out of me. At least, I thought it did. Tonight I wasn't so sure.

It reminded me of the stray kitten I had once rescued from the street outside the apartment. We weren't supposed to keep animals, so I called Pet Rescue to come and take her. After they had gone, I missed the little thing, and wondered why I hadn't made a case for keeping her. For months afterward, I felt this vague guilt, except one day passing a pet shop, I realized it wasn't guilt at all. It was simply that I would have liked a kitten for myself. I was lonely.

This was much bigger, obviously, but the principle was the same. Now that Dan was threatening to leave, I decided that I wanted my marriage to work.

The brief encounter with Ronan had sorted out a lot of the nonsense in my head and made me clearer about my husband. Excitement, drama, that heart-pumping, skin-tingling desire, was not for me after all. It had led me down too many relationship side roads in my life and was no more than a temporary, unsettling dynamic. When your emotions are being squeezed, you are filled with this passionate certainty. Something that is so powerful that it affects your body. Your stomach churns, you heat up, and you think—what is this if it's not love?

Newsflash, Tressa—it's a little thing called sex.

It can dress itself up as passion, but when you come right down to the nuts and bolts of it, it's just sex looking for its own way.

That ten-second revelation had taken me from the idealistic fantasy of wild passion, to the sometimes dull but always safe love of the married woman. A ten-second revelation that it had taken me thirty-eight years to get to.

Maybe I had paid a price in settling for one without the other.

Or maybe, just maybe—you had to choose. In which case, I chose Dan.

Dan was the safe option, the easy option. He was honest, reliable, and would never let me down. Dan made me feel good in a manageable, everyday way. I may not have always felt good about him, but I always felt good about *myself* when I was with him. This was what I needed, after all. This was right.

And now I had screwed it up.

*   *   *

I DIDN'T go up to bed last night. I stayed up cooking, then lay down on the sofa with a throw around me. I must have slept, because I was woken by Dan in the kitchen.

Dan is a tall, broad man—heavy with muscle. His noise is usually soft and muted like tomorrow's thunder. This morning he was clattering, the stressed sound of metal on metal, doors slamming. He was defiantly preparing a cooked breakfast, even though it was unlikely he was hungry. Even though it was my kitchen and he hadn't a clue where anything was. The thought of that dared a smile out of me, and a slither of fondness. If I held onto that, perhaps everything would be all right. Perhaps I could ride through this disaster on a chariot of love.

OK, who was I kidding with the chariot? A skateboard then—but it was worth a try.

I caught him picking a potato cake from the top of my pile. I kept my voice light and sunny and said, "Hey buddy—hands off."

He gave me a look that said he was gone.

The innocent, affable, harmless husband I thought I had was no more. The one I assumed I could afford not to love, because he was this bottomless source of innocent adoration. That meant he would forgive everything, right? I was the complicated, passionate one, he was what? Earth to Tressa—reality check. What *did* you think Dan was—a stupid, worthless fool?

That's how I had treated him. And his look said that he knew it.

He dropped the golden sphere as if it were rotten and went back to the pan.

I had the nerve to feel hurt. "There's no need to be like that."

He stared up at me from under his bed-head hair. His eyes were hard and mean. Impenetrable. He looked like he hadn't slept all night. Alarm and lust fizzled through me simultaneously.

"To be like what?"

Dan was being openly confrontational. I had tried to break the ice by being playful and light. Work through this unpleasantness in a gentle, jovial way. And now he was responding with anger.

That was not very mature, I thought, not very helpful. I didn't like this game and I wasn't going to play it.

"Forget it."

"Forget what, Tressa? Forget that you slept with somebody else, or forget the marriage?"

He was being unreasonable now. Making me out to be a slut.

"I did *not* sleep with him."

"Kissed, fucked—whatever. That's not the point."

"Well, it is the point, actually. I could have slept with him and I didn't. I chose you."

A sudden, speedy seesaw of triumph and doubt went whizzing up and down in my head.

"You *chose* me?"

"Yes . . ." And very stupidly mistaking his tone for a positive one, despite Gerry's sage advice, despite knowing I was in the wrong, I added with gravitas, "Yes. I chose you."

He raised his chin and said, "Fuck you, Tressa."

Then he walked out of the room.

The pan was smoking on the gas, so I leaned over and switched it off.

My head felt heavy on my neck, and I realized I was exhausted. My mouth tasted like there was a dead mouse living under my tongue and when I reached up to move my hair out of my eyes, it was matted and dishevelled.

I looked and smelled a mess. At age thirty-old-enough-to-know-better, I had been a bit unfaithful less than a year into my marriage. And I had chosen my husband.

Lucky Dan.

There was a patch of grease on the hob from last night's frying, so I went to the sink to wet a cloth. As I was there, I thought, what the hell am I doing worrying about a patch of grease when my marriage is falling apart? My face turned into my chest in a silent grimace; a line of fat tears dropped straight into the sink. A wedge of self-pity dislodged itself from my throat, and as it made its escape, I realized I hadn't even said that I was sorry.

Thirty

I could not let go of Niamh.

When she was twenty-five she announced that she was moving to America. It was 1964.

She didn't ask, or consult or defer to us in any way. She just announced it, as if our feelings didn't matter. As if she wasn't ripping out our hearts; as if now that she had taken everything we had to give her—a good upbringing, endless love, an education, gifts of money, clothes, a car—she was quite happy to leave us behind and go on about another life. I could scarcely believe her capable of such an act of selfishness.

I was furious. And you might assume that I wasted no time in telling her so.

Of course, I knew that I was being completely unreasonable, but I was not able to stop myself. I was afraid. Afraid that the miles would forge a distance between us, even though I had evidence to the contrary, because it was only after Niamh had moved away from Achadh Mor and up to Dublin that we had become friends.

I held on to her too tightly while she was growing up. All through her childhood and adolescence, we fought. She was feisty.

I saw myself in her and tried to contain her, to keep her safe. By the time she left for university to study English, I was exhausted from fighting with her. We disagreed on everything, her clothes, her hairstyle, her boyfriends. When she went into Swinford to the cinema with her friends, I would shake with fear until she came home again. James always offered a voice of reason, "She'll be fine, Bernadine. She's an intelligent, sensible girl." His attitude infuriated me. Sometimes, I wished he would be more authoritarian, keep Niamh prisoner, and scold her like other fathers did. Then I could be the gentle, easygoing parent and she and I could outnumber him, instead of it always being the other way around.

Niamh had thick wavy hair like mine and curves like a woman from the age of thirteen. Her bones were delicate and refined, like James's, but she had my large blue eyes. They were such windows on her innocence, her fear, her unsullied delight, her awakenings, that I often found it hard to look into them.

Niamh was artistic, messy, emotional, expressive. She was beautiful but uninterested in the way she looked; she was bewildered when people admired her—she inherited that humility from her father. She laughed readily, and her body was always open and stretched out in friendship. Her voice was loud and hearty, and her open passion gave voice to how I had felt all my life, but had never been able to express.

Sometimes I felt she was so perfect that I could scarcely believe she was a part of me, and my heart would collapse with fear that somebody might carry her away and hurt her. Other times, when she was being stubborn or spiteful, she reminded me too much of myself and I would struggle not to hit her.

In a corner of my mind, I was jealous of her joy, but my heart was hers completely. Though we became closer during the three years she spent in Dublin at university, I worried myself sick about her. It felt unnatural that I did not know where she was and what she was doing every minute of the day and night. I remember grating potatoes for boxty one afternoon and becoming so lost in a terrified reverie of what tragedy might have befallen her that I tore off the side of my thumb. Later that night, she telephoned and her father mentioned my accident to her.

"You should be more careful, Mam," she scolded me. I wanted to tell her how worried I was about her, ask what exactly she had been doing all day, and whom she had been with. But I didn't dare. I had learned that my instinct to smother her made her run from me.

So I waited for her to offer me information on the details of her life, greedily snatching each new fact and squirreling it away to help me build a picture in my mind. A vision that would help me know that she was safe, that would make me feel more involved in her life. In those years that she was away in Dublin, I learned to pretend that I thought she was a capable adult. I gave Niamh her independence, but in name only. I never believed in her ability apart from me. Reality told me she was an adult woman with a strong young body and a determined will. But if perception is truth, she was still an infant clinging to my breast, only truly protected and warm while in the cave of my soft arms.

In my pretending not to care too much, I was rewarded over the coming years with my daughter's friendship. Niamh got a place teaching English in a school in Galway. She came home every other weekend through choice, and those times were the best we ever had together. We became closer then, and she felt able to share more details about her life, although she surely omitted things that might hurt or distress me. Watching Niamh mature as a woman gave me more pleasure than watching her grow into an adult. The speed at which a child grows is alarming; you grieve one passing stage to another with barely time to enjoy in between. But from her late teens to mid-twenties, Niamh turned from a headstrong girl who I worried for daily into a warm young woman.

She started to paint, and I was astonished by her work. Powerful splashes of nothing in particular, but I loved them and I told her so. She started to bring home friends. Sunny, interesting young people who admired my cooking and appeared interested in my opinions. One was an English boy with hair down to his shoulders who was studying law and said his wealthy mother had never cooked him a meal in her life. There was a girl from Dublin with a pale, terrified face who sang like an angel and entertained us after supper each night. James and I welcomed them as if they were our own children because they brought our daughter with them. Niamh was delighted that we liked her friends, but more delighted, I think, that they liked us.

I was infatuated by the fact that Niamh seemed to consider me so worthy of her friendship that she was proud to show me to her friends. The feeling between us moved on from the love of mother and daughter to a mutual respect. So much more than I had with my own mother. It felt a miracle that we should like each other as well as love each other. James cleared out one of our old cowsheds and put a skylight in the roof to make a studio for Niamh to paint in, and it was after she had been painting there every weekend for about six months that she announced she was moving to New York.

I was devastated, and I did react badly. But ultimately, I knew I had to let her go.

A SHORT time before she left, we rented a caravan in Enniscrone and all three of us went there for a week, to say our good-byes. I

sat on the dunes one windless day, and watched as James and Niamh walked the strand arm in arm, like lovers. She teased him
into rolling up his trousers and taking off his shoes. As I watched
them jump the shredded lace of the tiny waves, I felt my heart
tear open that this chapter of our lives would soon be closing. We
were family, we three, and I thought we had arrived. I had always
hoped that our family might grow, if Niamh married, but had
trusted that, no matter what, we would be together, like this. It
seemed unfair to be adjusting again in the autumn of our lives.

A gentle breeze blew across the dull, muggy day—a whisper
from the sea flapped through from one ear to the other and made
me feel hollow. Once again, I stared out at the Atlantic in search
of a shadow from the other side. But there was only flat gray silk
spread out in front of me and then sky, sky, sky. The edge of the
world. Perhaps it was true and there was no such place as America
after all, and Niamh would never come back. Perhaps Michael
had fallen over the edge of the world. The end of the world.

Later that evening, Niamh and I made boxty, and she gently
coaxed the grater from me as she saw me grate the potatoes too
close to the edge.

We had only a few days, and I wanted to say so much. That she
had started her life as everything I had ever wanted, and then become so much more than that again. That I would miss seeing her
every week, that I wished I had looked at her harder, listened more
intently to her worries; that I was sorry for the years that I scolded
her; for not having shown her enough love, and for loving her too
much.

"I'm only going to America, Mam."

She took my hand and held it until I loosened my grip, then she
hugged me—taller, finer than I was now, or had ever been—and I
cried for her. With her long arms wrapped around me, she told me

not to be afraid, that America was only around the corner. I dabbed my eyes with a tea towel, and felt it as an old matronly act.

"Thanks, Mam," she said.

"For what?" I asked.

"For not asking me to stay."

NIAMH DEPARTED in the morning. She insisted that we not go to the airport to wave her off, but leave it as a normal good-bye. As if we would see each other again soon. As I watched her back, bag hooked over her shoulders, legs marching in her strong, confident stride, I felt angry again that she was leaving. For the rest of the day, I was irritable. James went swimming and brought his wet clothes into the caravan. Then he put muddy wellingtons on the clean floor. As I was starting to prepare supper, he decided he wanted a drink and I tripped over him as he reached for the icebox. I had a vegetable knife in my hand, and it sliced his shoulder by pure accident.

"You stupid, stupid old man!" I shouted, in fear of having hurt him.

I pushed him down on the corduroy cushions of the bench, and opened the cabinet above him to get the first-aid box. The short sleeve of his T-shirt was wet with blood, and I lifted it up and applied an antiseptic cloth to the small wound. James blanched and I looked at his face. Long and ghostly white, his eyes staring at me like saucers. They were full of sadness and fear.

Time and proximity had carved enough knowledge of each other's faces that we didn't need words. We looked and each of us was thinking that all we had left now was the other: he with a woman who seemed barely able to tolerate him, even after all these years, and I with a man who looked delicate and old, and whom I had never cared to love.

Yet James was the only person who could ever equal my love for Niamh. The sadness in his eyes was his grief that she was gone. The fear was that I would no longer need him, that my reason for loving him was gone. But, old and fragile as he was, I did need him. We had grown to be a part of each other. I had no choice but to be with him. Like two trees, resolutely separate but whose roots and branches have intertwined.

I was stuck with him, and had no choice but to accept it. All other excuses had been pared away.

Thirty-one

When I realized I had not said I was sorry, it was a great revelation to me.

I waited for Dan to get dressed and come back downstairs, then I ambushed him with my apology. "Dan, I am really, *really* sorry about what happened."

He ignored the apology and walked out the door, saying, "I don't know what time I'll be home. Don't bother cooking." It took me the whole morning to talk myself through the rage.

God, I hated him. The self-righteous pig. He was milking this for sure—not accepting an apology? How low could you get? All I had done was kiss Ronan—hardly more than a handshake in this day and age, and at least I had been honest about it. What did Dan think? I was a virgin before I met him? It's not like Ronan was a complete stranger. An old flame; these things are complicated. If he couldn't be bothered to work this out—well, we might as well forget it.

The parting shot—*"Don't bother cooking."* That finished me off altogether.

Fact: I cooked for him every single night, the lucky bastard.

Fact: The way he threw it away—as if he was doing me a favor, letting me cook for him.

Fact: He was living in the 1950s, a woman cooking a hot meal for him every night, and him not even noticing, the mollycoddled, unappreciative ass. He *so* did not deserve me. Apologize? To him? He should be apologizing to *me* for taking me for granted. I'd be gone when he got back. Packed. I'd move back to the apartment. There were plenty of people I could stay with while the sublet ran its course. No dinner? I'd give him no dinner—*ever again*! Let him come home every night to an empty house, and see how he liked it. To this fabulous kitchen, *my* kitchen, empty, unloved, unused.

Somewhere around that point, in my thinking about the empty, unloved kitchen, I managed to turn back around. Having whipped myself up into a frenzy of justified fury, I slowed the blades down to mill gently around the horrible truth again. This was my fault. Dan felt hurt and betrayed, and he was bound to snap.

What I had to do was take control of this situation and create a solution. I had to make it clear to him that I knew how wrong I had been, and how very sorry I was. No excuses, no "buts"—just an unreserved apology. Dan *would* forgive me, and everything would be all right. We could get back to how things had been before, except that this time, I would appreciate Dan properly, because I had learned an important lesson about commitment, fidelity, and marriage.

I had been drawn to Angelo and Ronan because I was looking for an answer, and now I had found it.

Wisdom. What a fantastic thing it is when it finally hits you.

so i went and bought the ingredients for a shepherd's pie—Dan's favorite. And, significantly, I made another batch of boxty cakes. I could tell that morning that he had been almost fatally attracted to them, which was why I had taken his final rejection of them so personally.

I kept my spirits up for the rest of the day. In between preparing dinner, I got around to weeding a ferocious patch of tangles near the lettuces that I'd been avoiding and painted a few plant pots. I did some ironing, potted some seeds, and lined the kitchen drawers in gingham oilcloth: jolly, housewifey things that made me feel virtuous and homey.

I set the table with a posy of garden flowers delicately drooping from a glass tumbler, and used retro mint-green plastic-handled cutlery for a Doris-Day-pleasing-her-man style. The potato cakes were for nibbling while the cheddar cheese crust was toasting on the shepherd's pie. Normally, I would do a light dessert with such a heavy main, but tonight was Dan's night, so there was a comfort food dessert of apple tart and—the ultimate compromise for me—Ben & Jerry's.

I am not one of nature's self-pampering females, so styling my hair and applying makeup is usually an either/or decision. That evening I did both and put on a print dress I had worn on our honeymoon. I dusted my arms with a glittery powder my friend Doreen had given me on my wedding day.

Seven o'clock came, then eight, and there was no sign of Dan. It was OK, I told myself. He had to come home sometime. It doesn't matter how late. I'd be waiting; I'd be ready for him.

At eight-thirty, he came in.

My heart was thumping ten to the dozen. I was all excited and shaky, and in a weird way it was like I was falling in love: a powerful, messy feeling, where I didn't know if I was terrified or elated. It was anticipation, I suppose. Knowing that soon, one way or another, this mess would be resolved.

"I told you not to cook," he said, and went straight out back to the garage.

I stood there, momentarily paralyzed with shock. I was a satirical photo still from a 1950s advertisement with my perfect dinner, my fancy table setting, my dress and lipstick. An image on a spoof postcard. I looked down at my arms, and they were glittering ludicrously—like I was an alien lifeform. Then it hit me. I was being an alien. What was I doing groveling like this? All I had done was try to be true to myself. Life was a journey, marriage a learning process and this incident with Ronan had just been part of that. Dan would just have to get over it.

I left the mixer on and followed him out to the garage.

"Don't you walk away from me like that," I snapped.

"I said not to bother cooking." He was standing over an engine on the bench, but had not changed into his work clothes. He was pretending to work. Hiding.

"So I have been slaving all day, trying to make things better, trying to say 'sorry,' and you are just going to walk away from me."

He didn't look up. "Whatever. I told you not to cook."

My day's efforts, frustration, disappointment tumbled out and I shouted, "I cooked because *I love you!*"

Dan looked up from the bench, and for a second I thought he was going to fold me into his arms and make everything better. Then I saw his eyes were flat and cold.

"No, Tressa. You cooked because it's what you do. I'm just the excuse."

His hands were gripping the wooden corners of the bench and his chin was shaking with fury. I felt very afraid suddenly and fell into a childish sobbing.

"How can you say that? How can you be so cruel?"

I knew he was right. I always cooked my way through crises.

Apologized with a batch of iced buns or a pile of buttery potato cakes. I was an expert in comfort food.

When Dan had told me not to cook, he had meant that it was going to take more than a batch of boxty to ferry me out of this fix.

So it was time to beg.

"Please, Dan—I can't stand this. I am so sorry. Please say you forgive me. Look at me."

He stopped working, but would not look up. His arms made a straight triangle with the bench and his eyes were closed. He was trying not to cry. I thought I might be getting somewhere.

"Please, Dan. Look at me."

He looked up, and his eyes flew across me briefly, then back down again.

"I can't, Tressa. I can't look at you."

It wasn't until that moment that I truly realized what I had done. I had planted a picture in Dan's head of me with another man. It was making him crazy. Dan didn't hate me. He loved me, but he couldn't stand what I had done, and that was all that he could see when he looked at me. Me having sex with another guy.

"I didn't sleep with him, Dan."

"You kissed him."

"Yes. But I didn't sleep with him. I swear I didn't."

I stared hard at the top of his head as his face was stuck firmly on his boots. He looked up briefly.

"You have to believe me, Dan. I did not have sex with Ronan."

Finally, he turned away in disgust. "Jesus, Tressa."

It was the first time I had used Ronan's name. The guy I hadn't slept with now had a name. I had to be firm, so I didn't back away. I had to keep talking. I wasn't going anywhere, until this barrier between us had been dismantled.

"We have to get past this, Dan."

He shook his head, and now it was his turn to be sorry as he looked up at me, and his eyes were filled with tears.

"I don't know if I can, Tressa . . ."

"But it was just a kiss . . ." the petulant wail came out of me before I had the chance to stop it. Dan shook his head and busied himself again to indicate the discussion was over.

Dan went out. He did not say where, but I think he went to his mother's house. And I was alone in the kitchen we had made together, wondering if I had ruined our marriage for good. When he wanted it, I was unsure. Now that I was sure, he moved away from me, and all because of my stupidity.

But there are no easy answers, and maybe no answers at all. All I could do was wait and waiting is the worst thing. Waiting is just doing nothing, and I am a doer. I wanted to make things better. I wanted to make things work, and it seems that I couldn't do either of those things without Dan. Making a marriage work is something you do together.

Isn't it?

I had no choice now. I had to accept that I had hurt Dan, and I couldn't make that go away. I couldn't undo what I had done, and I couldn't really make it better. I may have had the power to hurt him, but that didn't mean I had the power to take that hurt away. If he wanted to hold onto it, I couldn't wrestle the bad feeling from him.

Like he said, I couldn't cook my way out of this one. But I could still cook. And I guess that's just what I had to do. Keep going. Keep doing my thing and just accept the way things were for the moment. Do what my grandmother used to do when something bugged her: Throw her hands in the air and offer it up to God.

Loyalty

The most expensive gift a man can give you is his pride.

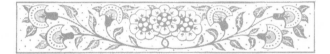

Slow Roasted Clove Ham

To get the salt out of a good ham and a delicate flavor into it takes time and patience, but a decent joint will then last you a few days.

Take your 3- to 4-lb joint and soak it in cold water for up to twenty-four hours. If I was cooking a ham for Sunday dinner, I would put it in to soak on the Saturday afternoon. Keep changing the water every few hours.

Next day, put your joint in fresh water and bring it to a boil. After that first boil, change the water again, add a bay leaf and a slither of onion to it, and allow the joint to boil slowly for three quarters of one hour. While the joint is on its second boil, prepare a roasting dish by lining with tin foil. In a teacup, mix 2 teaspoons ground cloves, a dessert spoon of honey, and a pinch of brown sugar. Add boiling water to the top of the cup and stir until everything is dissolved. Put your boiled ham on the foil and cover in the best mustard you can afford. Then pour your cupful of mixture over it, seal the foil around it, and bake in a medium to hot oven. For the last half hour of cooking time, unwrap the foil, baste the joint in its own fat, spear with a dozen or so whole cloves, and leave to crisp. Serve hot with boiled potatoes and cabbage, or cold, as you like it.

Thirty-two

In the summer of 1979 I saw Michael Tuffy again.

I also saw the Pope.

If the apparition of the Virgin Mary in 1879 was the first miracle at Knock, the Pope's visit in 1979 felt like the Second Coming. The whole of Ireland, and much of the world, was looking at us. Emigrants flocked home in the thousands, Americans with the vaguest relative connections rang ahead, looking for beds. We were at the center of the universe, where it was all happening. It was a magical time.

Achadh Mor, our sparsely populated, sprawling parish, was usually invisible. There was no obvious drama in our scenery. Tourists who ended up here thought they had taken a trip back in time. Even after a wrong turn, they rarely ventured onto our winding boreens, where our small farming communities were carved into the landscape. Cheery new bungalows perched hopefully on the edge of ancient, bleak bog. Old homes beside them, no more than stone sheds. Two-story farmhouses, windows like hollowed eyes, some patched shut with chipboard, made virtually derelict by bachelor farmers barely surviving their parents' deaths. The melancholy was broken in the summer, when the sun shone.

When the hedgerows were heavy with fuchsia, banks of orange monbretia, and cheeky hollyhocks, there was nowhere more beautiful. Yet while we now enjoyed all the modern conveniences— washing machines, televisions, and their like—Faliochtar (our townland, which is within the Achadh Mor parish) was still an outback. There were still women between my mother's generation and mine who refused to get electricity. Men lived alone in cottages with no toilets. We were still a hidden people, not *in* hiding but rather living in an older part of Ireland that many of our countrymen would sooner forget.

The Pope's visit gave us our moment in the spotlight.

The shrine had been there all of my life, and most of my mother's, too. The Virgin Mary had appeared to fifteen local people against the gable wall of St. John the Baptist Church in 1879.

Pilgrims traveled to the church from all over Ireland and talk of miracle cures was commonplace in our homes. "He was carried there on the back of a cart, and he walked home to Limerick!" "He crawled on his belly to kiss the gable wall, then sprung up like a frog!" If you were living in Ireland and looking for a miracle, Knock town was the place all right, but it had little benefit for those of us who lived in the area, except for keeping us entertained.

Until Father Horan came along. James Horan was an energetic priest who had previously served in our neighboring village, where he had built a huge parish hall. Dances were held there, and many a Mayo marriage was made in St. Mary's Hall, Toreen, throughout the fifties. When Father Horan was sent to Knock in 1963, the shrine was simple: a few statues, offerings of weathered crutches of the formerly afflicted left as mementos against the gable wall.

Over the next ten years, Horan built the place up to colossal proportion. Raising enormous sums of money, he had the gable wall encased in a glass chapel with giant marble statues depicting the scene of the apparition. He built a huge church to accommodate a crowd of forty thousand, and it sat at the center of rolling lawns, like a well-appointed spaceship. Watching the transformation of Knock was like a miracle in itself. A modern feat of mismatched architecture incongrous against our barren, rural backdrop. I was a bit cynical and secretly wondered how many of the miracles were real and how many a result of the spiritual mania the Blessed Virgin seemed to inspire in my guilt-ridden peers. But whatever you thought, nobody could deny the energy or commitment of Father Horan. As the centenary of the apparition in Knock drew in and the pontiff announced he was coming, even the atheists were quieted by his achievements.

THE WOMAN who had first set her cap at James, Aine Grealy, was around at that time, having come back to Faliochtar from a career teaching in Dublin when her mother fell ill in 1972. She was unmarried and clearly unhappy about the fact, because she made it her business to flick moments of misery in my direction, whenever she could.

"Michael Tuffy is home—you'll be wanting to see him."

I am a country woman; I don't mind gossip. In fact, liking gossip is a prerequisite for living in a small community. You gossip about your neighbors and they gossip about you, but there is a code. A good gossip requires subtlety. A story is made all the more interesting with a gradual, reluctant release. But there should always be a particular gentleness when you impart information that directly relates. You give all the information you can, without assuming anything or searching the other's face for a reaction. Aine was always smart when it came to academic matters, and pure thick in dealing with people.

It was a few days before His Holiness arrived, and our small church was thronged with irregular churchgoers, hungry for news from the altar. There were shuttle buses to the basilica, picking up at the local shop, Rogers, on the morning of Sunday, September 30, and people were being discouraged from keeping vigil in the surrounding fields overnight. For any of the older generation who were disinclined to brave the weather, St. Mary's Hall in Toureen would provide television coverage and light refreshments all day.

After Mass, Aine pushed her way over to me at the door, and made her statement within earshot of everyone, beadily scanning my face for evidence of a reaction. I ignored her, as if I hadn't heard, and she would have surely repeated her statement more loudly, if James had not hurried me outside.

In actual fact, I did not ignore her deliberately, rather she had propelled me into a state of shock. James had not heard what she said, or at least if he did he passed no comment, but was irritated by my distractedness as we took off in the car.

"For God's sake, Bernadine, are you listening to me at all? I've volunteered to work in St. Mary's for the day. The crowds will be terrible at the shrine itself, and Father Kenny has asked me to give a talk on the stories of the fifteen."

I caught my reflection in the wing mirror, and felt sadness wash over me. Sadness that here I was, in my sixties and yet so easily overcome by romantic reverie; that the decades had robbed me of my beauty and forged lines that suggested wisdom into my face, yet my stomach was fluttering like a silly schoolgirl's.

James went on, "I've put you down for serving refreshments between eleven and two in St. Mary's, if that's all right. You can do later if you like, but . . ."

"No."

For more than forty years I had held my love for Michael Tuffy as sacred. He had abandoned me, tried to embezzle from my family, and had dishonored my name. But as sure as a part of me had died when I learned the truth about him, another came alive at the thought I might see him again. Aine had harbored a grudge all this time, and gotten me.

Michael would be here to see the Pope, and the Pope would not be appearing at St. Mary's Hall in Toureen.

"I want to go to Knock."

"But the crowds will be terrible, Bernadine, and I've already said that . . ."

"I'll go alone, then."

"No, no—if that's what you want, I can cancel."

But this was something I had to do without James.

"I'll go on the bus. Cousin Mae is going with the Ballyhaunis ICA. I'll tag along with them."

"No, it's fine. I'll just tell Father Kenny that we've changed or minds and . . ."

"No, you go to Toureen. It's important. I'll be grand with Mae and the girls."

There was a moment's stand-off while James interpreted my protestation. The Pope's visit was history in the making, and it was an event that husband and wife should experience together. Yet his wife wanted, for some reason, to go without him.

James was hurt, but I couldn't care. True love had beckoned and I had no choice but to follow.

Thirty-three

When things in my life are uncertain, I fall back on the food of my youth. My grandmother's baked ham is wonderful for that. A huge hunk of meat, slowly simmered then slathered in honey, pricked with cloves, and roasted in a hot oven until it is crisp and tender. It is not fast food, but a joint of ham will last for days. Two of you will get one hot meal, a lunch, and suppertime sandwiches out of it. Proving that, sometimes, putting your time into something will pay dividends.

Doreen had been my friend for fifteen years, and though I hadn't seen her since my wedding, she had remained a constant. An eternally forty-one-year-old fashion editor. Stick thin and irrepressibly stylish, with a tongue as sharp as her nails, she was possibly the very last person I would have picked as a best friend. Yet Doreen got me my first break as a food writer after she discovered me working in a diner local to her magazine offices. I was floating through my post-college early twenties, looking for a career path, and she was careering toward middle age, trying to stay thin. To the distress of her couturier, Doreen developed a lunchtime taste for my clove-roasted ham on rye, and felt compelled to call me out on it. Such temptation was surely the work of the devil.

"I've gained nearly four pounds," she squawked over the counter at me.

I knew who she was. Doreen Franke was a high-profile columnist and her style musings on everything from shoes to restaurants were legendary. So I told her I wanted to be a food writer, and we struck a deal. She talked me up to some key editors and I left the diner.

Over the coming years, I was to become responsible for a colossal two-inch addition to her waistline, but then Doreen only ever ate when I cooked for her. Apart from the occasional cocktail party canapé, I more or less kept the woman alive.

People were often surprised by our friendship. Doreen was older than me and reputed to be an unscrupulous bitch. But I never felt that way about her. Doreen was cutting, but I found her humorous. She could be exhausting in her unassailable wit and dramatic delivery, but she was always entertaining. As our friendship spilled into years, I discovered that the icy fashion queen had a warm heart that she took great pains to disguise.

We had some things in common. Where Doreen was an appalling style snob, I reserved my snobbery for food. "Although," as she often said, "*how* you can differentiate between one type of pasta and another is beyond me."

"That's because you don't eat enough of it."

"Enough? Honey, I haven't eaten pasta since *1977*."

Doreen spoke in italics, and her minions copied her mannerisms as well as her clothes. So did half of New York, apart from me. I kept wearing my Levi's and "classic" John Smedley fine-knit sweaters bought mail order from England, despite Doreen's pleading.

"I am so bored looking at you in those what-do-you-call-them?"

"Jumpers." I always used my mother's Irish term for this particular item of clothing.

"This is a new one, right? What *is* this color? It's like something you'd see leaking from a child's nose."

"Pea green."

"Green is something you *eat*, darling, not wear."

"But I'm Irish."

"*Especially* if you're Irish. God, do you know nothing?"

For my part, I derided Doreen for disappearing when she stood sideways, and inspiring eating disorders in the nation's youth.

Doreen was a relationshipphobe. Married briefly in her early twenties, she had long since declared the concept of sharing one's life with another to be overrated. "Honey, I can barely stand to share a plate of sushi—but a bathroom? Eugh!" She nonetheless prevented me from going down the path of confirmed spinsterhood. "You're not stylish enough to get away with being old and single, and besides, you can cook. You *have* to get married!"

Doreen kept me trying. She was deeply unimpressed when I first started seeing Dan.

"Slept with your building superintendent? Have you *lost your mind*?"

It was one of Doreen's top three rules on how to run a successful sex life as a single woman in Manhattan: Wax every six weeks whatever the weather, always tip other people's doormen, and never, *ever* sleep with your own building super.

"It had been so long, Doreen."

"So, now all of a sudden you're a sex maniac . . ."

"I don't know what came over me."

"I know it's tempting, Tressa. They're male, they're on hand . . ."

"I think I like him."

"Oh Christ—you've done it more than once."

"Last night."

"At night!"

"I like him, he's, he's . . ."

"He's a building superintendent, Tressa. You stay friendly, at Christmas you tip. You do not date them. Your manicurist dates them. If you must have sex with them, you do it in the afternoon in the laundry room, and you only do it once."

"Well, he makes me feel good."

"You're just desperate, that's all. You're lonely. Whatever. Put an end to it now. It will end in tears. Believe me."

It ended in marriage.

Bluntly, Doreen did not think that Dan was good enough for me. If I had been 100 percent sure myself, none of her doubts would have been an issue with me.

Doreen had called me on my decision to marry Dan in her own unique way.

"You've been seeing him *what?* Five months?"

"Nine."

"Well, that's a lie, honey. March, I was dragging you off to the D & G party. Then you start this 'convenience fuck' thing with your super . . ."

I knew that breaking the news of my engagement to Dan was going to be an impossible conversation, because Doreen knew me inside out. She could smell I wasn't entirely convinced about Dan, and she was going to milk it. But though I wasn't sure marrying him was the right thing, I was less sure that it was the wrong thing.

As Doreen herself had once said, "Being divorced is not the same thing as being terminally single. Once you've been married and divorced, you *know* being married is not such a big deal."

It would have been too easy for Doreen to assure me that somebody better than Dan was only around the corner. So I eyeballed her and told her I was totally sure. "I love him," I said. It's the last line of defense. The Holy Grail of the single girl. Beyond the endless lists of pros and cons, the cappuccino-fuelled analysis: Will I, won't I? Is he, isn't he? The neurotic, nitpicking, navel-gazing, soul-searching quest for perfect love.

"We're getting married. I love him." It was a mystery solved, job done, the end of the line. The question, solution, resolution all rolled into one. I hoped that if I said it often enough, it would come true.

Doreen couldn't argue with that, although she didn't for one second believe me. But she sat back and smiled. "I suppose you'll want me floating up the aisle in front of you in green chiffon?"

She helped me organize the wedding, and was the perfect companion on the day. She found her own way of being nice about Dan—largely focussed on how he looked, which made him blush like an embarrassed schoolgirl and me feel like I was marrying a Chippendale. But I swallowed it. That was just Doreen's way, I told myself. She had a wicked sense of humor, and I had enjoyed it long enough at other people's expense so that I could hardly be prissy about it when it was pointed at me.

Since I moved out of the city, Doreen and I had been busy building new lives. But since I was the one who had found a husband and left Manhattan, I suspected that Doreen was feeling left behind. She did not want or need a man—but she had become dependent on me for whatever small emotional sustenance she did need. Since my wedding, she had fallen back on her gay fashion friends, and every time I rang her, she appeared to be recovering from one party or on her way to another. I sensed she was exaggerating how fabulous her life had become, and could not find the words to tell me she missed me.

But since things came to a head with Dan, I found myself missing her.

Doreen and I have seen off several presidents, Day-Glo jewelry, shoulder pads, nouvelle cuisine, cigarettes, and many boyfriends together. We reviewed restaurants, "did" Florence, hosted each other's birthday dinners, schmoozed each other's mothers, interviewed each other's latest flames, and, on one terrifyingly drunken night, waxed each other's armpits.

She made me laugh like nobody else and more than anything right then, I needed to laugh. I needed to break the bad spell poisoning my home, and there was no witch better than Doreen for cutting through the shit and telling it like it was.

So that afternoon, I e-mailed her and invited her to slum it out in Yonkers for the weekend.

Thirty-four

'm off now, Bernadine," James shouted from the door. "There'll be a bus leaving the Church of the Apparition at five o'clock, if you want to leave early and come on down to Toureen." Then, on my giving no reply, he repeated, "Bernadine?"

James came into the bedroom, and found me fussing through my wardrobe looking for a coat.

"What are you doing? Mae will be here in a few minutes."

It was nearly twelve, and my husband was full of excitement. He had been watching the pontiff's visit live on television that morning.

"Come and watch, Bernadine, Bishop Eamon Casey is on," James had called earlier. "Jesus, but he's a great man altogether—such confidence. Come on, Bernadine—you're missing it all!"

I could not bear to watch. The day before I had watched, with disbelief and despair, the size of the crowds in Dublin and Drogheda. Tens of thousands of people stretched across miles; they were all jubilant, hymn-singing faithful, sure that they would get a good view of St. Peter's successor as he whirred through the clouds in his helicopter, like an orange eagle. The TV cameras caught him up close, his hands raised in greeting and benediction—

but that proximity was just a false promise. If the pontiff himself was just a white dot to the thousands there, in reality what hope had I of finding Michael Tuffy in such a crowd?

For the full week before, I had been trying to talk myself out of seeing the Pope's visit as a backdrop to my own childish fantasy that Michael and I would be the two whom fate would mysteriously draw together through the crowded fields. We had spent a lifetime apart, yet the greater part of me still wondered if Michael and I were destined to be together. With the Pope there, God was sure to be in attendance. And fate was very much God's remit.

"What coat should I wear?" I said to James, holding aloft a navy rain mac, and a hooded cardigan that Niamh had posted me from New York.

"Wear the mac," James said. "It looks like rain."

He was right, of course, but I decided to wear my daughter's gift from New York. For luck.

AT THREE P.M., as the pontiff's helicopter landed to the side of the basilica, the crowd let out a welcoming cheer. Four hundred and fifty thousand individual bodies seemed to merge into one giant mass of devout delight. Exultation.

Four hundred and fifty thousand—and me. I had never felt so alone in my life.

Utterly underestimating the vastness of the crowd and its sheer volume, I had left Mae and the others at the coach park and wandered ignorantly into the crowd to search for Michael. I knew I was behaving out of character. Still, I walked and walked, expecting the crowd to dissipate, but it grew thicker the further in I walked. Within moments I was lost in a forest of bodies. I could not find my bearings, I had no idea of north or south. The familiar landscape of Knock was gone and all I could see was the grass under my feet and people crushing around me on all sides. The gray sky seemed to descend on us. It was one of those days that struggled to overcome dawn and turned to twilight soon after lunch. My cardigan felt clammy and was pulling down on me from a damp hem. The early beginnings of my arthritis (a condition I associated with old age and therefore denied) began to tug at my knees. I wanted to sit down.

As if by magic, a hush went over the crowd as we heard the *clack* of helicopter blades overhead. Silence ruled for a second while we took it in: Was it really—could it be? Then everyone was whooping and shouting. The noise was deafening. Four hundred and fifty thousand people cheering in our special guest, welcoming a new dawn of hope for the future, celebrating the newfound prestige of our country, our county, and the blessed, holy townland of Knock.

I pushed my way angrily through the thick soup of people. I thought I would never escape that crowd. The rain was a soft, damp mist that made my clothes itch and stuck inside my nose, making it hard to breathe. I don't know how long I walked, but it was farther than it had taken me to get in, and I was despairing. Eventually, weeping with frustration and fear, I grabbed a stranger and said, "Which is the way out?"

He signaled me to grab his coat and dragged me through the final thicket of hopeful head strainers. The road outside was cordoned off, but I must have looked dreadful because the man put me in the care of a steward. He found a stool and sat me by the door of St. John's to wait for the Toureen bus. It was a four-hour wait.

They say there is no fool like an old fool, and through those four hours, there was no one felt more of a fool than I. I was drenched to the skin, my knees stabbed at me, and my very bones creaked with damp. I remember thinking what a stupid old woman I was and what a cruel thing love is when it robs you of your good sense, your propriety, your dignity. It could hibernate inside you forever, then a smell, a name, a memory could prod the peaceful sleeping beast and make it howl with hunger. I thought of the bag of baked-ham sandwiches I had packed that morning and left with Mae so that if I met Michael Tuffy I would not be carrying a plastic grocery bag with me. She, and all the ICA, would be enjoying them now with their flasks, cozy in their rainproofs and sensible wellington boots. Other women our age were watching us all from the comfort of their homes, or in the hall in Toureen with friends. I was here, alone in an unsuitable cardigan meant for a much younger woman, my feet frozen in a pair of flimsy fabric shoes, looking for an old sweetheart in a crowd of nearly half a million.

EVENTUALLY, THE bus came and the crowd that had gathered around me all struggled on board, anxious to escape the rain and get stuck into a nice hot cup of tea in St. Mary's.

"Wasn't he fantastic, though!"

" 'The goal of my journey,' that's what he called us."

"He came as a pilgrim, like the rest of us, that's what he said."

"Ah, but sure, he has great humility. He's the Pope, what d'ye expect!"

Everyone was buzzing, and I smiled weakly back as they bantered and recalled the Mass in every euphoric detail.

I had not achieved the goal of my journey.

I took a window seat and looked out as the bus crawled its way past the knickknack shops and postcard stands. Hotels promising soup and sandwiches for under one pound. The hunger had gone off me. I was beyond it.

I wondered then, would I ever get beyond that promise made and broken, no matter what age I got to be?

Thirty-five

Waiting for somebody to forgive you is slow emotional torture. It had been three weeks since the Ronan business and things were far from resolved. Dan moved back into our bedroom, but would lie next to me like a frigid schoolgirl, terrified I might touch him after I made a couple of aborted attempts to seduce him. I tried to be patient but after a few days playing the reformed, ashamed hooker, I snapped, "Jesus, Dan—I've said I'm sorry!" He gazed through me with a look of anguish to illustrate that I would never know or understand the depths of his pain.

I didn't know why I was still there.

Why *was* I still there?

Maybe it's because I knew there were two ways to get salt out of ham. The first is to do what Bernadine did and leave it to soak, let the salt release itself slowly, then rinse it clean and soak again. Rinse clean and soak as often as you can, for as much time as you can spare, and the salt will eventually out.

The second is to boil it really fast in Coca-Cola.

Both methods work, but I think the first one tastes better because you have to wait for it. My belligerent self would argue it should taste exactly the same, but the point is I always take the harder option when it comes to food, and the easy option when it comes to relationships. So I was trying to do it the other way around. Every time Dan and I had a brief toxic exchange, I rinsed it off and started again. Maybe I was imagining it, but things seemed to be thawing.

On the other hand, maybe my thermometer was just adjusting to the cold. Or maybe I only want something when I think I can't have it. Now that Dan had withdrawn his love from me, I missed it. The irony is that now that I had finally grown up enough to appreciate his qualities, I'd managed to turn the gentlest, nicest man in New York into a hardened cynic.

Surprisingly, Dan made no fuss when I announced Doreen would be coming for the weekend.

"That'll be nice," he said flatly, then lied, "I like Doreen."

Dan claimed to like everybody. For example, he claimed to like Doreen but actually she made him feel uncomfortable. They are from planets that make Mars and Venus look like near neighbors. Both are great people, but in such different ways that I find it almost impossible to reconcile their presence in a room together.

Why had I invited Doreen up for the weekend while Dan and I were in the throes of a marriage crisis?

In fairness, it had to be done sometime. Doreen was my best woman after all, and Dan was, despite appearances to the contrary at the moment, my husband. If nothing else, I thought, she could give Dan and me some distraction. Gerry proved an unwitting mediator while we were building the kitchen, and perhaps Doreen would fill the same role. The way things were right then, it was a straw worth clinging to.

THE HOUSE was really taking shape, just as our relationship seemed to be falling apart. The irony of that was not lost on me.

As I prepared the place for Doreen's visit, the experience was made all the more pleasurable by the fact that I knew Doreen would subject every detail to her built-in style radar. It was a challenge that I enjoyed rising to. Especially as I needed a challenge I could control: Like, did the scented candle in the guest bedroom coordinate with the hand soap in the guest bathroom? I had no control over my husband's feelings, so I was catching my attention up in meaningless details—feathering the edges of cotton napkins, arranging Moroccan glasses by bedside tables, and hanging fresh herbs to dry in the kitchen. Hoping that the bigger things, like unfinished paint work, wouldn't be noticed. The same tactic went for Dan as I tried to convince myself that the ludicrous minutia of good housewifery—like changing the blades on his razor, ironing his boxers—would eventually add together to heal what had happened. And I was resentful when he didn't notice my unasked-for efforts, as if he believed ironed underpants were his birthright. Ultimately, I'd been looking for reasons to hang my anger on, something outside of myself to blame for all this frustration and shame.

DOREEN ARRIVED in the early evening and it was awkward. Not between her and Dan but, strangely, between her and me. I guess that was because we hadn't seen each other since the wedding.

"This is all rather precious," was the first thing she said when she entered the kitchen and picked up a floral milk jug I had rescued from Eileen's vast and largely ghastly collection.

"The jug or the kitchen?" I asked, not really wanting the answer.

"Is there a correct answer to that question?"

We gave each other a sardonic smile, but mine lacked commit-

ment and hers lacked humor. Cruel wit had once been our intimate language, that we could take it from each other was an illus-
tration of how close we were. Suddenly, I felt like the wit was
missing and only the cruelty was left. Maybe I was having a crisis
of confidence. I didn't want my house to be fussy and precious but
I wasn't confident enough to defend it against Doreen's cutting
style review.

So I didn't ask again, and got on with preparing our supper, a
ludicrously fattening carbonara with roasted garlic and Parma
ham and a salad fresh from the garden. Dan was puttering in and
out of the kitchen and at one point rewarded me with, "That
smells good, honey."

Doreen raised her eyes to heaven and I was immediately con-
scious of our folksy homeliness, even though the pleasant communication was a minor breakthrough for us. Aside from that brief
moment, Dan kept out of our way for the first few hours, as
Doreen entertained me with gossip about friends and colleagues.
After we'd eaten, Doreen threw in a couple of unnecessarily
graphic sexual anecdotes, designed to shoo him away from the
table in embarrassment. Which they did.

"Marital bliss?" she quipped, after Dan had excused himself to
go and meet Gerry for a beer.

I hadn't realized I needed to talk until I had my old friend in
front of me, asking. It all came tumbling out of me: my lack of
certainty about Dan, kissing Angelo and Ronan, how I had ruined
everything and just wanted things to be OK with my marriage. It
felt good to get it all out in the open, and I realized how much I
had been carrying around in my own head for the past few
months. Doreen nodded sagely for the time it took me to get
everything off my chest and her face was full of genuine concern.

She opened another bottle of wine while I was talking, and kept our glasses filled. I always took responsibility for our food, she for our drink. It felt old and familiar. Safe.

When I had finished, Doreen reached over and took my hand; it felt small and fleshy, like dough caught between her long manicured fingers.

"Do you want to know what I think, Tressa?"

The relief of my confession over, I suddenly saw how drunk Doreen was. I had been talking and she had been drinking. Now it was her turn to reveal. And instinctively, I knew this was a confession I did not want to hear. Before I had time to come to my senses and shout *"No!"* she said, "You have to leave him."

I recoiled swiftly, but not physically. She squeezed my hand with drunken emotion and said what she had wanted to say since the day I had told her I was marrying Dan. Everything I didn't want to hear. Everything I had myself feared was true.

Dan wasn't good enough for me. He wasn't "the One." I should never have had doubts. Doubts are bad, they mean you have made the wrong choice. I shouldn't have been "settling." There was no need to compromise; I should have had more respect for myself. I wasn't even forty yet, there was plenty of time. I should follow my gut instincts and leave now. So Ronan was a shit, but there were other Ronans out there who would make my heart beat and my stomach somersault. I deserved that. I was a passionate woman, blah, blah . . . deserved to have *all* my needs met . . . blah, blah . . . madly in love soul mates . . . blah, blah, blah.

When she started, I was scared. I thought, I can't listen to this, it's too close to the bone. But as she went on, I realized: There was no nerve being hit. And then I thought, *Actually, Doreen, this is bullshit. Dan is what I need; he is what I want, what I deserve.* Because suddenly I saw that life, love, and marriage are actually a whole lot simpler than this nitpicking, navel-gazing quest for the perfect man. I wanted, needed, deserved to be loved. Doesn't everybody? And Dan loved me. He deserved me to love him back, and I was endeavoring to do just that. It wasn't always easy, because I seemed to be naturally attracted to flaky, unavailable jerks but suddenly, knowing the love of a good man and then coming so close to losing it was curing me of that particular obsession. Maybe my natural predilection for dangerous men was changing or maybe this was what mature love felt like. And how much self-respect would I have if I traded in a perfectly nice man to go stand back in a bar in Manhattan waiting for some Hollywood cupid to throw arrows at me?

After all, Mr. Right only feels right until he does something wrong.

I let Doreen finish, then disappointed her by saying I was tired and it was time to go to bed. No dramatic bag-packing exits for me. She drained her glass and patted my arm as if to say, *You sleep on it, girl—I know you'll do the right thing.*

Dan came in late and stumbled into bed. He was drunk and for once forgot that he hated me, so we made tired, sloppy, ordinary love. He curled away from me afterward and put his arm out to pull me in, but I settled it back onto his belly, then hung back and watched his broad, muscled shoulders slow into the heavy rhythm of sleep.

"I love you," he said as he finally dropped off.

"I love you, too."

He always said it first.

SOMETIMES AN act of love is not what you say, but what you don't say, and Dan was saying nothing.

"I mean, Dan, how can you *never* have read William Faulkner. That's *ludicrous!*"

It was Saturday lunchtime, and the weather was nice, so Doreen and I were sipping Pimm's in the back garden. Dan was drinking beer and had taken his shirt off. Doreen realized that morning that I wasn't going to take her advice. In retaliation, she had returned to her "stupid but cute" attitude toward him.

"Still, who needs literature with muscles like those?" and she leaned over to give his bicep a squeeze.

Dan was mortified, but went along with her.

In life, loyalty is something that you earn, and Doreen had more than earned my loyalty over the years. But marriage is a rogue state with its own rules, and one of them is pledging your loyalty to somebody before you can be fully sure that they deserve it. You mess with him? You mess with me. That was the new rule. A husband is instant family. He gets the loyalty of a blood tie without doing any of the work. Except poor Dan was working for it, too.

"Oh yessss—you bagged yourself a regular Hemingway here, Tressa."

Doreen laughed and patted him on the cheek with one hand, while the other reached for her cigarettes.

Doreen had been really bitchy all day, but I knew it was her own insecurity at play. She could see that, despite everything I'd told her, Dan and I were on our way to being settled. And it unsettled her for some reason. It was what she had always said she wanted for me but now that she saw me with it, it felt alien to her.

I was in the midst of a marriage crisis, just keeping myself afloat by trying to second guess my husband's emotions and keep my own in check, and I didn't have time for self-obsessed and, let's face it, just plain mean girlfriends anymore. So did Doreen have my best interests at heart here?

No, I didn't believe so.

Was she flexible enough to make the adaptation necessary to be a supportive friend to Tressa the married woman?

Seemingly not.

Oh, and plus? She was pissing me off with her bad-mannered attempts at humor.

"Don't talk to my husband like that, Doreen."

"Like what?"

She raised her eyebrows at me, falsely incredulous.

"In that patronizing tone; he's not a child."

Dan talked over me with, "Hey, wait a minute, honey. It's okay . . ."

I was irritated with him butting in, but at the same time, I heard his old softness in the word "honey" and I knew I couldn't back down.

"No, Dan, it's not . . ."

In a show of emotional intelligence, my husband said, "I'll make coffee," and bolted at full speed toward the kitchen door.

"I can hear what you are trying to do, Doreen," I said, "and it is *not* OK."

"You are a fool, Tressa, and I am not going to be spoken to like this," Doreen said simply, and walked toward the door. On reaching it, she turned, rather grandly, saying, "I'll send a car later for my things." In that stylish gesture I realized, yes, I was going to miss this woman, this friend in my life, but the hard truth is that fifteen years of friendship can be flushed when the stake is a marriage.

Even a short, shaky one like mine.

Thirty-six

didn't even bother looking for James when I got to St. Mary's Hall, because I knew he would be caught up in some responsibility or other. So I was surprised when I found him waiting for me at the door. The hall was not as packed as I had expected it to be. There were chairs along the walls, not all of them taken, and there were tables dotted across the vast dance floor. Four large television sets sat on trestle tables on the stage. It was a predictable crowd, our neighbors in age and locality were largely here.

I looked around to see who I might sit with. Rather, in the humor I was in, who I might *not* sit with. I spotted Aine Grealy right away. She looked across and waved me over enthusiastically. She was up to no good, and it was only then that I saw who was sitting with her.

Michael.

I lost my balance, but James, who had appeared beside me, caught my arm.

"Would you like some tea, dear?"

James spoke into the muted murmur of village curiosity. The room had quietened by half, the polite pretended to talk while others openly stared. There was not a sinner in the place who did not know the connection between Michael Tuffy and me. And if there were any gaps, Aine Grealy had spent all day filling them in.

I started to shake, and gripped onto James's steady arm. He did not let me go, but glided me across the floor towards his lifetime's rival.

"Aine," he said. "I wonder if I might ask you to help me prepare my talk. There're a few translations that could use your expert opinion."

He gave her no choice but to peel herself away, although she no doubt consoled herself with spending an hour sharing her brilliant brain with my husband.

Michael stood up and held out his hand to greet me. As I sat down on the seat next to him it was all I could do to keep my breath from exploding out of my mouth. If I opened it to smile at him, it would surely draw back over my cheeks in a shocked sob and then everyone would know. Even him. Especially him.

I had never in my mind's eye envisioned Michael as an old man. The last time I had seen him, we had both been young and full of vigor. I had watched myself age, and in the evidence of getting older, I had pushed my handsome young Michael further into my memory. As decades passed, I let him rest in the place of dreams where the young stay beautiful forever. As the years moved on, I stopped wondering.

Now he was here. He was wearing a brown suit that was out of fashion, and a blue shirt that did not go well with it. Much of his hair was gone and his face was lined. The blue eyes remained.

He was my own Michael. The same as that first night we had seen each other in Kitty Conlan's parlor, and I had known we were meant to be together. The years had passed like a moment, as if he had just turned to pick a flower for my hair, and now I was sixty. I knew from his eyes that he didn't care I'd aged. I knew I looked the same to him now as I had then. We had grown older, yet the beauty we had seen in each other when we were young had seemed to simply mature, like exquisite wine.

Eventually I said, "Michael Tuffy."

He smiled at me. Broad, brave mischief.

"You look the same," he said.

I shrugged and looked away. I was afraid to hold his eye for too long.

We sat looking forward for a moment, not needing words but locked together in our world as we had always been. I had questions to ask, but there was time enough for that. He leaned over to me and I could feel his breath next to my ear. Like the warm breeze on the beach in Enniscrone the day I dreamt I saw him.

"Do you remember how we were, Bernadine Moran? Do you remember how it was then?"

I started to close my eyes to conjure up my private summer meadow daydream that I might share it with him, but as my lids folded down, I saw James across the room.

He was shuffling his feet, half talking to Aine and half looking back at me. His agitation broke my spell. Then, for one second, I caught my husband's eye. He looked tired and nervous. No sparkling shots of blue, no grand desires, no dreams, no jokes, no promises of passionate delights. Just worn, worried, everyday James.

And I knew I had to get up from my chair and walk over to him. Because however much I loved Michael Tuffy, still and forever, a promise is a promise. James had kept his promise to me and been a good husband. If I answered Michael Tuffy's question, I would be making a choice. And whatever my heart told me, I had to be loyal to my husband. He deserved my love, but the least I could give him was my loyalty.

I took one last look at my one true love. I held my hands tightly in my lap as I scanned his face good-bye.

"No, Michael Tuffy," I said. "I barely remember it at all."

I stood and walked across to James. His face relaxed in relief, and he took my hand and held me by him for the rest of that afternoon.

Michael, I saw, left shortly afterwards.

I believe he returned to America, although I never heard of him ever again.

Trust

You don't have to feel love to give it.

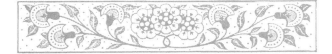

Pobs

Your mother was a fussy eater when she was a child, and on days when she would not trust to my cooking, I would feed her a slice of bread mashed into a cup of warm milk, with a sprinkle of sugar on top. As her taste developed and changed, she would always return to a cup of "pobs" as comfort food. It was the only recipe I could ever get your mother to master, and I know you were virtually reared on it yourself.

Sometimes we can only stomach the simplest of things. This is food for the very young and the very old. As it is only at the very beginning and the very end of our lives that we have answers, I have come around to thinking that, with all of the fuss we make over food, perhaps all any of us really needs is bread, milk, and a little sugar to sweeten it at times.

Thirty-seven

I was staying in a hotel in South Beach, Miami. Everything was warm and candy colored, even the women in their string bikinis. I was speaking at a conference there and the manager had upgraded me to a suite overlooking the beach. Somewhere behind the clamor of the *Vogue* fashion teams ordering breakfast on the patio beneath my balcony, I could hear the sea.

I missed Dan.

I didn't think I would and I wasn't sure why I did.

It's just that in the past year, my new husband had grown on me. I noticed when he wasn't here—his clumsy lumbering ways, doing those things I hated, blowing his nose, using hillbilly words, and drinking instant coffee. I didn't feel madly in love with him. But a small, slow miracle had occurred inside me so that he no longer annoyed me as much as he used to. Maybe that counted for something, or maybe my standards had dropped and I should have been worried. But I found a kind of freedom in shrugging stuff off, and I was going to stick with it. Tolerance is an unfashionable quality—but I found that being irritated wastes an awful lot more energy than you think.

Dan was over the Ronan thing. Kind of.

He didn't exactly dance a jig when I said I'd been invited to Miami for work for a few days. I asked him rather than told him, although I don't know what I would have said if he had said "No," which, of course, he would never have done. He said something much worse, which was, "I trust you."

There was a menu of potential fights to choose from:

For starters, "Well, gee, *thanks,* honey for allowing me to go to work and earn a living."

Then a meaty entrée, "Can we *please* put the 'my wife's a slut' card to the back of the pack now?"

And for dessert, that old family favorite, "I never should have married you in the first place!"

The thing that really drove me crazy is that I completely trusted Dan. I *knew* he would never betray me in the way I betrayed him.

Trust is nothing when you have it. It's bread and milk. Basic. There's no glamour, no emotion, no drama—you just trust and that's it. Trusting someone is boring. It's a nonevent. But take it away—try living without trust—and suddenly your relationship is plunged into a living hellhole. I've been there, and I have seen my friends live with men they didn't trust, men who lie. Not little "no, you don't look fat in that" lies, but terrifying "working late while really I am banging my secretary" lies.

I always thought you had to be really crazy about somebody not to trust them. Actually, you just have to be with somebody who is untrustworthy. Like somebody who really *would* feel up your friend under a dinner party table. Or somebody who never says "I love you" first.

Dan deserved my trust, but I didn't deserve his. I would have liked it. It would have made my inner life easier, and made me feel like I was a nicer person. But I didn't have it. Not all of it, or not yet. Dan had always known that he loved me that bit more than I loved him. When I betrayed him, it shifted the balance too far in my direction.

"I trust you," was my punishment for the past and my challenge for a future together.

So I was standing in front of two hundred food industry executives about to deliver my wisdom on memory and food, when the shithead Angelo Orlandi walked right up to the front of the theater and plonked himself down in front of the podium. He was minus Jan and wearing dark glasses so I couldn't see his eyes. He started to look around the room as I spoke, like I was boring him. It unnerved me, and I stumbled over a couple of sentences.

When I was finished, he walked over to the side of the stage, standing almost directly beneath me. I was sorely tempted to bury my heel in the top of his head. Not for the first time, I wished I had worn stilettos to work.

"Hi, Tressa."

I hate men. Behind me, I had a smug husband saying, "I trust you" when he so did not, and in front of me I had a lecherous, manipulative ex who probably wanted a fuck, and would probably be just crude enough to ask me straight out for one.

"You free for dinner?"

Same thing.

"Where's Jan?"

"She's not here."

Then he gave me this thoroughly-delighted-with-himself grin.

I couldn't be bothered with this man anymore. He was an insult to the principle of marital trust. I found him so appalling that he could no longer tempt me.

So I looked at one of the richest, cleverest, and most admired men in the food industry in America and I thought, What is it that I hate about you so much? Then I saw it, clear as the blue Miami sky. Angelo lacked integrity. And the reason I could see it with such clarity is because I was married to a man who *had* integrity so I knew when it was missing, and in Angelo Orlandi, it was missing in spades.

Angelo had high standards when it came to organic farming and food politics and arugula and slow-roasted garlic sauces. But he had no integrity in his marriage, with his wife, with the human being who was supposed to be closest to him. And I realized, in that moment, that integrity of that sort was the only kind that counts. Or rather, it's the only kind that counted for me. Great men, good men, humane, heroic, brilliant, history-making men shit on their own doorsteps all the time. And that's fine. I just didn't want to be married to one of them and, thankfully, I was not.

So Dan won. He won the stupid test I had set him before the Orlandi weekend. That it had taken me this long to figure it out was no credit to me, yet it was so simple. You make a promise, and you keep it—not until you don't feel like keeping it anymore, not until you got bored or restless or someone more exciting, more interesting comes along. You say you are going to do something and then you do it. In the same everyday way that we do things that we don't feel like doing, like getting up on a frosty morning to do a photo-shoot with a photographer you hate because you have a deadline to meet.

The same goes for living with the same person day in and day out for the rest of your life. You don't always *feel* like doing it, but you do it because you said that you would. And that, I realized, is how love grows.

"Go home to Jan," I said.

Angelo looked at me like, "What is *that* supposed to mean?"

*   *   *

I WENT straight upstairs to phone Dan. I had a compulsion to tell him that I loved him. Say it first. Without analysis or thinking about whether I really, *really* meant it or not. I just wanted him to hear it. I wanted to give him that.

I stepped on an envelope that had been pushed under my door and opened it impatiently, assuming it was something to do with tomorrow's work schedule.

It was a typed hotel memo, marked URGENT:

"There has been an accident. Please call Gerry."

Thirty-eight

There are so many things about marriage that are never spoken of either within or outside it.

Although nobody ever said it, it was understood that the death of a first wife in childbirth could be the making of a man. He was free to marry again, and it was often the second wife's dowry that made his fortune.

Similarly, the death of the man of the house could be viewed as a relief. There were those families with a dozen children, a two-room cottage, and no privacy for a wife to object to her husband's advances. Some women would send their husbands to the pub with the week's housekeeping, praying that he would get so drunk that he might fall and hit his head on a rock and be found dead in a ditch in the morning. There would be weeping and wailing and genuine grief. But there would also be a widow's pension that would see the elder children through school and the younger ones fed properly.

I never suffered hunger or indignity at the hands of my husband and yet, at times I had wished him dead. In the early years of our marriage, I fantasized about it. What would happen if some terrible tragedy should befall him? Then Michael would come back and marry me, the young widow.

I could have been forgiven for such thoughts during my youth and given the circumstances under which we were married, but as the years went on, I continued to harbor the occasional petty death wish, whether over a pompous comment or a query as to how I had prepared the ham, as it was not as much to his liking as usual. Right up into my fifties, when I was fit and strong and still perceived myself as an attractive woman, at times I would look at James and think that if he were to die, I might have ten good years left to make another life for myself entirely.

You might assume that contentment is the right of the elderly, but you'd be wrong. Peace of mind does not come with time or age or routine. It masquerades as a product of luck and personality but in fact, serenity is hard won through prayer and perseverance and an understanding of hardship.

For some people, hardship is a husband who beats them or the death of a child. Others will search for and find hardship in an everyday rain cloud.

The trick to contentment is knowing when hardship has passed, and appreciating its absence for every moment that it is not there. I was never content with James because I was determined not to be. I looked at him and saw what he was not. What he never could be.

WHEN THE doctor told me James was dying, the shock was harder for my having wished him dead.

There is so much you can say about a person dying, yet there is so little worth saying. We get caught up in the language of disease, use it to distract ourselves from the truth of what is happening; we become experts in diagnosis, in treatments, yet cannot say the only thing worth saying, which is that soon this person will not be with us anymore.

James had a heart condition and bowel cancer. He was seventy-eight; the doctor talked about cell growth and breathing patterns and blood pressure. In the year he was sick I learned to use a syringe; I cleaned and fed him like a small child and, towards the end, like a baby. I would not let a nurse into the house or see him suffer the indignity of being fed or washed by anyone but his own wife.

When you and Niamh came to stay during that time your mother and I fought. She wanted to tend him and I would not let her. Niamh called me a "stubborn old bitch." I never told her then that James thought he was her hero. He could not have borne his daughter seeing him as reduced as he was.

"Read to him," I said.

They say that it is not until you lose both parents that you finally mature into an adult. But a life partner dying brings home the inevitability of your own death. There is nothing that can prepare you. I wondered, but wouldn't say aloud, if Niamh would be here to nurse me when my time came. Or who would comfort me at the end of my life?

James kept saying it, "I am dying. I am dying," and I kept swatting him back like a kitchen bluebottle.

"I'm not afraid," he said, "I've made my peace. I just want to know that you'll be all right. Bernadine . . ."

To the end, even in the morphine-induced throes of his pain relief, James said my name, "Bernadine," as if I were the answer to a prayer. The great love of his life.

*   *   *

WE LIVED a year like that: me watching him so closely that I could not see him anymore. I saw only individual details like the fine membrane of his skin as I changed his drip, rheumy eyes that needed cleaning, a mouth peeled back in a noiseless scream as the periods of ease that the morphine gave him became shorter. I shaved him, washed him, trimmed his hair and nails. I changed his sheets every two days, his pajamas every day. When people came, I put a shirt and a tie on him and covered the bed in Foxford tweed rugs to take the bare, bedridden look off him. I aired his room and filled it with flowers, and I banished the smell of death from our house.

You can study death, you can talk about it, you can know it is going to happen, but nothing can prepare you.

When you care for the dying, you don't absorb the things you so desperately want to remember after they are gone: their voice in whispered prayer, a hand that grips, eyes that move across you, a chest moving up and down in breath. Life to the end is a series of small miracles you can only appreciate after your beloved is gone. The instant the miracles cease, you wish you had looked harder, treasured the gift of life itself.

You wish you hadn't wasted so much time wanting more.

Thirty-nine

I had not truly realized how attached I was to my life back in Yonkers until I became completely cut off from it over the next few hours.

I am cell-phone dependent—I use it for everything from keeping a diary to taking pictures to reminding me of my to-do list. It always irritated the hell out of Dan that I seemed constantly distracted by my "little buzzing box," as he called it, so when I accidentally dropped and smashed it the day before my trip to Miami I decided, as an experiment, to live without it for a few days. Just to prove to him that I could. "Cell phones are for emergencies," he was always saying to me. Good call, Dan. Now there was an emergency, and I had no cell.

I got straight onto the hotel line and called home. It kept switching to voicemail and I thought the line was engaged until I remembered that I had bought a dinky retro phone unit the week before. Discovering it had the wrong cable fitting I remembered, with shocking clarity, that I had forgotten to plug the old one back in and neglected to tell Dan about my mistake so there would be nothing ringing in the house. I wasn't panicked about the home phone because Dan had a cell, too, and I was diligent about keeping it charged. But I was in Miami—so Dan's cell was dead as was, of course, the chaotic Gerry's, which also switched immediately to voicemail. Starting to get desperate, I rang Eileen's house, certain that she would know what was going on. The phone was answered after half a second by one of Dan's infant nephews who gurgled prettily at me before dropping the receiver on the floor and wandering off. I could hear the noise of adults talking in the background and frantically shouted, "Hello? Hello?" to no avail. This was a common occurrence in the Mullins household, and as their visiting rota was so vigilant, Eileen barely used the phone. It might be days before the mishap was discovered. Kay's cell phone number was in my phone, as was every other number that might lead me to finding out what had happened. Addresses, too, so I couldn't even call information. I memorized nothing—no need when you have a buzzing box to hold all the information you need, right? God was clearly conspiring against me, so in a state of rising panic tempered by pure frustration, I rang the airport and booked myself on the first plane back to New York.

My head was spinning with dreadful possibilities all the way back. I had no idea what had happened, did not know if Dan was dead or alive. I went through every scenario in my head. He had fallen off that cursed bike, perhaps he had decided to refelt the garage roof like he had been threatening to do for weeks, or—Jesus—there was major electrical work going on in the house. Please don't let him have got himself electrocuted.

What did "accident" mean, anyway? It could mean he was dead. "There has been an accident," that's what they say in the films. No. "There has been a terrible accident," is what they say when someone has died. He wasn't dead—was he? No, surely Gerry would have said. Or not. It's not the sort of thing you'd leave with a hotel receptionist: "Husband dead. Please phone home."

If it was really serious, Gerry would have told the hotel, and they would have interrupted my talk.

I flagged a steward and ordered four whiskies. I threw them down back to back and slept my way out of my panic.

I was nudged awake five minutes after landing to an almost empty plane. My head was thumping as I made it to the taxi stand, and my heart joined in with it as the line snailed along and I wondered whether to faint my way to the top of it. Once in the cab, I didn't know where to go. A hospital, but which one? Did the accident happen at home or in Manhattan? I decided to go home first.

My hands were trembling so hard I could hardly get my key in the lock. I fell in the door, weak with dread, and made my way toward the back of the house. If there was a note, it would be on the kitchen table. There was a faint sound of voices to my left so I opened the door to the living room and walked in.

The TV was on and Dan was asleep on the sofa. His head was back, his mouth was open, and there was a perfectly healthy man's snore emanating from it. He had one of my good patchwork quilts tucked in under his neck, and it looked out of place with the surrounding bachelor debris: three Domino's Pizza boxes, an ashtray with a couple of half-smoked reefers, and a pile of Budweiser cans.

Some kind of an unholy rage rose up in me.

"What the hell is going on!" I shouted.

Dan leaped up in shock, then recoiled in pain. As the blanket fell aside, I saw that his arm was in a sling.

"Ouch!"

"I thought you were *DEAD*!"

He looked kind of annoyed himself, cradling his hurt arm.

"Sorry to disappoint you!"

I sensed Gerry loitering behind me, and I swirled on him like a dervish before he had the chance to retreat.

"And you've got some bloody explaining to do . . ."

"I'm sorry, Tress, I swear—I tried calling you again, but my cell phone was dead and . . ."

I had never felt so angry in my life. My extremities were fizzing.

"Don't blame Gerry, babe, it was my fault. I took my eye off the road for a second and there was this piece of wood or something . . ."

"Next thing—wham, he goes down and I'm a coupla' hundred feet behind him on the Harley and I go 'shit!'"

"And I went down and next thing I remember I'm . . ."

"Shut up, the pair of you!"

I didn't recognize my own voice, it came out in such a roar.

"You are both in *so much* trouble."

I caught Dan giving Gerry a cheeky schoolboy wink and realized, for the first time since I came in, that they were both more than a little drunk. That sent me right over the edge. I can't remember what I said next, but it was a boiling stream of consciousness that contained references to the fact that I was not his mother, that they were both like children, that I was a very important person who did not appreciate being dragged back up the coast for no good reason; and that I had always said that that bike was a death trap and he was never going out on it again. Never. *Ever.*

Dan was nodding and trying to look contrite, but I saw his eyes flick across Gerry, who was standing behind me, and the beginnings of a smile form on his lips.

Hateful bastards. Laughing at me.

"Is that arm broken, Dan?"

I needed to assess the seriousness of his injury in order to calculate whether I could reasonably add to it.

"No it's . . ."

". . . fractured. Just hairline," his partner in crime butted in. Abbot and Costello.

I stood there, literally hopping from foot to foot, I was so mad. I didn't know what to do with myself. I wanted to bang their two heads together.

Then I had an idea.

"Right," I said, "that's *it!*"

They followed me out to the garage, where I picked up a hammer from Dan's tool shelf and swung it in an arc at the side of the bike, tearing a huge lump down one side. There was a joint, horrified gasp from behind me.

I did not care. This was a revelation—violence felt good.

So I swung again. The two men shouted, "No!" and Dan grabbed the hammer, while Gerry threw himself at the wheels of his beloved Kawasaki and begged its forgiveness for having put it in the path of a madwoman.

I turned and accidentally belted Dan's bad arm.

"Ow!" he yelped.

"I thought you were dead!" I screamed, then I caught his eyes with my own collapsing, angry face. We stood for a moment, our eyes glued to the other's in the shock of strong emotion. I was brought back to that first afternoon we slept together: my disbelief that this handsome stranger desired me, the unthinking, simple way that Dan fell instantly in love with me, and his solid willingness to follow through on it.

If you'd asked a girl like me, *What more could you ask for?* I would always think of something. But I didn't want to lose him, and I hadn't realized I cared so much. Neither had he.

Dan walked over and put his good arm around me. Even with one arm, he was strong.

"You can trust me, baby—I wouldn't go dying on you. Not yet, anyway."

I realized then that while I had virtually no trust in my *own* judgment, I had always, and could always, totally trust Dan.

I knew then that he was the only man in my life I would ever believe in that completely. My husband.

Forty

ames died on a Tuesday. I remember it because I had been studying the weather, looking for hardship in rain clouds. The summer had been swinging between terrible slashing storms that would make you afraid to leave the house and glorious sunshine that made the humble hedgerows vigorous and colorful. This day was neither. It felt airless and flat, a plain day where everything looked like itself. No beauty, no pain—just as it is.

And I remember thinking nothing in particular, only what an ordinary day it was, and noting that no day could be more ordinary than a Tuesday, which falls neither at the beginning, middle, nor end of the week.

James looked so sleepy that morning that I decided to forego the day's toilet routine and let him doze. I gave him his painkillers in the mid-morning and fussed around the room chatting about something stupid—the Munnellys' vegetable-digging cat, I think it was. It was one of the new things I did when James got ill. I became chatty, pouring out a constant stream of pointless words to fill the space left by his weak silence. Sometimes he raised his hand to indicate I was annoying him. But this day, I could tell he was enjoying listening to me. Not to the words surely, but just to the sound of my voice.

For lunch I had mashed some potatoes through with bacon and cabbage. James was barely eating now, but I was determined, and every day, I prepared him proper food and worried and nagged when he didn't eat it. I would not give in.

On this Tuesday, I did give in to him. He asked me to prepare warm milk and bread for his lunch. He said the single word, "pobs," as a child would.

As I fed him, sitting on the chair next to his bed, I talked my tittle-tattle. My silly verbal nonsense balanced out his physical disability; as distraction from the humiliation of napkins and spoons and liquidized food, I would turn myself into a mindless gossip.

"So I said to Mary—start again and this time I want details. Tell me what did he say to you—then what did you say to him . . ."

I wiped James's mouth, and as I did, he raised his hand and took my wrist.

I raised my eyes to heaven to indicate that I understood him telling me to stop the story before he lost his mind, and I half stood up.

James shook his head and tried to grip my wrist harder, failed, and it slid down my arm, but he did not let go. He wanted to speak, but seemed unable.

"What is it?" I said, then started to work down my list, "Apple jelly? Tea? The paper? Do you want me to read the paper? The television?"

James shook his head as if he could not speak, but his face was alive and I could tell there was energy in him. I got irritated.

"Speak up, you silly old fool. Tell me what you want."

James rested his head back on the pillow, shut his eyes, and spoke. It was barely above a whisper, but I heard him clearly.

"Tell me you love me."

I was stunned.

James had broken the understanding that had existed between us for over fifty years; our unspoken contract. He was my husband, but my heart had always belonged to another man. James knew that. The night his mother died, James told me he loved me. I had never said it back. It was understood from that day on that when I didn't say it to comfort him then, I was never going to say it. Now he was dying, and it felt like a manipulation more than a request.

James's eyes stayed closed as he repeated his request, quieter still, almost as if to himself. Beyond meek, beyond hopeful in the face of my silence: "Tell me you love me, my only Bernadine."

I knew he was waiting for me. Of all of the things I had ever done for James, this was the only thing he had ever wanted. Perhaps because it was the one thing he knew he could never have. The alarm on the bedside cabinet went off to indicate it was time for his drugs. We both started, but before I stood up to busy myself, I had a sense that I should stay sitting for one moment longer, a feeling outside of myself, like I was being held in the chair.

I looked at this man I had known all of my life, this man I did not love, but with whom I had lived for longer than my mother, my father, my child. This man who I had married as a stranger, yet who had become my oldest friend. The person I had tried to keep myself hidden from, and yet who knew me better than anyone.

I did not go and fetch his tablets, but sat instead and noticed for the first time how frail and withered he was. James was barely in the room. The robust, elegant schoolteacher, soldier, father, husband was gone. All that was left was this barely breathing sliver of soul, asking for love. Not asking if I loved him, or had I ever loved him, but just to say the words, "I love you" to him.

Once. That once would be enough to set him free.

In that moment, what had been impossible all my life now seemed so simple. I did not have to love James to tell him I loved him.

I just had to say the words.

"I love you."

Briefly James opened his eyes and his mouth closed around my name for the last time.

IN THE moment he was gone, there was a revelation.

As I had said the words "I love you" to my husband for the first time, I realized they were true.

I held him for one hour and I said the words "I love you, I love you, I love you" over and over into our empty room. And I imagined them carrying his soul in a stream of words out through the window and way up to heaven—how many words does it take to carry a soul to heaven? How many "I love you's"?

It should have felt like I was saying it too late. But it didn't, and that was the greatest revelation of all. James had been the love of my life. Not what I had wished for, not what I had dreamt of— but wishes and dreams don't live in the real world. James had been my life. My reality.

Love can live in your mind and your heart, and it can be anything you want it to be. My love for Michael Tuffy, bar that first glorious summer, was a fantasy. What I shared with James truly belonged to me. Love that lives in the world, love that has to sacrifice, compromise, share, endure. Tangible, tough, tender love, this is the real thing. Love you can touch, that can comfort and hold and protect you, love that smells and tastes familiar, if not always sweet.

The legacy James left me was his trust. He never faulted me as a wife, a lover, or a mother—although I was lacking in all three. He had faith in my love for him, even though it remained unspoken for all of our life together. James saw love in my sense of duty towards him and although I would never dare admit it, he was right. I look at the shooting bag I had embroidered with his initials, the antimacassar I crocheted for his chair, now imprinted with the shape of his sleeping skull—and I think that each thing I made him, each scone I baked, each crust I cut, each lettuce I grew, contained perhaps no more than a pinprick of love. But it was enough.

James had gathered each gesture and banked it away so that in the end of his life I knew he felt loved by me. He just needed me to say it before he went. And I believe he knew that I needed to say it, too.

James had been the love of my life, because I had shared my life with him. It was no more mysterious than that. My husband had been my bread and butter, my sustenance. And Michael? Well, he was just jam.

THEY SAY there is no such thing as a perfect marriage, but there is. A perfect marriage is one where two people live together for most of their lives until death separates them. There is no such thing as an easy marriage. And when it comes to love, we have somehow come around to believing it should happen with ease.

The differences between men and women are what set our hearts alight, but the similarities are the fuel that keeps us going: warmth, companionship, bearing witness to another's grief—the original joy and pain of being human. Married love is the gold at the center of the rubble after the fire has gone out. It can take years to find the hidden treasure, but the search is what is important, and when treasure is too easily found how can you be sure it isn't fool's gold?

What my marriage taught me is that real love is only what you give. That's all. Love is not "out there," waiting for you. It is in you. In your own heart, in what you are willing to give of it. We are all capable of love, but few of us have the courage to do it properly. You can take a person's love and waste it. But you are the fool. When you give love, it grows and flowers inside you like a carefully pruned rose. Love is joy. Those who love, no matter what indignities, what burdens they carry, are always full of joy. James was happy in our marriage because he gave me his love. And in the end, despite myself, I *had* loved my husband. Reluctantly and never absolutely.

But what in life is ever absolute?

Except death.

Commitment

*You can make a commitment to love,
but you cannot truly love
without commitment.*

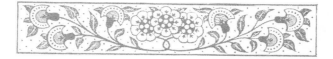

Modern Irish Stew

This is not my grandmother's recipe, but my own. Because sometimes, no matter how much pleasure you get from somebody else's work, there is no replacement for a recipe that you have developed yourself.

Serves 2

You will need

Rack of lamb (around 6 cutlets)
3–4 shallots, chopped
1 clove garlic, finely chopped
1½ cups lamb stock
2–3 sprigs rosemary, leaves removed and chopped
2 handfuls tiny new potatoes
8 small whole baby carrots
red wine

Brown the rack of lamb for 3 minutes on each side in a hot pan. Remove from the pan and throw in your shallots and garlic for 1 minute, then remove. Throw the hot stock into a saucepan and add potatoes, carrots, and rosemary, then bring to a boil. Place rack of lamb on top, cover, and simmer for 15 minutes (rare) or 20 minutes (medium rare). Remove rack of lamb and the vegetables with a slotted spoon and place in a shallow casserole dish. Cover with a tea towel and leave to rest for 5 minutes. Meanwhile, reduce the pan liquid by a third (on a high heat for 2–3 minutes). Once reduced, add a good slug of red wine and leave on high heat for another 2 minutes. Take off the heat and cover with a lid to keep gravy hot. Slice the lamb into six cutlets, place 3 on each plate, and spoon the spuds and carrots around them. Add the red wine sauce just before serving.

Accompany with buttered, wilted white cabbage sprinkled with thyme. (Finely chop a quarter of a head of white cabbage, simmer over a very low heat with 2 knobs butter for 10 minutes, adding a little of the red wine. Add thyme 2 minutes before removing from the heat.)

My darling Tressa,

It may be old fashioned for me to believe, in this day and age, that you will ever choose to get married. And while my instincts have led me astray many times over the past seventy years, I feel certain in my belief that you, of all the people I have known, will find lasting love. My hope for you is that my story, as true as I am able to write it, will help you hold onto that love when you do find it. Because it has taken me all of this time to realize that there is nothing in this world worth speaking of more than love.

Since your grandfather died, I have become more clearly aware of the connection between food and love. Not having him to cook for anymore, I turned away from my kitchen and to his old desk in my need to record the details of our marriage. In these pages, he has come alive to me again and I have found great comfort in that.

You are probably wondering why I chose you as my audience rather than your mother. All I can tell you is that sometimes it is difficult to be absolutely honest with your own child. I was able to love you as my grandchild yet enjoy a light, friendly freedom I never had with Niamh. It may have seemed, as you grew older, that your mother envied the closeness we enjoyed; our mutual love of cooking, the easy immediate way we could talk and joke together— but I know Niamh better than anyone and I know that she reveled in it too. You may pass this on to her if she asks to read it, but I doubt she will. Niamh knows all she needs to know about my story because she carries the truth of it in her blood. Your blood and mine is diluted so I feel freer to speak the truth out.

If you never marry, you may never read this—but I hope you do. We love best by giving of the things we love best. In my marriage, I moved from one recipe to another and through them learned the lessons I needed to love. I would like to think I am leaving some legacy behind in teaching you my kitchen skills and telling you my story. Use them both to love more thoroughly, more generously than I did.

I hope that your husband is everything you have ever wished for. But mostly, I hope that he is kind and that he loves you. They are the only two things that matter in the end.

Love and every happiness, Grandma Bernadine

Forty-one

The first year of my marriage didn't work out quite how I planned it, in all sorts of ways.

The photographs of our kitchen, which *New York Interiors* magazine had shot months before (and we had more or less forgotten about) hit the newsstands. The response to our customized cupboards was astounding, and I was suddenly overwhelmed with requests to design kitchens. Except that everyone wanted a one off "original" like ours. Dan had an idea. He called Gerry and the two of them started calling in favors. They borrowed some muscle, big wheels, and started trawling around salvage yards and building suppliers. Before I had time to really figure out what was happening, the three of us were running a kitchen design and manufacturing company called, of all things, Eclectic Kitchens. We sold the apartment in Manhattan, trading it for the lease on a showroom, and less than three months in business we were short-listed for a new business award. It has been the craziest, busiest, scariest, and most profitable experience of my life. Dan and I spent our first wedding anniversary in a tiling factory formulating our new range of retro colors. And here's the craziest thing of all: *I loved it*. It was the perfect end to the first year of what continues to be the biggest adventure of my life: marriage. When we got home that night, there was a package waiting for me from my mother. The covering note said that she was passing on my grandmother's memoirs, which she had held onto all of these years, following Bernadine's request that they be sent to me on my first wedding anniversary. I didn't tear the package open immediately, as I want to savor her story properly as I have been doing with my memories of her recipes throughout the past year.

I found the first year hard because I asked too many questions. Questions are the sign of an active, intelligent mind, a filter you rinse your ideas through before you make a decision. But sometimes the filter gets clogged and then it becomes a barrier to the truth. The truth is that while I was busy wondering if I loved Dan enough, measuring him up against ex-boyfriends, being attracted to other men, sweating, deliberating, agonizing about my decision to spend the rest of my life with him, our marriage was just marching on anyway.

We moved home, we renovated a house, we negotiated around family, we built a kitchen, we entertained new and old friends. We lived, ate, slept together. Dan was busy just being my husband and despite myself, I had been a wife to him.

An adoring, generous-spirited wife? No. The words "grudging" and "duty" spring to mind, but I guess it's a start. I thought that you could not make a commitment until you were truly in love. What I know now is that you cannot love truly until you have made a commitment.

I like to have all the answers up front, before I decide if a risk is worth taking. But with relationships, it just doesn't work like that. Being in love has a shorter guarantee than a kettle, and in the long run can be a lot less use in a marriage. Better to be armed with a dose of blind faith, so that when the love runs out you can believe it will be back again. Because it will. What I have learned this year is that married love is never complete or finite. It has to be elastic, adjustable. If you become too attached to a way of loving, the beautiful buzz, the thrill, you'll have no way of replacing it when it's gone. Marriages are custom made; you just jiggle them around until you find a way to make them fit.

They say the heart rules the head, but sometimes it works the other way around. I was a grown woman when I married Dan. I married him because his heart was big and brave enough to take me on. It needed to be, as I discovered that my own heart was small and wretchedly weak. Lucky for me, Dan's heart wouldn't let me go. He told me once that he loved me enough for the both of us. It frightened me at the time, and I comforted myself with the fact that it was just a figure of speech. But it wasn't—and I sure am glad that it was true. Do I love him now? Yes, but don't ask me to put a 100 percent tag on it because I don't know if that mysterious gap that craves certainty will ever be filled. In my most self-brutalizing moments, I still wonder if I married Dan just to not be alone. I wonder then if marriage is about love at all. Perhaps it is just the dance two people make, when they move quietly about the same house. Perhaps it is not how I feel about Dan's little foibles that matters, but the fact that I know about them at all. Perhaps intimacy is not just loving everything about him, but knowing everything about him—and staying anyway.

This is my last chance at love not because I am too old to meet anyone else, but because it is just time to stop. Stop running, chasing this moving target I call happiness, and get happy with what I have got.

Dan is not the right guy or the wrong guy. He is just my guy. My husband. The one I chose on the day I chose him, and right now, I plan to go on choosing him for the rest of my life.

In the meantime, I am going to clear some space in my life to read my grandmother's memoirs. Maybe I will discover what it was that kept Bernadine and James together for so long and perhaps my marriage to Dan will be different from theirs, but just as good. Like my Irish stew.

Wisdom

There is no magic recipe.

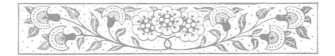

Glossary of Irish Words

Aul	old
Boithrin	(*baureen*)—lane
Craic	fun
Cupla focal	(*coo-pla fuckel*)—couple of words, chat
Ludarman	(*lude-ra-mawn*)—idiot
Muinteoir	(moon-chore)—teacher
Poitin	(putcheen)—poteen, strong alcoholic drink distilled from potatoes
Pioneer	member of the Pioneer Total Abstinence Association of the Sacred Heart. Group that shows its dedication to the church by abstaining from alcohol, living out the message of the Gospel through sacrifice. Their catchphrase: "Promoting Sobriety for a Better Society"
Spraoi	(*spree*)—fun or sport—a name given in Achadh Mor at that time to a party thrown in somebody's house. *Spraois* were often held by local women who derived fun out of matchmaking, and although many romances were made there, few ended in marriage.

Acknowledgments

hanks to the women whose practical and emotional support enabled me to write *Recipes*: Theresa Gilroy, Deirdre McGreevy, Renee Kerrigan, Sabine Lacey, Dee Hanna, and Sheila Smyth. Also our community in Killala, especially Joe and Rose McGivern for all their hospitality and help. To fellow writers Helen Falconer and Pat McCabe for their support and friendship.

I have been so lucky in the generosity and integrity I have experienced in those people who work directly with me: my agents Marianne Gunn O'Connor and Vicky Satlow; editors Peternelle van Arsdale, Imogen Taylor, and Alison Walsh; and my trusted reader, Una Morris.

Thanks to those people who helped with my research: my aunt, Maureen Murrey, and wonderful cousins Kathy and Michelle for their hospitality and friendship. Thanks also to Maureen Nolan, John Kilkenny, and Joe Byrne for sharing their stories and ideas with me, and to Colm Nolan and Jean Spence for recording my grandmother and bringing her to life for me again.

To my mother, Moira, whose love is a constant source of encouragement and inspiration.

Lastly to my husband, my hero, Niall: Thank you for giving me all the time in the world.

A Note About the Recipes

The recipes in this book were either handed down to me through the generations or given to me by various Irish women.

A recipe is a true gift, and I would like to acknowledge the generosity of those family members and friends who coughed up their culinary secrets.

The gooseberry jam and rhubarb tart recipes were developed from my memory of recipes by my maternal grandmother, Ann Nolan. Granny had a taste for sour food and loved the tart flavor of both gooseberries and rhubarb, both of which grew in her garden.

Honey cake I developed myself with advice and encouragement from my cousin Mary Nolan, whose husband, Michael, keeps bees.

The fairy cakes are the recipe of my pal Una's mother—Marie Morris. Marie has a plethora of grandchildren and their hangers on (including my own son) traipsing in and out of her house and they all know where the Tupperware containing her famous fairy cakes lives. As do I!

Brown bread—Anna McGreevy from Kilkelly was a mine of information about breadmaking at that time, and the individual, chaotic nature of how each woman developed her own recipe. Inspired by our conversations, I make my own bread every other day and am still finding my way.

Porter cake—Margaret Galvin's Christmas cake is legendary and I am so grateful to her for allowing me to use this fantastic recipe. So grateful in fact that part of me is pained to see it published as it really is so special. If there is one recipe in this book worth trying, this is it.

Boxty—this traditional recipe reminds me of my paternal grandmother Katy Prunty's kitchen. A social center-point in Longford, Granny was a priest's housekeeper before she got married, and a fine traditional cook. Her daughters, Angie and Maureen, continue the tradition in Killoe and New York, respectively. So many recipes from them I would love to have included— boiled fruit cake, corned beef—but this boxty is in memory of her.

Honey Roasted Clove Ham—my mother-in-law, Renee Kerrigan, upstages me every Christmas with her ham, and now that I know how much work goes into it, I'm happy to take second billing!

Pobs—milk and bread soup. The name "pobs" appears to be exclusive to the west of Ireland although it seems that this suppertime "filler" was common food. In the south of Ireland and elsewhere, it is called "goodie."

Irish Stew. A truly modern recipe from a real foodie. My sister, Christine, developed this recipe especially for this book. It is as unique and delicious as the lady herself.

The author would like to
invite you to collect your
special recipes on the
following pages.